V4
VENGEANCE

THE FIRST IN THE JIM WILSON SERIES

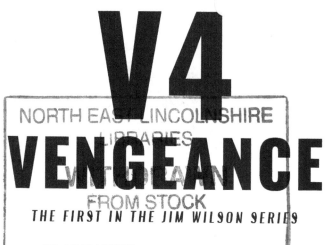

NIGEL SEED

ASTOR
+BLUE
EDITIONS

V4 VENGEANCE

Copyright © 2016 Nigel Seed

Typography © Astor + Blue Editions

The right of Nigel Seed to be identified as the author of this
work has been asserted.

This Edition Published by:

Astor + Blue Editions LLC, 1441 Broadway, Suite 5015,

New York, NY 10018, U.S.A.

www.astorandblue.com

Publisher's Cataloging-In-Publication Data

SEED, NIGEL. V4 VENGEANCE

ISBN: 978-1-68120-057-6 (Paperback)

ISBN: 978-1-68120-058-3 (ePdf)

ISBN: 978-1-68120-059-0 (ePub)

ISBN: 978-1-68120-060-6 (Mobi)

1. Naval—Fiction. 2. Retired Royal Engineers search for historic German

U-boats—Fiction 3. Thriller—Fiction 4. World War II—Fiction

5. International Crime—Fiction 6. Military—Fiction

7. England, Germany, New York City I. Title

A catalogue record for this book is available from the Library
of Congress and the British Library.

Cover Design: Kate Murphy

This book is dedicated to the memory of that exceptional author John Gordon Davis who generously shared his knowledge of the writing craft with me and many others.

1944 Western Germany

Oberleutnant Hans Gehrlich watched through the thick armored glass window of the control bunker as *Feldwebel Weine* supervised the final refueling out on the ramp. As he watched, the men stopped the pump and secured the filler cap on the rocket. Weine checked their work and took a last careful look around the launch area for anything that might impede the weapon launch. Satisfied, he turned to the bunker and saluted, the usual signal that everything was ready.

Inside the bunker, Gehrlich scratched the stump of his left arm through the cloth of his uniform jacket, as he watched Weine move out of the danger area and into the crew bunker. He watched the fireproof steel door close and turned to the operators sitting at the control desk before him.

He gave the order, "Prepare to fire," and then turned to the drab, bespectacled man in civilian clothes standing just behind him. "*Herr Professor*, since you were part of the team that designed and built the weapon, would you care to give the order?"

The civilian smiled and said, "Thank you *Herr Oberleutnant,* to strike a blow for the Fatherland would give me great pleasure."

He took the half step forward to the command position as the *Oberleutnant* stepped back. They both stared through the small slit windows for a second or two at the stubby winged missile sitting on the launching ramp. The fir trees around the clearing, that hid the launch site from allied aircraft, swayed gently in the breeze and the two operators waited patiently.

"It seems a long time since we developed these flying bombs," said the Professor, "so much has happened since then. Sadly not all of it good for our country." He sighed and turning to the two operators gave the launch order.

The pulse jet mounted on the spine of the missile roared into pounding life and settled down to the rhythmic pulsations of the engine. The holding clamps released and the missile accelerated rapidly up the ramp and into the gray, forbidding sky. With the danger of a launch explosion past, the two men stepped outside the safety of the command bunker and watched the missile, looking like a small aircraft, climb and disappear into the overcast. This one seemed to be working well, unlike the last that had burned out its engine and nosed into a field no more than a kilometer from the launch ramp.

"Another gift for Mr. Churchill," said the uniformed *Oberleutnant*.

"Indeed," said the Professor. "Just a pity we will not know which part of London it lands on. It has the range, but at this distance not the accuracy we might wish for. We can but hope it will be on something the British value highly."

They turned away and the officer escorted his distinguished guest toward the staff car waiting under the cover of the trees.

"These longer range rockets are allowing us to continue to operate, even though our launch sites in France have been overrun, but it is a shame we cannot put a bigger fuel tank on them and give the Americans a taste of war in their own country," said Gehrlich a little sadly.

The Professor stopped. "Why the Americans particularly?"

"They have been shielded from the true meaning of this war. Their cities are untouched and their civilians carry on making money as usual. Plus, of course, I owe them for this," he said, indicating the stump of his left arm.

The Professor nodded, "Yet you still serve your country. My compliments. And I can tell you that the *Führer* has had the same thoughts. He issued a directive, some months ago, to prepare two new weapons to visit death and destruction on the cities of the USA. One system will be ready in just a few days and the other is also nearing the end of its development. One day you will have your wish as our weapons bring down our vengeance on the Americans."

Chapter 1

The Present Day – Southern England

His head would probably not fall off if he kept it still but the urgent need to find a bathroom was making that impossible. He sat up in the narrow single bed. The room spun around him and he thought there was a very real possibility that he was going to be violently sick. He managed to get to his feet by levering himself up on the bedhead. Slowly, so as not to disturb the monster in his head, he stepped forward. As his foot touched down the throb in his head made sure he knew this was not going to be a good morning. Holding on to the wall, to stop it moving, he made it to the communal bathroom. He managed to stand at the urinal even though the room was definitely in motion. That task completed, he struggled to the sink and rinsed his face. My God, the creature in the mirror looked rough, as rough as he felt. The skin was pale and the eyes were seriously bloodshot. He was far too old to be drinking in the Sergeants' Mess. Still, that would not be a problem from now on. This morning he was still Major Jim Wilson of the Corps of Royal Engineers, respected by his men so that they laid on a special formal dinner in the Sergeants' Mess to say goodbye to a mere company commander. By this afternoon he would be another unemployed civilian, courtesy of a government that knew the cost of everything and the value of nothing. He managed to make it back to his room in the overflow annex of the Officers' Mess. He checked his watch, once he found it under the bed. He needed to get a move on. He had an appointment with the Colonel in less than half an hour.

The shave was painful and the cleaning of his teeth a challenge to keep yesterday's festivities down. The shower helped and he could almost stand the sunlight as he stepped out of the building and walked across to Regimental HQ. He had decided to wear civilian clothes this morning. No point stringing out the pain of parting from the Army after nearly sixteen years. Where had the time gone? He had served around the world, as Royal Engineers do. His experience was varied and deep.

He had commanded an armored engineer company in combat, had run the drone troop with its UAVs, been part of airfield construction teams, commanded a Tank Landing Ship down at Marchwood and even been a Chemical Warfare Instructor at the Royal Military Academy Sandhurst for a while. His company was well run and effective. Commanding tough and intelligent soldiers had been a wonderful experience, even if it had cost him his marriage. His belly was still flat and he could still keep up with the young soldiers on the physical fitness tests, though probably not this morning.

Yet the last three promotion boards had passed him over for advancement in the rapidly shrinking Army that was now smaller than it had been since before the Napoleonic War. Opportunities were drying up and that had been enough for the bean counters to identify him for compulsory redundancy. Well, he was in good company, some damned fine soldiers had been kicked out over the last few months.

As he entered the front door of the imposing HQ building he acknowledged the salutes of a number of senior NCOs waiting outside the post room. Now why weren't they with their soldiers at this time of the morning? Not his problem anymore.

He made his way carefully up the stairs and headed for his Commanding Officer's office. The young female corporal in the outer office smiled at him as he entered. It was sympathy and nothing more.

"He's waiting for you, sir. Go straight in and I'll bring the coffee."

He could have kissed her, coffee was badly needed and the sooner the better. He pushed the door open. Lieutenant Colonel John Whittaker was behind his desk shuffling the normal pile of papers expected of a battalion commander; he pushed them aside grateful for the interruption.

"Well Jim, I see the Sergeants' Mess gave you a good send off last night."

Jim smiled weakly and sat down without waiting to be invited. He really needed that coffee now. John nodded indulgently. They had been friends for years and John's promotion at the last board had not affected that, at least in private.

"You weren't playing your whisky game with them again were you?"

Jim started to nod but remembered the pain that would cause. He was famous in many parts of the army for being able to recognize any scotch whisky put in front of him by smell and taste. It was a completely useless talent, but it amused the Sergeants' Mess every Christmas.

They would search high and low for the most obscure whiskies from the outer islands and the deep glens to try to beat him. Last night they had trotted out as much as they could to finally catch him out and he was paying the price this morning. The coffee arrived and the young corporal had the good sense to bring a large pot and two decent sized mugs. The pain killers were tucked discretely at the edge of the tray. This girl was a treasure. John let him get the first coffee down and made a point of not noticing the tablets.

"Well Jim, I will be sad to see you go and I am certain B Company will miss you. At this point I am supposed to talk you through the party line about it being for the good of the service, but even if you didn't have the hangover already I think that might make you vomit. Jim, the government has royally screwed up, I only hope they realize and bring you and a lot of others back before the Army loses all its best talent."

He didn't comment; he knew John meant well, but he could not imagine coming back after this had been done to him. The bond of trust, so important to soldiers, had been broken. There was more small talk and he got up to leave. John came round the desk to shake his hand, but had the compassion not to slap his back. His head was not up to that yet. As he left he went to give the packet of pain killers back to the Corporal.

"Keep them, sir," she said. "I think you need them more than me."

He nodded his thanks and immediately regretted it.

At the top of the sweeping staircase he looked down into the foyer. Company Sergeant Major Ivan Thomas was standing there, waiting for him. He had a sheet of folded white paper in his hand, which was quivering. When CSM Thomas quivered that was usually the sign of an impending verbal explosion. He was probably the best soldier Jimmy had ever commanded, but he had a fierce temper. It had cost him at least two promotions over the years. He walked down to meet him.

"Well Mr. Thomas, the end of an era for me and now you have to train up a new company commander to your standards."

"Not really sir," he said and handed the white paper over.

Jim read it and looked at the CSM with disbelief. "They've made you redundant too? But you've only got, what, less than two years to a full pension? That's criminal."

The CSM nodded, "Not just me sir, about a third of the Senior NCOs got the same letter this morning. That's what we were summoned here to collect."

Jim put a hand on the man's immaculately ironed shoulder tabs "Ivan, I am so sorry. If I can ever help let me know."

They shook hands and the CSM gave him his last salute as an officer. He walked out of the Regimental HQ and stood with his back to the large oak doors, taking his last look out across the empty parade square with the neat white stones around the flag pole. He sighed then squared his shoulders and walked down the wide stone steps and got into his car. With a last, sad look around the barracks he drove out through the gate and into an unknown future.

He had no home of his own to go to, that had gone to his wife in the divorce settlement. He had received the papers halfway through his last overseas combat tour. He didn't blame her. She had stuck it out with him for longer than he had a right to expect, but the Army was a harsh mistress and demanded sacrifice. Some women managed to live through the separations and loneliness, others gave up. Maybe if there had been children things could have been different.

His younger sister had offered him a bed at her home in East Anglia until he sorted himself out with a permanent place to live. He couldn't do that until he found a job and during a recession was the wrong time to be looking for a new career.

The drive through the fen country was uneventful. Miles of flat country rolling beneath his wheels with canals and drainage dykes by the side of the road. He pulled into the driveway of the classic English thatched cottage that looked like it had been there for two hundred years or more. In truth it was a modern prefabricated kit that arrived here on the back of a fleet of trucks five years ago. The inside looked just as rustic with massive exposed beams and large, black, iron fixing pins, but with every modern convenience and modern wiring. Although it did look convincing as the evening mists rolled in from the North Sea.

His sister stood in the small porch waiting for him. She smiled, but the nervous entwining of her fingers gave the lie to that greeting.

"Hello Jimmy, You've just got time to wash up before dinner."

"Hi, Sandra. Everything OK with you?"

"Yes everything's fine. We're looking forward to having you with us."

Now that was a lie and they both knew it, but he could do nothing to help until she asked.

Dinner that night was the usual mixture of inconsequential chatter from his sister and grumbles and moans from his brother-in-law, with the customary barbed comments about the army. At least the conversation with his nephew, David, was pleasant as always. He was a fine boy. It was sometimes difficult to believe that the sour-faced man sweating at the head of the table was really his father.

The next morning he rose early and ran through the fens in a long circuit of obscure pathways he had discovered over the years, scaring birds out of the reed beds as he passed and listening to the protests of the white beaked Coots in their water side nests.

No point letting his belly grow and hang over his belt like his brother-in-law. Returning to the house, he showered and shaved. Wiping the misted mirror with the towel he checked his reflection, no beer belly, a full head of hair with just a touch of gray starting at the temples, and clear blue eyes that did not need glasses yet. After breakfast he scanned the newspapers and the Internet for jobs. Not many and even less for a man who could destroy bridges, build airfields and command troops in combat.

He walked down to the village pub for lunch. Now there was a building that really had been in place for well over a hundred years. Some of the locals looked as though they had been on the original building crew. They knew him from his leaves between combat tours over the last couple of years. He had stayed with his sister after each of his recent deployments in the Middle East and the permanence of these uncomplicated people had calmed him. They acknowledged him with nods or a quiet raising of a sunburned hand from a scarred, oak table. Even the black Labrador by the fire only managed to slap his tail twice before drifting back to sleep in the patch of sunlight from the window.

The barman had his pint of locally brewed beer on the bar by the time he reached it. He was tempted to ruin the moment by ordering something else, but that would not be fair to kind people.

The barman looked at him with a raised eyebrow, "The usual?"

Six months since he had last been here and when he said "Yes," the Plowman's Lunch was straight out in front of him. Crusty, warm bread from the village bakery and rich, tangy cheese from local farms. Pickled onions from somewhere with a sense of humor. He always left them.

In the afternoons, to keep in trim, he rowed his nephew's small boat though the waterways of the Norfolk Broads. Occasionally he dangled a line in the water to try to catch a fish or two and to have an excuse to stay away from the poisonous atmosphere in the house.

His routine was set. On the weekends his nephew David ran with him and egged him on to run faster, teasing him with comments about his advanced age. But on school days he ran alone with just the birds scattering from the reeds for company. In the afternoons he carried on with his fruitless job search. This enforced tedium went on for nearly a month until the day when his sister was waiting for him as he ran back into the garden.

"You've had a phone call. No message, but they left a number and they want you to call back."

"Who was it?"

She shrugged "They wouldn't say, but they did say it's about a job."

The signs were there in her expression; he was outstaying his welcome. It was probably his delightful brother-in-law being a pain in the neck, as usual, about his presence. He showered and then rang the number she had taken down.

The phone was answered quickly, "Ah Major Wilson, thank you for ringing back. I think we should meet. I have an employment opportunity for you."

"That's interesting, but could you tell me a little more about it?"

"I do not want to discuss it over the phone, but since I will pay your expenses, what have you got to lose?"

"I'm not sure I want to drag myself all the way down to London for nothing and I'm wary of secrets. How legal is this?"

"It's far from being nothing, Major. You will not infringe a single law of this country and if it's successful you may even be making a little bit of history. I promise you it will be worth your while to listen to my proposition."

Despite his misgivings, Jim was intrigued and allowed himself to be persuaded to meet. They discussed places of mutual convenience and decided to meet in London at the Thistle Hotel located on Victoria Station. The man on the phone refused to give him a name. Odd.

"And by the way, it's not Major Wilson anymore, in my view that's reserved for Golf Club secretaries and I don't play the game."

He heard the chuckle from the other end of the line as the phone went down.

Chapter 2

As he came out of the tunnel of the Underground, Victoria Mainline Station was the customary mad crush of commuters dashing this way and that to get to whatever dreary office they worked in. His shirt felt clammy from the heat in the underground tunnels and the moist breath of the crowds in the train. At least he had been spared this nightmare for the last sixteen years. He hoped the proposition he was heading toward did not involve anything to do with traveling on the London Underground. He was not keen on enclosed spaces at the best of times and ones filled to overflowing with people who were overdue an appointment with soap and water did not thrill him at all.

Finding his way to the hotel located in the corner of the main concourse, he wandered through the winding passages to the reception area and waited as a family from Wisconsin checked out. The piles of baggage they were trying to manoeuver were impressive. Eventually he made it to the desk and announced himself. The desk clerk nodded and turned to the letter rack behind him. Turning back, the harassed receptionist wordlessly handed him an envelope with his name on it and turned to deal with the next client.

Inside the envelope was a single sheet of paper that simply asked him to go to room 504. It seemed a strange way to conduct a job interview, but he was still prepared to investigate almost anything that might allow him to escape the rapidly growing boredom and awkward atmosphere in East Anglia.

He walked to the lift and went up to the fifth floor. The corridor carpet was a little threadbare in places, unlike the reception area which had been at a high standard. Finding 504 he knocked on the door and waited until it was opened by a nondescript man in a cheap charcoal gray suit, with a white shirt that had seen better days and a plain blue tie. His sallow complexion added to the feeling of bland grayness. He could have been any one of a thousand middle-grade civil servants scurrying through the station below.

"Ah there you are, Major, do come in." He stepped back and made way for Jim to walk through. "Would you care for a coffee or something to eat?"

Jim shrugged. "A coffee would be welcome."

He was trying hard to work out what this man did for a living and why he would want to talk to him. The lack of any identifiable accent didn't help. With the coffee poured and handed over, the man in the gray suit sat down.

"I must apologize for the mystery," he said, "but my client is a very private person. Until you accept the proposition I am about to put to you, there is no need for names. I do apologize, but my client was very clear on that point."

"Well if your client is trying to intrigue me, it's working. So make your pitch and we'll see where it takes us."

The anonymous man nodded, "Have you done much sailing in your time in the Army?"

"A reasonable amount when I could. I found being out on the water was a damned fine way to relieve stress."

"Did you ever sail round the Baltic from the British Kiel Yacht Club, which I understand was an Army-run club in Germany?"

Jim thought that an odd question, but said "Well, yes I did. BKYC was a very pleasant place to sail from, especially around the Danish islands."

"Indeed. I don't like the water much myself. However, while you were there did you hear the legend of the lost U-Boat base?"

"I did, but you have to realize that there are legends of mysterious hidden bases all over Germany and soldiers love tall tales. So I wouldn't put much credence in it. Why do you ask?"

"Could you tell me which version of the legend you heard?"

Jim cast his mind back. He recalled sitting in the bar, nursing a cold beer, looking out over the yacht club moorings talking to the club coxswain one summer evening when life in the British Army was simple and pleasant. He repeated the old story he had been told about the Germans taking a number of their bases underground to avoid the intense allied bombing. The huge U-Boat pens on the French coast had been bombed heavily and severely damaged by larger and larger bombs. As those bases were liable to be overrun or at least cut off after any invasion, a base had been ordered near to the main *Kriegsmarine* naval base in Kiel.

This one was to be concealed by being dug out under a hill rather than being built of huge concrete blocks, that could be seen through a bomb aimer's sight. To aid the camouflage, the entrance was to be beneath the water so boats could only enter and exit when submerged. Kiel was in the British occupation sector after the war and considerable effort had been put into finding the base. None of the locals knew anything definite although there was much speculation and the entrance was never found. The legend was that the entrance had been collapsed as the war ended to prevent the Allies gaining the technology and secrets that the base contained. The British Military authorities had decided it was all wishful thinking and had forgotten about it.

The undistinguished man was taking notes. "And how do you feel about the legend?"

"As I told you, soldiers tell tall stories about hidden bases and secret weapons factories all over Germany. When I was stationed in Detmold a supposedly secret room was found in one of the barrack blocks. It had been walled off because the floor beams were damaged, but the discovery fueled an epidemic of rumors for months and stories about the artifacts found in there got wilder and wilder with every telling."

"So do you believe the story of the U-Boat base?"

"Well the Germans are a very industrious people and they did construct underground factories, but to house U-Boats the place would have to be huge and should have been well known to local people. So no, I don't believe it."

"Logically you are right of course, but my client has come into possession of some wartime German military documents that indicate this base is a reality."

"Really? Fascinating, but what has that to do with me?"

The gray man looked out of the window then turned back to him. "My client is a collector of sorts and he is fascinated by that period. Luckily for him he has the money to indulge his interests. He wants to find that base. More accurately, he wants you to find it for him and if possible, to recover any interesting finds for him."

Jim sat back in his chair and studied the man opposite him. "Why me?"

"We have been looking for a particular type of man for this job. I have read your record. You have all the experience we would need for a task of this sort. A tour in command of an Unmanned Aerial Vehicle troop, commanding a Tank Landing Ship and a lot of time in units using heavy plant, which I assume means big diesel engines and generators. Ideal for our needs. Your annual reports indicate that, as well as being a good engineer, you are a determined and effective officer although on occasion you have had some difficulties with authority. You have just been badly treated by the British government and would probably not object to recovering the artifacts without troubling the German government. Plus, you need a job. Running through the damp fens of East Anglia every morning cannot be very satisfying for a recently retired Army officer of your quality."

"How the hell did you get hold of my records? And how do you know what I do at home?"

The anonymous man smiled. "Oh dear, Major, you are still a little naïve. Money can buy anything in this world and there are still people in the Army who admire you and have your best interests at heart. The two things combined produced the records for me. Checking up on you and how you pass your time was the matter of a couple of phone calls and a little observation by people who make a point of not being noticed."

Jim was quiet, thinking about what he had just heard. He suspected the story was still nonsense, but being paid to work on a search project in that part of Northern Germany was attractive. He had a great affection for German food and beer and he might even manage a little sailing round the islands. Plus, the gray man was right, sitting on his backside in the fens of East Anglia was doing nothing for his self-esteem, almost any job was better than imposing any further on his sister and her damned husband any longer. The spirit sapping boredom persuaded him to take the plunge.

"I'm interested. So what does this job pay? And how are we going to handle the legalities of removing this equipment? Some of this stuff, if we find it, could be quite big."

"At the end of the war the Allied Powers deployed teams across Germany to search out equipment and technology that they commandeered as part of war reparations. The British team was called 'T Force' and Kiel was in the British area. If they had found the base they would have stripped it bare. You will just be finishing their work for them. The German government would probably argue so we do not intend to tell them until the artifacts we find are out of their territory."

"That's theft."

"Not really. The people who owned the equipment we hope to find are long dead and the present government knows nothing about it. In any case I will be handling the legalities with a team of very expensive lawyers, so you have nothing to worry about."

The salary on offer was generous and all expenses would be met. He could hardly refuse, particularly since this was probably a wild goose chase anyway. Besides, how could the loss of obsolete wartime equipment bother the Germans of today?

"I'm not sure you're right about the Germans, but we'll let that slide until I've found the base shall we? When do you want me to start and what do we do about a team to work with me?"

"We thought you might like to start immediately and the team is up to you. Make it a small team of people you can trust implicitly to keep their mouths shut. The salary for them will be almost as good as yours. We will pay you monthly, in advance, so there is no suggestion of you being let down. How many people will you need?"

Jim thought for a moment about what the search might entail and said, "Just two and I know who the first one is. What about specialist equipment? I don't know what I will need yet, we might even need ground penetrating radar or something similar."

"Whatever you need will be supplied. I am your logistic support, if you will, if you phone me and tell me what you need I will tell you where to collect it from." He stood and held out a hand. "Do we have an agreement?"

"We do, but who am I working for?"

"I think the Army has an expression for that being on a 'Need to Know' basis. When you need to know you will be told."

They shook hands and Jim started to leave. He was still a little surprised at suddenly being plunged into this adventure, but very glad to have something useful to do, at least for a while.

"One moment, Major. This is the phone you need to contact me. It has my number programed in. I will answer it day or night. You will find that it is something called a Tri-Band phone and works anywhere in the world. There is also an anonymous email address in there for you to use if you need it."

Jim took the box with the phone and turned to leave still wondering quite what he had got himself into. He paused in the doorway and looked back.

"You do realize this is all fantasy and legend, don't you?"

"Possibly, but indulging rich men's fantasies can still be profitable don't you think?"

Chapter 3

Back in the Fens his sister tried hard to disguise her relief that he would be moving out. She was OK, but he suspected that fat insurance salesman she married had been bitching about him again and making her life more of a misery than usual.

A call to the chief clerk back at the barracks got him the address for Ivan Thomas and confirmation that he had been discharged from the Army three weeks previously. He was living up a mountain in North Wales on a small sheep farm he had inherited from his parents. Directory enquiries could find no phone number for the address so he would have to go himself.

The drive to North Wales was long and tedious, although once he got off the motorways and on to the winding Welsh roads he could appreciate the handling of the old Austin Healey sports car he had inherited from his father and which had become his pride and joy. It was all that was left of the old man's life after all the debts were settled.

He was quite cheered up by the time he arrived in the small slate gray village at the foot of the mountain. He took a room in the pub rather than try and find Ivan's place in the dark. He asked around the bar for directions to the Thomas place and was rewarded by gales of laughter. He had forgotten for a second quite how common a name Thomas was in Wales. He described Ivan. In a small place like this everyone knew everyone else's business and they all knew about Ivan coming home. Over a couple of pints of good Welsh beer he even found out that he had originally been called Ivor, a good Welsh name. He wondered what that story was.

There was no road up to the farm, just a rough track. A Land Rover in four wheel drive might make it, but the dips and rocks would have the oil pan out of the low slung sports car in seconds. The walk would do him good after the long drive yesterday so he set off up the hill. It was a long steep climb and despite his recent efforts to keep fit, he was starting to breathe a little deeply as he rounded a bend and came in sight of the house.

It was a small building with a couple of even smaller sheep barns alongside it, all made out of the local gray slate. Tucked back into the hillside it was sheltered from the worst of the wind, but as he looked it over he thought it must be bleak in the winter when the snows came. The path sloped gently up to a gate into the yard and as he walked on, he saw smoke from the chimney. Ivan was at the gate as he reached it. Even in the grubby blue farmer's clothes and rubber wellington boots he had the clear eyes and bearing of a professional soldier.

"Morning sir, what brings you to this center of vice and depravity?"

They shook hands, "Hello Ivan, I've got a job offer for you."

They went into the farmhouse. It was small and sparsely furnished. Ivan's parents had lived very simply. The big, chipped, brown enamel kettle was heating up on the wood-burning stove. The gleaming stainless steel weight bench in the corner struck a jarring note, but Ivan, it seemed, was not going to let the remarkable power in his arms fade.

"Thought you would like a brew when you got here. I was expecting you a bit later. The big breakfast at the pub usually slows people down a bit."

Jim looked around, there was no phone. "How did you know I was coming?"

"This is North Wales boss; there are no secrets up here. Particularly when an Englishman arrives asking for me."

He did not elaborate and Jim thought it best to leave it at that. Over the steaming mug of tea he looked at Ivan. Even in the dirty overalls he was wearing to renovate the farm, there was an air of authority and confidence about the man. The twenty years of soldiering was deeply embedded in him.

Jim explained the job he had been given and asked Ivan to join him. The Welshman was just as bored as Jim had been and was probably starting to feel lonely stuck up on the windswept hillside. It took only a moment for Ivan to say yes.

"But you do know this is a wild goose chase don't you?"

"Probably, but the money is good and we get to work in the fresh air in Germany, all expenses paid."

"Fair enough, when do we start?"

"As soon as we find another team member. I think three of us should do and if we are going to be digging into a hill we need someone with the right experience. Any ideas?"

Ivan thought for a while "Quite a few spring to mind. Pete Magee for one, he is a hell of a guy with a bull dozer if we need to do some digging. Andy Davidson knows that area well, I think his wife is from Kiel. But I think there is one man who might suit us down to the ground. Do you remember Geordie Peters? A sergeant in 4 Troop, in A Company."

"Was he the black guy who pulled the stunt with the bulldozer during that ambush?"

"That's him. Every man in the regiment wanted to buy him a beer after that one."

Jim nodded. "Apart from raw guts, what's so special about him?"

"He's a qualified welder, he did tours on the heavy plant teams, driving and maintaining every kind of heavy construction vehicle and he did four years as a coal miner round Newcastle before his pit was closed down and he joined up. Bit of an expert on controlled explosions too, if I recall rightly. He was the one that got sent on the intensive Arabic course before our last tour in Iraq. In six months we never found an Arab who could understand Arabic with a Geordie accent."

Jim recognized the description of the big troop sergeant. "Oh yeah, got him for sure now. Can we get him?"

"I think we can. He was discharged at the same time as me, so unless he has been very lucky he will be borderline suicidal with boredom by now."

Ivan paused and looked at Jim. "Look, before I ring Geordie, are you sure this isn't going to be just a glorious waste of time? Are we being paid up front or only on results?"

"It may well be a waste of time, but we are being paid monthly in advance. So win, lose or draw we don't lose out."

"That'll do for me. I just hope they have *Herforder Bier* where we are going."

Despite being halfway up a Welsh mountain, Jim's mobile phone picked up a weak signal. Checks with directory enquiries revealed that around the city of Newcastle phones were far more common and they had Geordie's number in minutes.

Ivan used the company phone Jim had been given and called the Newcastle number. Geordie was in the house watching a daytime TV chat show and bored out of his skull, especially as his actress girlfriend, Sam, had been working abroad in a successful stage play for the last three weeks and would be away for at least the next three months.

Ivan had hardly finished outlining the job before Geordie agreed to be part of it. Jim had his team.

Ivan packed up his old Army rucksack and was ready to go within the hour. He had made it clear that farming sheep on a mountainside had little attraction for him. He tidied round the house, washed the tea mugs and they stepped outside.

"Aren't you going to lock the door?"

Ivan shook his head. "There hasn't been a lock on that door since the house was built by my great, great Grandfather. Besides it would make it awkward for people to check on the place."

As they walked down the hill toward the village Jim said, "So how did you become Ivan instead of Ivor?"

"Originally it was a nickname from when I got back to the regiment, after I did my Russian language course at Beaconsfield, but after a while I got to like it and made it official. Makes me quite exotic around here."

"I would have thought just joining the Army would make you exotic here?"

"No, not really. This is hard country; the farms can't support many people, so the men from here have been going off to the Army for hundreds of years just to make a living."

They walked on. As they came in sight of the village Ivan said, "The acoustics in this part of the hill are famous here, just listen."

He launched into a very competent rendering of the great Welsh anthem "Men of Harlech." His powerful voice echoed off the rocks and cliffs and sounded like a platoon of men walking with them. Jim couldn't carry a tune in a bucket, but appreciated the fine Welsh voice beside him. He smiled; it felt comfortable being back with this highly capable soldier. Even if the search was fruitless, this was going to be fun.

Chapter 4

They drove back to his sister's house to leave his precious Austin Healey sports car in the back of her garage. Before he covered it with the tailor-made cover he gave the white and red bodywork a wash down to remove the splattered insects and polished the chrome detailing. They spent the night in the two single beds in the guest room. His brother-in-law was as welcoming as ever despite knowing it was only for one night. Having two military men in the house gave him even more excuse for his customary snide remarks about the Army during dinner, while resting his fat belly on the table end.

As they arrived at the train station in the morning Ivan said, "So tell me boss, what stopped you from giving that unpleasant git your sister married a good smacking?"

They were still smiling about that as they got on the London train. They met up with Geordie on the platform at Kings Cross station. Jim recognized the ex-Sergeant from halfway up the platform, leaning up against one of the large stone roof supports, scanning the sweating, pushing crowd rushing past him to the underground station entrance and managing to look relaxed and alert at the same time.

Geordie drew himself up as Jim approached, "Morning sir. Nice to see you again."

Jim shook his head, "Not sir anymore, Geordie. The Army has dispensed with my services just like you."

"OK, boss. Where to first?"

Geordie and Ivan shook hands and the three men set off for the car park. Jim had called the night before on his new phone, to the programed number, and asked for a long wheel base Land Rover fitted with a winch to be waiting for them. The gray man might be a bit over excited about his secrets, he thought, but he was as good as his word. The three well built, purposeful men walked together down the platform toward the car park. They exuded an air of determination as they moved and the scurrying crowd of commuters cleared before them.

The brand new vehicle was waiting in the parking area behind the station with an apprehensive salesman beside it. The thin London sunshine reflected off the glossy blue paint as the three men opened the rear door and threw their bags into the back. They inspected the vehicle while the salesman hovered nervously. Once they were satisfied he signed over the vehicle with all the paperwork they would need for driving all over Europe and then gave them a large sealed envelope. Whoever was paying for this jaunt certainly hired efficient people.

In the pack of information provided was a booking on the Channel Tunnel train for that evening. There was no point hanging about, so they set off toward Folkestone to meet up with the vehicle train to France. Driving the big heavy Land Rover through London traffic was a challenge. Ivan drove and kept up a steady stream of colorful invective about the people of London who seemed to be possessed of a mass death wish. He reserved his most pointed comments for the drivers of the black taxi cabs that dodged around them. Once clear of the city Geordie took over for the more relaxing drive to the Channel Tunnel.

Jim sat in the front passenger seat slowly reading through the information that had been in the pack with the vehicle paperwork. As he finished each sheet he passed it over his shoulder to Ivan, in the second row of seats. They were to drive to Folkestone, load the Land Rover on the train and disembark in Calais. Once out of France they were to drive through Holland and Germany toward Kiel. Hotel accommodation had been booked for them about three hours out of Calais. Satnav coordinates for the hotel were given. Next morning they were to drive to Kiel and again accommodation had been booked for them for one night in a hotel. From then on they would be staying in a small secluded villa for which a door key and more Satnav coordinates were included. Equipment would be waiting for them in the villa. Once they checked it they were to call for anything else they needed.

Within the pack was a heavyweight white envelope sealed with wax. How very dramatic, Jim thought. He opened the envelope and found that it was a translated overview of the documents that the mysterious client had acquired. There were four close typed pages of witness statements that concerned the base and claimed that it existed. None of the documents would have proved anything if taken in isolation. It was all legend and speculation, but interestingly a few pointed to an area by the river just a little way north of Kiel.

More substantial were the documents concerning the supply of food from warehouses in the city. The food was collected in *Kriegsmarine* trucks, always at night and no destinations were given. The document showed that the orders were signed personally by Admiral Karl Doenitz. Now that was interesting. Why would the head of the German Navy U-Boat fleet bother to sign off on ration requests? Jim looked through the sheets; this was a lot of food at a time when Germany was struggling to feed the population. OK, so that explained the Admiral. His signature would give these ration demands a high priority.

The next document was an exclusion and evacuation order with another English translation clipped to the back. It was a type-written instruction with space left for including the name of the recipient. It instructed whoever was given it to pack up and move out of his or her house immediately. They were instructed to wait at their gate at a certain time and they would be collected by *Kriegsmarine* vehicles and taken to a "place of safety." Why would the *Kriegsmarine* be interested in transporting people to safety, they must have had other priorities during that part of the war, surely?

There was a small map on the next page with a number of houses marked. These appeared to be the ones that were known to have received the instruction to vacate. Not all the houses on the map were marked, but those that were made a large semicircle next to the river. He grabbed the witness statements from the back seat and went through them again. About a third referred to the same general area, the rest described places up and down the river with no consistency.

He looked over at Ivan who was still running through the papers with a small smile on his face. It was all circumstantial, but it was tantalizing. He watched Ivan put down the last paper and break into a wide grin. He felt it too. This might not be quite the wild goose chase they had expected.

Chapter 5

The drive to Kiel on the fast, efficient German Autobahns was uneventful and they found both of their hotels without difficulty. After the second night and a solid German breakfast, they found their way to the villa. As expected, it was secluded with thick hedges around it. Even a nosey neighbor would have to walk quite a way up the track to see them. Between their villa and the initial search area they noticed a *Schnell Imbiss* food stall by the side of the road, providing good German sausages and coffee. That would serve nicely for breakfast each morning.

They checked through the equipment they had been provided with. There wasn't much. Presumably they would work out what they needed if and when they found anything. With time on their hands they drove around the area to orientate themselves. At the end of their wanderings they came to the area indicated on the paperwork they had been given.

Not shown on the simple map was the large hill that took up most of the primary search area. They parked the Land Rover and climbed out. They walked up to the top of the hill through an open field that seemed to be mostly used for grazing sheep. As they crested the top they were faced with a fine view of the wide natural harbor and across it to the sprawling city of Kiel. Away to the north a short way they could see a tall white tower. Geordie asked what it was. Jim remembered visiting it years ago when he had been here on a sail training course.

"It's the memorial and museum to the U-Boat service of the *Kriegsmarine*. Really quite impressive. They even have a U-Boat on the beach that you can walk through. I think it might be worth a call in there on the way back to the villa."

They spread out and wandered the hill. There was nothing there. No concrete, no doorways, no roads. Nothing. After an hour of wandering and looking they climbed back into the vehicle and drove out to find the U-Boat museum. As Jim had remembered, the museum was impressive and a reminder of the remarkable courage of the U-Boat crews of the Second World War, so many of whom had not come home again.

They sat, that evening, watching a German football game on the TV and sipping a cold beer. Ivan was the first to bring up the subject when he said, "OK boss. There's nothing where we were thinking the base might be, so where do we look next?"

They couldn't admit defeat that easily so they went back to the papers they had been given. The stories that had been collected indicated that the Germans had selected a hill by the waterside to hollow out to build the base. So they sat at the kitchen table poring over detailed maps of the area and identifying hills that might be big enough.

Geordie managed to cut some hills off the list when he tapped the map. "So how tall is a U-Boat from keel to periscope?" he asked.

Ivan looked at him. "Why the hell would you care?"

"Well, bonny lad, if the sub has to be submerged when it enters the base the water has to be deep enough for it to do that."

It was so obvious and they had missed it. Next morning a rapidly acquired nautical chart of the river showed depths and eliminated hills where the water offshore was too shallow. Jim was quite impressed. That logic had escaped him. Geordie was starting to earn his pay. The next few days were spent wandering the hills that looked promising. There was nothing. They hiked up and down and around getting nothing but muddy boots for their trouble. Ivan was getting irritated by the lack of progress.

They took a break, sitting on a bench overlooking the water.

Ivan turned to Jim. "Boss," he said, "if the U-Boats had to sail through the front door of this base that door had to be pretty big, but even so they must have had navigation markers to guide them in. I wonder if we have more chance of seeing something from out on the water?"

It was worth a try. They hired a small motor boat and spent the next few days cruising slowly up and down the shore looking for any sign of the massive doorway that would be needed, or any marks built on the bank to guide the skippers in. Again nothing. They had found not a single sign that there was any truth in the rumors and legends of the lost base. The strongest indication that this was just a fantasy was that nobody knew about it after years of legend. None of the many hundreds of builders and laborers, who would have been needed, had ever come forward to tell his tale.

Starting to get despondent they decided a night out in a bar with real people might clear their heads. They found a *Gasthaus* on the edge of town and ordered beers. The menu was not large, but looking at the plates in front of the diners around them, the food seemed substantial and inviting. The beer was cold and the waitress attractive and friendly. Geordie's eyes followed the waitress around the room as she delivered the food and beer to the various customers.

"You'll have to stop doing that soon, Geordie, with your wedding getting closer."

"Ivan, I may be on a strict diet, but I am still allowed to look at the menu. Sam knows fine well that I would never let her down."

"You'd be a fool if you did. Sam's way too good for you in the first place."

Geordie smiled contentedly. "Can't argue with that."

The meal went quietly with all three of them lost in their own thoughts. Halfway through a very well prepared *Jaeger Schnitzel,* Geordie put down his knife and fork and said, "I've just remembered something."

The others looked at him and waited.

"Do you remember the guy who played Baldrick in the Blackadder series on TV?"

Jim could not see where this was going, hopefully not to some rehashed Blackadder joke about cunning plans.

Geordie went on, "I've forgotten his name but ..."

"Tony Robinson" Ivan volunteered.

"Why aye, that's him. Anyway, once Sam had gone off to the States and I was stuck in the house watching daytime TV, I saw him fronting some archeological program, digging up Roman ruins in somebody's back garden. They had some electronic kit for detecting anomalies underground. Even if there was not much there, they could see where the ground had been disturbed. It was like one of those ground penetrating radar units, but a hell of a lot lighter and easier to use."

"Like a mine sweeper?"

"Similar, but it didn't need to be metal. Stone or even disturbed earth showed up and when they overlaid it on a map you could see how it fitted into the landscape."

Ivan pushed his plate away. "OK, so what are we looking for?"

The light went on for Jim. "Vents!"

"What?"

"Vents. Any kind of industrial facility where they are running big diesel engines, like those you find on a sub, has got to be able to get rid of the exhaust fumes. The best place to do that would be at the top of the roof because warm air rises."

Ivan had it now, "So if we get one of these detectors we just check the tops of the hills and see if there is anything buried?"

"Seems like a good place to start. OK, Geordie," Jim said, "we have someone who will get it for us, but we need to tell him what to get. What's it called?"

"Away boss, you know us simple Geordies don't do big words."

An enthusiastic Internet search that night revealed that what they were looking for was used in a technique called Archeological Geophysical Survey and the item they needed used Electrical Resistivity Tomography. Even if they had no idea what that meant they could now describe the equipment they needed. A call to the gray man caused a slight sucking of teeth from the other end of the line.

"Give me a couple of hours," he said.

It took a little longer than that, but the next afternoon they were on their way to the Archeological Department of the University of Kiel, on the far side of the city. The professor who met them was almost a caricature of an Archeologist with untidy white hair, dirt under his chipped finger nails and a sunburned face. He did not seem over pleased to be lending his delicate equipment to these three large men, especially as they declined to tell him where it was to be used, but the generous hire fee had convinced him. He was helpful though and offered to loan one of his graduate students to operate the equipment for them. They declined and accepted a two-hour course of instruction instead. With the equipment loaded they headed back to their villa. The next morning they would be back on their target hills to start all over again.

As they drove, Jim was thoughtful. "We are becoming too noticeable," he said, "our employer clearly wants this search to be secret. If we are seen wandering these hills again with this equipment people will start to ask questions."

They could not make themselves invisible so decided that misdirection was their best course of action. A call to the gray man had the right material on the way to them in short order, with no questions asked.

The slow methodical search of the first two hill tops revealed nothing significant on the equipment. The third hill was going the same way until Ivan's turn on the monitor.

"Stop there and mark it!" he yelled from the square, white tent where they had set up the computer monitors on folding tables.

The others inserted a small red flag in the ground to mark the spot and then returned to the tent. Ivan was waiting for them. As they came through the tent flaps he pointed to the rectangular shapes that the monitor screen was showing they had detected. For the first time they had something other than legend.

They returned to the small flag they had used to mark the spot where the shapes were seen. The continuing electronic search was concentrated around it in close, logical sweeps pacing slowly forward and inserting the probes of the detector into the ground at each step. Within the hour they had marked out the extent of the anomaly under the soil on top of the hill. Large rectangular shapes bounded an even larger rectangular dark patch on the scan. They did not have the experience to work out what the various shapes might be from what the computer screen showed them, but they were certainly too regular to be natural.

They stared around them. There was nothing to indicate there might be anything below them. The hill top looked like the rest of the sheep pasture. The only way forward was to dig.

Three feet down, having worked up a good sweat, they hit dressed stone, then the cement between the stones and then the heavy duty metal plate that must be the largest dark rectangle of their scan picture. Two hours later as the evening started to close in, they were sitting together on the stones with their feet dangling over the large metal plate that was now clear of the earth that had hidden it since the end of the war. All three men were running with sweat and out of breath from the digging. But all three were highly elated. Jim heaved himself up and went over to his pack. Pulling out a small blue plastic cool box he walked back over to the structure. The cool box held three cans of cold local beer.

"There you go gents. I have been carrying these around for days just waiting for this."

They sat on the edge of the structure and drank the beer while they contemplated their prize.

"OK boss," said Geordie, "any idea how we lift that bloody great sheet of steel?"

"Oh Geordie, don't tell me all that engineering training Her Majesty paid for was a waste? That's why we have a Land Rover with a winch and an angle iron frame."

"Oh right! An angle frame tripod over the hole with a pulley wheel to direct the cable and we are home free. Sorry, boss, wasn't thinking."

"Well gents, do we open her up tonight or wait for morning?"

Ivan put down his empty beer can and crushed it, then said, "My vote is for now. If there is nothing under there we can move on to the next hill tomorrow."

Geordie nodded his agreement and they set to work. The advantage of working with ex-Royal Engineers is that no long planning sessions are needed when a practical problem has to be dealt with. The angle iron tripod was out of the Land Rover and assembled in short order with the heavy pulley wheel slung beneath it. The Land Rover was moved into position by Jim and the wheels chocked while Ivan and Geordie finished tightening the heavy bolts of the tripod. Geordie checked that the winch was free to rotate and then helped Ivan heave the winch cable out and loop it over the pulley so that the hook at the end was just touching the heavy steel plate. They dug around at the edge of the plate with a shovel and a crowbar until they found the recess the engineers had used all those years ago to hold it as they dropped it into place. They forced the hook into it and started very slowly to winch in.

The steel plate had been down there a long time and had no intention of moving. The winch cable was vibrating and humming with the strain. They were just about to give up and try something else when the dirt and corrosion holding the plate closed surrendered and it flicked up a few inches. Jim stopped the winch quickly so the hook would not slip out and allow the plate to fall back. They secured the hook more carefully and continued with a slow steady pull from the Land Rover winch. Geordie and Ivan slipped angle iron bars in to hold the plate as it rose progressively. Eventually the plate was braced fully open with the spare angle iron beams and they looked down into the hole they had opened. The sky was almost completely dark now so no light shone down into the cavity below them. Ivan fetched the yellow, right angled flashlight from the vehicle's tool kit and they lay on their bellies with their heads over the hole while he shone it down.

"See anything?" asked Jim.

"Not much. There are some shapes down there, but this light isn't powerful enough at this distance."

"Tell you what though. It stinks in there."

"After nearly seventy years without ventilation I'm not surprised."

"How deep do you reckon that is, boss?' asked Geordie.

Ivan reached out and dropped his crushed beer can in to the hole. It seemed a long time before they heard the sound of it striking metal.

He looked up, "Judging by the time to fall and using my mathematical genius I would say it's approximately chuffing deep."

Jim nodded, "We need climbing ropes to get into there and something to help get us back out again. We will need to get ready for an abseiling expedition tomorrow. Our contact should not have any trouble acquiring climbing kit for us."

They dropped the steel plate back into place carefully and disassembled the tripod. They had earned their salt today and despite the tiredness were extremely pleased with themselves.

Chapter 6

The next morning found the team on top of the hill with wet trouser legs from the dew on the grass, but with the tripod and pulley assembled. Jim checked and found that the almost flat top to the hill meant they were not visible from the roads and farms around them. Once again the winch cable was hauled out of the drum on the front of the Land Rover and looped over the pulley, the heavy duty hook was forced around the edge of the plate and the sheet of steel was dragged up. There was considerably less resistance this time, but it was still an effort with a hatch cover of this size. Once the steel sheet was secured firmly in the open position with angle iron beams holding it up, climbing ropes were tied securely to the front of the Land Rover and dropped into the darkness below.

Jim and Ivan had decided they would descend with Geordie providing safety cover from the top of the hill in case anything went wrong. Wearing caver's helmets with lamps and carrying lightweight back packs of equipment, they prepared to lower themselves over the edge with Jim taking the lead. As he dropped below the hatchway he stopped and looked back up.

"Have I ever told you how much I dislike dark enclosed spaces?"

The ropes disappeared into the darkness below him and he dropped slowly and carefully down. They had tied a stopper knot at the end of each rope to ensure they did not slide down too far and start a sudden free-fall, which, with the lack of visibility was some comfort. Jim felt rather than saw the huge space vanishing into the silent darkness as he slid down into the forgotten night of the hill. The helmet lamp showed indistinct shapes below him. As he dropped further into the past these became clearer.

The first shape below him started to resolve into something large and black. A conning tower appeared below him with periscope tubes and antennae pointing at the top of the cavern. He was dropping on to the rear deck of a large submarine. He slowed the descent even more and was soon standing on the metal gratings of the boat to the rear of the conning tower. He checked the grating beneath his feet. It was dry and sound. He swiveled his head to let the helmet lamp sweep around to check for hazards. As far as he could see there were no sharp upright poles or anything else that could ruin Ivan's day as he dropped in. He opened the patch pocket on the leg of his trousers and pulled out the small VHF radio. Thumbing the transmit button he called back up to the surface.

"OK Ivan, you're next to drop into history."

He saw Ivan's legs appear over the rim of the hatchway high above him and then Ivan himself appeared swinging slightly as he slipped down the rope. Ivan's helmet light tracked around, but it was as weak as Jim's and the huge echoing space he was dropping into remained a mystery.

Beyond Ivan, Jim could see Geordie's head outlined against the sky as he lay on his belly staring down and breathing in the seventy-year-old air. From where he lay the helmet lights showed only tantalizing glimpses of what the others were seeing.

Ivan joined Jim on the aft deck of the submarine and unclipped his harness.

"We really must find the marble staircase into this place."

They walked to the edge of the grating and looked over the side of the boat. They saw no water beneath them reflecting their helmet lights back.

Ivan looked at Jim, "Dry dock?"

"Looks like it."

They walked toward the conning tower. This seemed to be a big boat by World War Two standards, but in the darkness it was hard to judge. They walked around the conning tower expecting to see the deck gun in front of them. There was a raised platform and a mounting, but no gun. Apparently the designers had changed their minds or the boat had not been completely equipped when the base was abandoned. They stood on the empty gun platform and looked forward.

In front of the platform, let into the deck they saw a large rectangular hatch, but strangely it had no external means of opening it. Forward of the large smooth hatch, two parallel metal beams were secured to the deck as permanent features. They walked forward between these beams and found that, as they neared the bow, there was a pronounced "up tilt" in them.

Jim looked at Ivan. "This looks a bit like the ski jump fitted to a small aircraft carrier."

"You think they were going to launch aircraft from this?"

Jim shrugged, "Who knows what they were going to do? The Germans were doing some weird and wonderful things by the end of the war."

They turned back to the conning tower still puzzling about the strange contraption on the forward deck. They passed around the conning tower again and made their way back to the aft deck looking for a way off the boat. If this was a dry dock there must be a gangway to the dockside somewhere, but there was nothing on the submarine.

Ivan shrugged off his back pack and having retrieved a more powerful flashlight, he swept it along the dockside. There was a gangway, neatly stowed on the dock with no way to reach it from the deck they stood on. He held the flashlight out as far as he could and shone it down to confirm there was no water below them.

They went back to the conning tower. Set into the side of the structure were rungs leading up. They climbed the rungs and Jim was the first to fling his leg over the top. Ivan followed close behind. They found themselves on the command bridge deck, intended for use during surface operations. Set into the deck gratings was a round hatch with a locking wheel in the center. Jim tried to open the deck hatch. The wheel would not move.

"Ivan, give me a hand with this."

"In a minute boss. I think you might want to see this first."

Jim stood and looked where Ivan was pointing. With the more powerful flashlight they could now see another U-Boat in a second dock. He stared. How big was this place? Ivan tapped him on the shoulder and pointed the other way. As he turned, Ivan moved the big flashlight to show him a third U-Boat sitting quietly in its own dock.

"Have you noticed something strange?" said Ivan.

"What? Stranger than standing on the deck of a seventy-year-old submarine that's sitting inside a hill?"

"Maybe not that strange. But I thought all U-Boats had a U and a number on the conning tower as their designation?"

"I think they did. Why?"

"Look again at that one," said Ivan pointing the torch.

The number was there, but not a U. The numbers on the side of the conning tower read V4-1. There was a stylized red fire breathing dragon painted below the numbers. He pointed the flashlight back at the other boat to read V4-3. Another dragon graced the side of this conning tower as well, this one was yellow. Heaving himself up on the guard rail he looked down at the conning tower of the boat they stood on. The lamp from his helmet showed V4-2 and a blue dragon breathing fire.

Ivan swung the flashlight round to look along the back of the boat. Even with the beam from this more powerful light, the wall of the base behind them was indistinct, although it looked as if there might be doors at that end of the dock. Looking forward was even more unproductive. From the conning tower the flashlight was picking up very little in the way of identifiable features. They returned to the hatch in the deck of the conning tower. Even with two of them heaving on the lock wheel, they could not move it.

"I suppose at the age of seventy it's entitled to be a little difficult," said Jim. "We probably need a good long lever to get this moving." They stood and looked around again.

"Looks like our employer has hit the mother lode down here. How he expects us to sneak these out without the German authorities noticing should be fun to discover. Anyhow, Ivan, can you grab the camera and start taking pictures? He will definitely want to see this."

Ivan took the digital camera out of Jim's backpack and started to take the photographs. He walked along the forward deck and took pictures of the deck rails, then the large hatch. The aft end of the boat seemed unremarkable. He walked all the way back to the vertical stabilizer that rose at the stern. This boat seemed to have two rudders, one above and one below. He dropped to his belly and slid aft. As he looked over he could just see the two bronze propellers and photographed them.

Below them, he could now confirm, was dry concrete. There was a ladder of rungs built into the end wall of the dry dock and he could now see a large rail-mounted lifting gantry with a crane cab slung below it parked at the end of the dock. Hanging from the gantry was a massive red, white and black Nazi flag.

This was clearly a well equipped dry dock; purposely built to service the needs of these specialized U-Boats. He returned to the base of the conning tower. Jim had been searching for another way into the boat without success. There was a further hatch set into the main deck, but it too was unwilling to open after lying undisturbed for all these years.

"Not much else we can do here, boss, these ropes are not long enough to drop us down to the bottom of this dry dock."

"OK, let's start back up. I've not been looking forward to this bit."

Again Jim went first. Using one of the descent ropes as a safety line, he clipped the two moving hand grips from his pack onto the second rope and started to pull himself up, with Geordie reeling in the safety line as he rose. It was a long climb and he was out of practice with climbing equipment. The ascender hand grips made the climb easier, but not easy. The muscles in his arms felt like they were on fire by the time his head emerged from the roof entrance near Geordie's feet. He was out of breath and sweating when Geordie helped him out of the hatchway. Despite the massive size of the base it was still dark and underground and his claustrophobia had been waiting for him to crack.

He had recovered slightly by the time Ivan joined them and he was immensely cheered to notice that, despite his strength, Ivan was just as red in the face.

They briefed Geordie on what they had found. He was keen to take his turn and go down as well, but they had to report in and he was promised the chance to descend the next day. The equipment was packed away and the steel hatch cover dropped into place. The tripod was disassembled and everything removed from the site. From the bottom of the hill no casual passerby would see anything. They drove down the hill and out onto the narrow lane that skirted it. By way of a small celebration, they called in at a roadside *Gasthaus* for a cold beer and a *Bratwurst* on the way to their temporary home. Geordie flipped through the photographs they had taken with the digital camera.

"Quite impressive," he said. "I'll look forward to seeing these on a bigger screen when we get them onto the laptop."

Back at the villa, they fired up the computer and downloaded the pictures from the camera. On the larger screen they were far clearer and they were eager to get back into the cavernous base tomorrow to explore further. While Ivan cooked a late supper, Geordie opened the cold beer from the fridge. If nothing else all this climbing was giving them an excellent thirst. Jim emailed the photographs to the gray man in London with a report of what they had found and a rough outline of what they planned for the next day. He also included a list of the extra equipment needed to survey the base, now that they had a better idea of what they were up against.

All three men were dog tired and were fast asleep seconds after their heads hit their pillows.

Chapter 7

By morning they had a return email detailing where to go to pick up the equipment they had requested. It took a couple of trips back and forth in the Land Rover to get it all in place. Much of it would be staying inside the hill once they had it positioned.

Ivan was the first to go down into the base and the extra ropes and floodlights were lowered to him. He positioned these out of the way on the submarine's aft casing. Jim and Geordie heaved the petrol driven generator into position and lifted it out over the entryway suspended from the winch pulley. Jim abseiled down, past the hanging generator, to be at the bottom to help with handling it when it arrived. The generator was dropped slowly onto the submarine and positioned in the center of the deck grating.

The extra climbing ropes were tied off to the conning tower and the two men clipped on their abseiling harnesses and walked backwards down and around the submarine pressure hull, then dropped down to the floor of the dry dock. Ivan picked up the beer can he had dropped when they first opened the roof hatch and tossed it into the corner of the large concrete basin. They looked around at the towering concrete walls which seemed to be in remarkable condition for their age.

From below, the submarine looked huge and menacing. The massive wooden blocks that it sat on were examined and found to be sound. They walked to the end of the dock; their footsteps echoing off the concrete walls and climbed carefully up the rung ladder in the end wall, checking, as they went, that time had not destroyed the iron or the concrete it was mounted in.

At the top they walked around the dock to the gangplank they had seen on their first visit. Using the rollers it was sitting on, they managed to heave it across the gap to the deck of the submarine. Jim went across first, with Ivan balancing his weight, and secured the inner end to the deck rings aft of the conning tower. The generator and the floodlights were moved across to the concrete dock and set up so that the central area of the base could be illuminated. The generator was

modern and quiet, and the floodlights were lightweight and equipped
with telescopic mounting poles. It was the work of less than an hour to
have lights strung out and the generator running. Jim looked up to see
Geordie's head hanging over the entry hatch waiting for the big reveal.
Ivan flipped the switch and the lights flickered on.

Even these lights could not fully illuminate a space of this size.
The ends of the dock area were still fairly dimly lit. He could see that the
boat they had originally landed on was in the center of the complex, with
another boat to each side of it. Beyond that in one direction was what
looked like another dry dock, but without a U-Boat in it. In the other
direction, beyond the submarine labeled as V4-1, was a wide concrete
area with equipment stacks, heavy looking wooden crates and work
benches. Above them in the darkness they could just see dangling lights
hanging from the roof gantries. Running across the whole space was a
tall moving crane mounted on tracks set into the concrete which at first
glance looked as though it had been designed for very heavy lifting.

Despite the urge to explore immediately, discipline took over and they
continued to bring down the supplies they needed to carry out a full
survey of the base. Extra generator fuel, food, water, tool boxes and oxy-
acetylene cutting gear were all dropped down and maneuvered across
the gangway onto the dock. To save their aching arms at the end of the
day they installed a Boatswain's Chair to lift them back up to the entrance when they finished their work.

After a couple of hours of hard physical labor they were out of breath,
sweaty and glad of a rest. They sat at the side of the central dry dock to
watch Geordie abseil down from the entrance high above, and wondered
if their faces had been like his when they first looked around at this
incredible sight. Geordie had brought down cheese sandwiches and a
flask of coffee for the three of them before they started to investigate.
As they ate their sandwiches, they stared in awe at the sheer size of their
surroundings, a place that had been lost to the world for seventy years. It
seemed a little inadequate to be eating something so mundane in a location of such remarkable historical significance.

Chapter 8

Naturally they all wanted to climb inside the submarines, but they decided to survey the base itself first to ensure it was not in a dangerous condition. They split up. Ivan took one of the big flashlights and headed into the workshop and storage area at one end of the base, Jim found his flashlight and took the area in front of the three submarines, and Geordie headed off toward the empty dry dock at the end away from Ivan.

Jim walked slowly along the dock, checking the condition of the concrete as he went and found himself looking down into yet another apparent dry dock. This one was much larger, with room for any of the submarines to move out of the individual dry docks and maneuver to line up with what appeared to be large exit doors on the far side, behind which there had been some kind of rock fall. There were winches set around the sides to assist with turning the boats which were unlikely to have bow thrusters and other modern conveniences. Jim was about to walk around to investigate the other side of the great doors when he heard Geordie's call echoing through the gloom of the great open base.

"Boss! Ivan! You have to come and see this!"

Walking back down the dock he could see Ivan approaching from the workshop area carrying something. Geordie was waiting for them. As they joined up Ivan handed Jim a dusty steel helmet of the type the Germans used during the war.

"What's so special about that? There's probably quite a bit of personal kit hanging about."

"Yes that's true, boss, but have a look at the helmet markings."

Jim turned the helmet over and looked at the badges on the sides. On one side, a Nazi eagle clutching the Swastika in a laurel wreath in its claws as expected, but on the other side were the angular silver lightning strikes on a black shield that signified the SS.

"There weren't any SS in the Navy as far as I know, so what the hell were they doing in here?"

Geordie stepped up and looked at the helmet. "I think I know the answer to that and you're not going to like it. Come away and look at this."

He led them along the side of the dock behind the U-Boats to the fourth dry dock. As they got closer they could see it wasn't empty, there was a pile of rubbish of some kind in it. It had been used as a dump by the look of it. Geordie led them to the edge of the dock, then after a pause he pointed his large flashlight down into the dock and turned it on. It wasn't rubbish. It was bodies, lots of bodies.

Looking down they could see skulls and hand bones sticking out of rough brown uniforms stained with the ooze of long decomposed flesh. Jaws hung open in an endless scream and empty eye sockets stared toward the roof high above them.

"Bloody hell! Who were they?" said Ivan.

Jim swallowed as he looked down, and once he had control of his feelings he said, "By the look of those uniforms they were Russian prisoners of war being used as slave labor. But how the devil did the Germans keep that a secret? The SS might have been ruthless enough for this, but the Navy people in here would have been pretty decent and they would have spoken about a massacre on this scale, after the war."

Geordie tapped his arm. "Sorry boss, but I can answer that one as well."

He led them to the end of the dock and pointed the flashlight down again. On top of the rough, brown Russian uniforms were blue ones. After the Russians were slaughtered, the *Kriegsmarine* men guarding them had been killed too.

"Charming!" said Ivan. "These SS types were truly princes among men."

"Well," said Jim, "now we know why none of the builders ever talked about this after the war, but I think that blows any chance of sneaking these boats out of here. We have to report this to the German and Russian military authorities so they can look after their own."

"Don't be quite so hasty Major," said a voice from behind them.

They spun round and Jim was pleased to see Geordie and Ivan instinctively move quickly left and right to make the group less of a target. Years of military training takes time to forget. Standing in front of them was the man in the gray suit from London, looking a little less neat after his climb down the rope from the roof entrance.

"Steady lads, he's one of ours," Jim said. The two ex-soldiers relaxed.

"Good timing dropping in while we were looking at this horror. Very dramatic entrance."

"Thank you," said the newcomer walking to the edge of the dock and looking down.

He took the large flashlight from Geordie and walked slowly along the edge of the dock, shining it on the tangled heap of what had once been men. When he turned back to the three engineers he was visibly affected.

"I understand your feelings, gentlemen and I share them. These men deserve to be identified if we can and then properly buried with the honors they deserve. But after seventy years I don't think it's all that urgent. They can be left where they are for a little longer." He looked back into the dock and then said casually, "I think they will forgive us if we delay that secondary issue for a few weeks, don't you?"

Jim could sense Ivan starting to quiver, another statement like that and the gray man was going to end up in the charnel house beneath them.

"I mean no disrespect," he continued, "but if we go public on this too soon they will be used as a political football and our employer will not get what he was seeking here. A short delay would be best for all of us, even for these poor souls."

Ivan calmed slowly and Jim could feel the tension go out of him.

"I think we need to talk. Would you care to join me for a walk round?" Jim asked.

"Certainly, Major, a guided tour of what you have found so far would be most welcome." They walked away.

Jim turned to the other two, "If you have finished your initial look round could you have a try at opening the conning tower hatch we tried yesterday?"

Better to give them a physical task while they were still angry, the extra adrenalin might help. He walked the gray man into the workshop and storage area away from the other two.

"OK. Couple of points to note here. First, never show disrespect to a dead military man while other military men are present, calling them a secondary issue is dangerous. No dead serviceman is a secondary issue to another military man. Second, never sneak up on people in a dark place. My two ex-soldiers there were ready to take you down until I recognized you. Three, you know more about this place than you have told us and that ends now. And fourth, what the hell is your name and who are we working for?"

The man looked at him, "Thank you for the pointers on military etiquette. I will be a little more circumspect around your two heavies in future. You may call me John Smith, for the time being and our employer is a Russian called Maxim Romanov. He is one of those unusual Russian Oligarchs who does not spend his money on football teams or huge houses in London full of young blonde ladies, though he does enjoy some of the finer things in life. As to the further information, I do know a little more, but Mr Romanov is keen to brief you himself tonight when he gets in."

"Fair enough, I will await his briefing with some impatience. Well, in truth, not much to show you yet. We had only just started to survey the site when you dropped in, Mr. Smith. We have found some SS equipment and the bodies you saw. At the front of the dry docks is a large maneuvering area for the boats, which is also dry. We haven't looked in the crates over there yet or inside those doors at the back. I assume the large crates we can see stacked up contain spares and equipment for the boats, but we will confirm that as we go. My guess is that those doors lead to workshops for servicing the boats between missions. And we are just starting to try and get a look inside our first U-Boat."

Smith nodded, "Do you need a German translator to work out what is in the crates?"

Jim shook his head, "We shouldn't need one. All three of us spent time with the army in Germany so we should have enough of the language between us to work it out."

As he finished speaking Ivan's powerful voice echoed from the conning tower of the middle submarine.

"OK boss, it's open."

They walked back to the center U-Boat. Jim pointed out its unusual markings as they crossed the gangway and climbed up into the conning tower. Smith seemed strangely unsurprised.

Geordie and Ivan were both red in the face and breathing heavily. Geordie held the stout metal bar they had used to persuade the hatch that, after seventy years, it was time to open.

Geordie smiled. "We thought our visitor might like to go down first."

Smith nodded and started down.

"Just in case of booby traps," Geordie finished.

Smith was back out of the hatchway and standing beside Jim in a second.

"You'll have to forgive them, Mr. Smith. Army humor can take some getting used to."

Geordie and Ivan were trying so hard not to laugh they were almost crying. Jim couldn't blame them, it was too good a set up to let it go by and they had done it well. He stepped forward and climbed down through the hatchway, into the upper control room, leaving Smith and the other two on the bridge deck. It was pitch dark inside the boat and the air was stale and smelled faintly of diesel oil. He switched on the lamp on his caver's helmet and looked around. Thankfully no bodies.

On the forward bulkhead he saw a dull brass plate. He ran his fingers slowly over it. No dust. This boat had been completely sealed for seventy years. He read the plate, 'U-3999, Typ XXII, Blohm und Voss, Hamburg. He dropped down the vertical ladder into the main control room and turned to look aft. On that bulkhead, above the watertight door, he saw a painted sign *Führer Befehl Wir Folgen*. He felt he had stepped back in time to those dark days when boats like this plied their deadly trade out in the cold waters of the wide Atlantic.

The inside of the U-Boat looked very much like the submarine he had visited on the beach at the Kiel U-Boat memorial. Though a little larger it was still cramped with exposed pipes and cable runs. The large instrument dials and control wheels at the various control stations looked archaic, but if they still worked would no doubt do the job. He glanced at the chart table.

The yellowing chart of the North Atlantic lying there was no surprise. The U-Boat's major combat area had been the North Atlantic for the full five years of the Second World War. They had nearly won the war right there by starving the British Isles of food and munitions. Nearly, but not quite. The American entry into the war had changed the dynamics of the Battle of the Atlantic and had saved the British, who were almost worn out by the constant pressure of the battle against the U-Boats of the *Kriegsmarine*. The U-Boats had never managed to overcome the combined fleets. Not for want of trying though.

As he turned over the Atlantic chart the second sheet he spotted was more interesting, a very detailed chart of the Hudson River right up to Manhattan Island. Now why would a U-Boat need that, he wondered?

He moved on slowly, looking around carefully. Aft of the control room was the Chiefs' Mess, then the galley and quite a decent sized storage room for food. Empty now of course, presumably they would have stocked the boat just before she left, to keep the food fresh for as long as possible. Next came the toilets. He must remember to call them "heads," though why the navy called them that he had no idea. The mass of pipes and levers needed to let them evacuate waste when submerged would take some working out.

He moved on into a bunk area. Not much room for each man. It must be quite difficult for a big man to even turn over in there, he thought. He had seen deeper bookshelves. No place for people, like him, with claustrophobia, here. Beyond the accommodation space was the engine room with the two huge, gray painted diesels and then the massive electric motors for use when submerged.

Further on he came to the aft torpedo room. Just two tubes and no space to carry any reloads, so weapons of last resort, he guessed. He moved back through the various compartments and noticed that, although there was a smell of diesel oil, there was no stink of sweat and unwashed bodies or rotting food. This must have been a fairly new boat when it was brought in here, all those years ago.

Forward of the control room he found the radio operator's position and the sound man's position, both looking very crude by modern standards. The wooden case of the Enigma coding machine sat on the desk next to the radio with a yellowing pad of paper waiting for the message that would never come. The next position almost had him stumped until he realized he was looking at a very early radar set, with oscilloscope dials.

Just beyond this technical area he found what could only be the Captain's small bunk room. It could hardly be called a cabin with its small size and curtain door. He stepped in. A battered naval officer's cap lay on the neat bunk with various papers and file folders scattered around it. There was a faded black and white photograph on the tiny desk, of a smiling woman and a small child with Heidi pigtails squinting into the sunlight behind the photographer. They were standing outside what appeared to be a Bavarian style house. He wondered if the girl was still alive and whether her daddy had ever made it home to her, or was he too lying in that obscene pile of bodies. He moved on.

The Officers' Mess was followed by a bunk area and then another, which seemed similar to the Petty Officers' Mess he had seen in the museum U-Boat on the beach. He had to heave at the half open water tight hatch to move further forward. This was different. A large space with two L-shaped steel rails running the length of the compartment.

There were hammocks stowed against the bulkheads. As he moved forward the lamp on his helmet picked out a trolley sitting with its wheels between the rails. Too small for a torpedo trolley although the semi-circles cut in the top frame were clearly to hold something of a similar shape. Against the curved walls of the compartment were a number of heavy duty air tanks that seemed to have no obvious purpose. He realized he was standing on some sort of hydraulic powered lifting mechanism, located right below the large deck hatch he had seen the day before.

He walked through the compartment and through another water-tight door into the forward torpedo room. Usually the largest compart-ment on a submarine, this one seemed small for the size of this U-Boat. As he looked around he could see the four forward torpedo tubes, but only racks for four reload torpedoes. That seemed a small number for the boat's main armament. Something to be puzzled over later.

He returned to the base of the conning tower and shouted up, "All clear, come on down." He waited until the other three were standing on the deck at the base of the ladder and then said, "OK gents, take a look around, but if you don't know what it is don't touch it and if you do know what it is don't touch it either. No souvenirs yet, just photographs."

He handed his caving helmet to Smith and climbed back out of the conning tower, grateful for the slightly fresher air of the underground base. He waited, leaning on the side of the conning tower, letting the others explore the boat without him. By the time they had finished wandering the boat and taking photographs, the day was done. Examining the rest of the base would have to wait until morning. They had an appointment with the mysterious Mr. Romanov.

Chapter 9

Back at their secluded villa they found two large, silver Mercedes saloons parked inside the tall, shielding hedge. The Land Rover and the small Fiat, that Smith had hired, were in a completely different league. As they entered the house they were stopped by a very large man in a roll neck sweater and black leather jacket. He didn't speak, and just blocked the hallway with his hand resting on Smith's chest.

A voice from the living area called through in what sounded like Russian and the large obstruction stepped out of the way; as he did so his jacket swung open just enough for Jim to register the shoulder holster and the butt of a serious looking automatic pistol. They walked into the sitting room to find a slim, smiling, young man in a well cut, but somehow ill-chosen suit sitting in the best chair. Another two large men in matching leather jackets were behind him. Jim checked and noted that both jackets bulged, just a little, under the armpit. Three bodyguards seemed rather a lot for a law abiding country like Germany.

The smiling, but strangely cold-eyed, man stood. "Welcome home gentlemen. I am Romanov."

They introduced themselves one by one. Jim was intrigued to note that Smith introduced himself as well. Presumably he had never met his client, face to face, either. The three heavies in the leather jackets had spaced themselves out around the room, with their backs to the wall. Whether this was for show or they really did expect their client to be attacked, it made for an uncomfortable situation and Jim noticed that his two men were keeping a wary eye on the bodyguards. Romanov waved the four of them into chairs.

"A long day for you, I imagine, gentlemen. Can I offer you something to drink? I have some rather nice whisky that I always bring with me when I travel, if you would like to try it?" All four nodded.

"Andrei! Five more whiskies!"

A small man in a dark suit appeared from the kitchen carrying a tray with the whisky bottle and the five cut-glass tumblers. He looked like the sort of man who was a past master at fading into the background to avoid being noticed. Jim looked at the bottle as Andrei passed him. A Macallan 12. Now that was a nice whisky. No water or ice was on offer so apparently they were to appreciate it properly. Andrei poured five generous measures and passed the glasses around.

Romanov raised his glass. "Your good health, gentlemen," then took a surprisingly large mouthful.

Drinkers of fine whisky usually savor the smell, the look and the subtle tastes of a good whisky; rather like wine drinkers, but with far less pretension. Jim sniffed quietly and then sipped. He looked at Andrei, but saw no sign that this was a joke. He knew this whisky well; it was a Famous Grouse, a good whisky in its own way but tasting nothing like a Macallan. Interesting.

Romanov put down his glass, "Now I expect that you wish to know what I know about the U-Boat base. My research agents spent a lot of time in dusty archives to make this possible. You have seen the documents I sent to Mr. Smith for you and clearly they were enough to help to find the base and to effect an entry. My congratulations for that, by the way. There will be a bonus in your salary this month. But now, tell me, how much do you know about the German V-weapons from the last war?"

Geordie was the first to answer. "They were Hitler's Vengeance weapons when the war started going badly. The V1 was the first cruise missile and was mostly used to hit London from France as that's a nice big target and they weren't very accurate at that range. The other one was the V2, a missile that was almost the equivalent of a modern ICBM. The Americans captured some and started their space program with them."

Romanov nodded, "That is as much as most people know, but there is more to tell. There was also a V3 which was a huge, smooth-bore cannon system that was also going to pound London to rubble. The first site was captured by the advancing allied armies before it was ready to use and the second site could not hit anywhere very important, but it was used. Interestingly, Saddam Hussein of Iraq also tried to build one to bombard Israel, but that was foiled by some Customs Inspectors in England who found the parts being shipped to him. The Americans also took some V1 flying bombs back for experiments and tested them in various launch methods, including from the decks of landing ships and submarines. They even built some copies of their own to continue the testing. Those are the ones that are commonly known."

He took another large mouthful of whisky from his crystal tumbler before continuing.

"There was also a multi stage missile that was a development of the V2 rocket and was called the A10. That was intended to hit New York and other cities, when launched from Germany, but it was never finished. The one very few people know about was the V4 which is what you have found for me. The V4 was to be the *Kriegsmarine's* contribution to Hitler's vengeance."

He paused and took another heavy swig from his whisky glass, which had been quietly refilled by his servant.

"The Germans could have won the war in Western Europe, but they abandoned the invasion of England and turned on my country, Russia. That was a foolish error, as we all know. They might have gone back to the invasion of England later, but America entered the war and changed everything. The V4 was the vengeance weapon to punish America. These submarines were designed to sail close to large American cities near the east coast and from their decks to launch modified V1 flying bombs. The terror would have been incredible. The US homeland was not prepared for war and no real precautions had been taken. They did not even turn off their lights in the cities, so confident were they that they were untouchable. Luckily for them, the war ended just before the V4 system could be deployed."

Jim was taken by surprise. The significance of the V4 markings on the conning towers had not occurred to him.

"But why are you prepared to spend so much money to get hold of these submarines? And it won't be easy to get one out, by the way."

"Major Wilson, you cut straight to the point. That is good, I like that. In the turmoil in Russia as the communist state collapsed and we moved to democracy, there were remarkable opportunities for men like me to make money, a lot of money. I have more money now than I could spend in a dozen lifetimes. So I want to use that money to re-build Russian pride in ourselves and our country. When my country was invaded by the Germans and their allies, millions of our people were slaughtered. There are crumbling monuments to our heroes all over Russia and the Ukraine. But nowhere is there a museum that shows the true extent of what we did. One of the finest armies from one of the most technically advanced countries in the world attacked us and we won. Our people are starting to forget what we as a nation achieved.

It was the Russians who stopped Hitler and it was not so easy. I want to tell that story to rebuild Russian pride in our history and achievements. One of these boats will be a major part of that."

Ivan leaned forward and said, "Hang on, sir. These boats never went to war, so how are they part of that?"

"A good question, my friend. If Russia had not destroyed the German army and drained their forces away from the Western front, the British and Americans would not have reached as far as they did, as fast as they did. These boats were mere days, maybe even hours, away from being ready and they would have launched from this base and their missiles would have rained down on American cities, killing many of their people. I want the Americans to understand that. They owe us much more than they ever knew."

Jim looked at his team. They were nodding. It was a good argument and the museum a worthwhile goal.

"You know about the bodies in the base, I take it?" Jim said.

Romanov put down his glass. "Yes, Mr. Smith called me about them. My countrymen were used as slave labor and then murdered to keep the secret. They will have a heroes' burial, all together, next to my museum on the Black Sea coast."

"That works for me, boss," said Ivan and Geordie agreed.

"OK, Mr Romanov, as you can see, on that basis, we have no problem carrying on working with you."

Romanov was pleased. "Good," he said and turned toward his servant. Jim was surprised to see him still there, his talent for fading into the background was very well developed.

"Andrei more of my good whisky for my friends!"

Chapter 10

In the morning they climbed into the big blue Land Rover and headed out to the base, leaving the large saloon cars behind. It was a tight fit as all three of the bodyguards insisted on coming along and crammed themselves into the drop down seats in the cargo area. As they drove up the hill track to the tent they had left on site; they saw three local teenagers wandering up from the other side. The bodyguards reached under their jackets and prepared to jump from the still moving vehicle.

"No! Stay where you are!"

Jim knew they didn't understand him, but his meaning was clear and years of command had given him the manner to get people's attention. They stopped the vehicle and taking their cue from Jim, all climbed out casually. Jim nodded to Ivan who steered the leather jacketed men away from the youngsters.

"Geordie, time for you to do your thing."

Geordie grinned and walked over to the inquisitive visitors. His German was good, if a little rusty, and soon he had them walking into the white tent.

"Will he hold them in there?" said Romanov.

"Nothing so dramatic. Wait."

After a little less than fifteen minutes the teenagers left the tent with Geordie following them, still inviting them back. They accelerated away from him.

Smith turned to Jim "How did you do that?"

"You remember those odd items that I asked for? Roman pottery, broken Roman pottery in fact. Well Geordie has just been telling them far more than they ever wanted to know about the significance of two-thousand-year-old broken Roman pottery. He has bored them away. They should tell all their friends how dull we are and with luck they will avoid us like the plague."

"But how does he come to know so much about Roman pottery?"

"He doesn't. He knows damn all about it, but Sergeants are famous for coming up with convincing stories to get themselves out of trouble. He has just woven them a little boring fantasy." Jim looked around, "Mr Romanov, can I suggest one of your friends stays up here for security? And please tell him to be discreet, we really do not want to attract attention."

Romanov called his men over and briefed one of them, then he and the other two walked up to the entrance hatch that was now open. Ivan and Smith had already gone down. The rest of the group followed quickly.

As Jim landed on the deck of the middle submarine he looked at the three Russians. All of them were staring around, taken by surprise by the sheer scale of the base.

"What would you like to see first?"

Romanov looked at him with wide eyes, "Everything."

The next hour passed with Jim showing the Russians and Smith around the base, pointing out the things they had found. They were quiet when standing by the fourth dry dock, staring down at a war crime. The maneuvering dock impressed them and they wanted to know how to make it work.

Jim explained. "We have yet to get in there and see what the Germans did to disable it. After that we can see if it is possible to bring it back to a working condition."

While the tour was going on Ivan and Geordie had continued their own exploration of other parts of the base. As Jim climbed back out of the conning tower after the inspection of the center U-Boat his two men were sitting on a crate by the gangplank, waiting for him.

"Hi boss. We've found all sorts of fun things. Can we leave these guys to play while we show you?"

"Is there anything we can send them off to look at?"

"Yeah. Over behind the crates on the workshop area there is a green metal door that leads through into what looks like it was the Headquarters for the base. Nice little Officer's Mess with a bar and some offices with desks that have papers scattered around. Quite a few bits of uniform lying about too, even one or two weapons. It looks like they all left in a bit of a hurry."

"That will do nicely." He turned to see Romanov coming across the gangplank. "Mr. Romanov I think we have found something right up your street. Geordie, will you show Mr. Romanov to the HQ complex and then come back to me?"

The Russians and Smith trailed behind the tall Englishman and went behind the stack of crates. Geordie reappeared moments later and they met at the rear of the dock basins.

Jim looked at his team, "OK gents what have you got?"

Ivan led the way to the large metal doors at the rear of the base. They had been heavily padlocked, but a large crowbar with Welsh muscle behind it had easily corrected that. He swung the door open and stood back. Jim looked past him and had to admit they really had found something. Lined up in the bay, on trollies just like the one he had seen inside the submarine, were row after row of V1 Flying Bombs. He walked in, counting as he went. There were thirty-two of them, with cradles ready for at least another twenty. He stood and looked at the size of the missile and its trolley, imagining the space he had seen inside the submarine.

"My guess is that each sub will take ten of these," he said turning to his team.

"Yeah, that was our guesstimate as well," said Geordie. "Quite a payload. Ten of these arriving in an unprepared city would have caused absolute chaos."

"That's not quite all, boss. Come next door."

Ivan led the way as they walked around to the next bay.

Jim looked above the double metal doors to read *"Der Atem Des Drachen,"* painted on the wall in Gothic script. The crowbar had done its work here as well. This bay was different. It was equipped as a laboratory of sorts. Nose cones that were clearly for the V1's were lined up along a wide wooden wall bench and in front of each one was an aluminum frame with a mechanism attached. Across the room were large steel tanks and in front of these were cases of round glass canisters set into yellow foam padding. The middle of the room was taken up with chemical apparatus. There were protective suits and goggles hanging on racks and large ventilators set into the ceiling. There was something familiar about all this. It took a second or two for the memories to click back into place.

"Oh my God. Do you know what this is?"

"We were rather hoping you would know," said Geordie.

"When I was instructing Officer Cadets at Sandhurst, one of the PowerPoint lectures had a picture very similar to this in it. It was of the early years of the Chemical Warfare Research facility at Porton Down. This is a laboratory for assembling chemical warheads."

"Very good, Major," said Romanov from the doorway. "We clearly picked the right man for this job." Romanov walked into the laboratory and looked around. His bodyguards stayed in the doorway, watching. "Yes, the attack the Germans were planning on New York was to be chemical. Hitler had always shied away from using chemical warfare in Europe because he thought the allies had better chemical technology and would use it in retaliation. Maybe even that madman was horrified by the gas attacks he had seen during the First World War? Historians have always thought that the 'D-1' model of this missile, with its chemical warhead, was developed but never went into production. It seems they were wrong. By this stage of the war Hitler was getting desperate and wanted to truly terrorize the Americans so overcame his own horror of chemical warfare. Apparently he thought the outcry would be so great that the US would pull out of the war."

"So what gas is this material intended for?" asked Ivan.

Romanov paused, looking at the tanks against the wall, then said, "My researchers tell me it was nerve agent. The Germans had been working on three very effective types, but all had problems. They were either too corrosive to store for long periods, or they deteriorated and lost their efficacy. This system was the solution, binary warheads. The nerve agent components were stored in different containers and were only mixed to form the toxic material as the missile had almost landed. It also made it much safer for the crews to handle. The missiles next door and these warheads, when launched from those submarines, constituted the V4 system and they were only days away from initiating the first attacks on New York when the Germans surrendered in May 1945."

"This lab is well named then," said Jim.

"What do you mean Major?"

"The sign above the door as you came in reads 'The Breath of the Dragon,' which also explains the designs on the submarine conning towers."

Geordie had wandered across to one of the large stainless steel tanks and tapped the dials. "Err, boss. According to this gauge this tank is still pretty full."

Ivan stepped to the second tank and tapped the gauge on that one, "And this one."

Jim turned to Romanov. "You seem to be remarkably well informed about these missiles, especially since they were so secret. You must be aware this is pretty risky stuff to handle. If you won't inform the German government, then we need a couple of very careful industrial chemists to deal with all of this and make it safe."

"I make it a point to be well informed before I commit to any enterprise, Major. And as for the chemists they are already on their way from one of my laboratories in Moscow. They should be here in a couple of days and should have made this safe by early next week."

Chapter 11

Back in the main dock area Romanov turned to Jim. "Major, I think it is time for you and your team to solve our major problem."

"Which is?"

"How are you going to get one of my boats out of here so that we can sail it around to my museum on the Black Sea?"

Jim thought about it for a moment, "The big problem is going to be opening the front door and flooding the dry docks without destroying them," he said. "The mechanisms are pretty old and we haven't even found out how to open the main entrance yet. Plus, the Germans may have left some nasty surprises for us when they moved out of here."

"Indeed. Then I think I would be happy if you started solving those two problems for me."

Jim nodded, "You have one or two other small problems to solve."

Romanov had been turning away but stopped, "And they are?"

"Those submarines have been there for seventy years or so. Seals could have dried out, if they weren't properly prepared and batteries will have deteriorated. A thousand things could fail and if you are underwater that's not what you want. It's lucky the base has stayed so dry or there could have been major corrosion problems as well."

"All true, Major, but once we are on our way and clear of German territory, there will be very little time spent underwater. But you are of course correct and I have hired some submarine engineering experts, who are also on their way, to check which of these boats is in the best condition and to carry out whatever maintenance is needed. I may ask you to help them later."

Romanov turned and walked away, back toward the V1 storage warehouse.

Jim turned to his team, "OK, you heard the man. Let's go and solve some serious engineering problems."

They walked along the docks between the submarines until they came to the large maneuvering dock at the front end. They located a set of rungs set into the concrete and climbed down. As they walked across to the huge steel doors they could appreciate the scale of this place even more. The vision and skill of the engineers who had built all of this was truly staggering. Their methods in using prisoners of war as slave labor was considerably less impressive and the treatment of those men at the end was awful.

They reached the doors and started to examine them. There was no water seepage around or under them, so presumably the other side must be dry. But it would be wise to check before opening them. If they got it wrong and managed to open the doors too quickly, the rush of water would be fatal to anybody in the dock and could well smash the inner dry dock doors protecting the three submarines.

Ivan climbed the gates and identified a valve wheel on top of the adjoining coffer dam wall. It hadn't been moved in a long time, but had been well greased before the base had been abandoned so a large amount of force from the big man's shoulders and arms persuaded it to turn. They heard the valve operate within the wall, but nothing came from the inlet tube. It was a fair bet that it was completely dry on the other side. Ivan walked along the top of the gates, the wall of the cavern came down almost in line with the exterior wall of the maneuvering dock. Beyond the gates he could see that the hill above appeared to have been partially collapsed into the entrance tunnel and concrete had been poured over that. Not a trivial task to remove safely. He dropped down another steel ladder to join the others.

"As far as I can see, boss, the doors are safe to open. That should give us a good look at what we are going to have to deal with."

They identified the gate opening mechanisms, and after considerable effort and the judicious use of some favorite Army swear words, managed to free them. The doors themselves did not move. Climbing back up out of the maneuvering dock they brought one of the dock winches into use. Reeling out the cable, they connected it to the dock gates and started to reel it back in manually with the long winch handle. The cable tightened, vibrated, and strained. Jim and Ivan standing in the bottom of the dock retired to a safe distance; a cable of that size would be a little too exciting if it snapped and started to whip around the concrete basin. Little by little the dock gates gave up and swung slowly open to reveal the mass of material they were going to have to shift. It was just short of overwhelming. Luckily for Mr. Romanov, Royal Engineers are used to destroying large things and the mining expertise from Geordie gave them a real chance of success.

They sat on the concrete floor of the maneuvering dock with their backs against the wall, staring at the pile of rubble in front of them that had to be shifted and wondering how deep it was. And even when they had blown it apart how the hell were they going to handle the huge mass of stone and debris, without heavy machinery like bulldozers?

Smith's head appeared over the dock above them, "Mr. Romanov was wondering how you were getting along?"

Ivan looked up at him, "Just peachy. We just need a couple of picks and shovels and we'll magic that lot out of there in no time."

Smith looked across to where Ivan was pointing, "Oh. I see your point. Can I help?"

Jim looked up and said, "Actually you can. We need three sets of SCUBA gear, an inflatable dinghy and a compressor. Then we can take a look at this from both sides to make a full assessment."

"No problem," said Smith, as his head vanished.

Geordie had been quiet for a long time. Jim nudged him, "Go on then, what are you thinking?"

"Not sure yet, boss, but something doesn't add up."

"Go on."

"Well, we know the people who built this were bloody good engineers. So why didn't they just collapse the lot? Why go to all the trouble of just blocking the water tunnel, unless they were intending to come back one day? Then the other thing, we've all seen demolitions and I've seen mining cave-ins. Did you ever see one that was watertight like this before? There is always some trickle of air or water between the rocks and rubble especially if there is pressure behind it like, I guess, there is over there. Yet, that is bone dry after seventy years. It just doesn't seem right somehow. See what I mean?"

They did, Geordie was right; a totally watertight, explosive demolition was unlikely and why go to all that trouble unless the plan was to come back to the base in the future?

The three engineers walked back to the rubble wall. Jim laid his hand on it and looked up. It was too neat. There should have been debris in the maneuvering dock, but it was clear. The walls of the base should have been damaged, but they were intact. Looking at it from here with a different viewpoint the collapsed walls look false, as though it had all had been staged to look more difficult than it actually was.

"Let's get outside and look at this. We're missing something," said Jim. He led the way back across the empty dock and toward the exit.

The exterior water gates to the maneuvering dock were lined up with the bow of V4-2, the middle U-Boat. By looking down from the entryway on the top of the hill they should be able to line up where the other end of the underwater exit could be found.

As they climbed out of the hatch on the hilltop, Smith met them and told them the diving gear was on its way.

"There's a narrow lane that runs through the trees between the hill and the waterside," said Jim. "Get it delivered down there, will you."

He turned back to the others. Ivan nodded; he had lined up the submarine bow and now knew which direction they needed to walk to find the underwater entrance, if it was still there. Using the Orienteering compass from his pack he led them in a straight line down the hillside, over a couple of wire sheep fences and on to the water's edge. While they were waiting for the diving gear to arrive they took a look around, but there was nothing to suggest a tunnel beneath them. Jim sat down on a block of concrete at the waterside to wait and contemplated the oddly shaped boulder between himself and the water.

"Ivan," he said as the big man approached, "have you ever realized you have been blind?"

"Not recently boss, what's up?"

"In front of me down by the water is a large boulder with a deep notch carved in the top and under my backside is a concrete block with a hole in it. What do you bet that if I fitted a pole in the hole and then aligned it with that notch, through my periscope I would have my boat lined up exactly on the tunnel?"

"Worth making it the start point of the search at least, boss. The truck is arriving with our gear, by the way," Ivan said, pointing along the track to where a white pickup truck was slowing down.

The pickup truck, driven by Smith, pulled up alongside them.

"Everything you asked for is here," he said. "I even got you a small dinghy with a compressed air cylinder instead of a pump."

The breathing cylinders were already charged as they unloaded them. They tested everything as they assembled it and then changed into the wetsuits.

"Do we need the dinghy yet?" asked Ivan, grabbing hold of the tightly rolled carrying case.

"No, not for the first dive I think. Let's leave it nicely packed away in case we need it later. If I am right the entrance is right under our feet, or at least not far away."

They continued struggling into the wetsuits by the side of the truck and then helped each other to put on the heavy tanks and weight belts. They then walked down to the water's edge and shuffled slowly backwards into the water to avoid problems with the fins they had slipped on to their feet. As usual, at this time of year, the water of the Baltic was much warmer than the adjoining North Sea, so the swim would be reasonably pleasant.

They swam a few yards from the shore and dived under the surface to find that the bottom had dropped away beneath them rapidly. It was an almost vertical drop into the depths. They paused at a depth of about ten feet to check that each of them was alright and the equipment was functioning before they began to descend further. They swam down until they reached the bottom and then turned toward the hill. After no more than a few minutes of pushing weeds aside, they found the entrance to a large tunnel. It could only be the one they were looking for. Keeping close to the bottom to avoid the weeds hanging from above, they swam in.

The weeds that had grown around the tunnel entrance stopped much of the surface light so the powerful underwater flashlights, which Smith had included in the kit, were very valuable. The lights showed that the walls of this tunnel were lined with large and solidly mounted square stones, so it was certainly man made. As they moved deeper into the tunnel they saw heavy scrapes in the stonework. Bringing a large submarine in through here was not that easy, then.

They moved on slowly checking the condition of the tunnel walls and roof as they went. The lack of tides and current in this area meant that the water had been kind and the tunnel was still in good shape. After swimming for more than three hundred meters, they reached the answer to the riddle. There was no rubble from a collapsed tunnel. Instead there was a huge single piece of steel with heavy angle cross braces bolted and welded to it, holding it rigid. They swam to the sides and to the bottom of this monster door. It was mounted in large steel tracks that held it rigidly in place and presumably gave it the watertight seal it needed. They found no sign of any controls that might be used to open it. Curiosity satisfied, they swam back out of the tunnel and into the light.

Smith was waiting for them on the bank, almost hopping from foot to foot with excitement. "Well, did you find it and can you open it again?"

"Oh yes. We just need to find the key."

They took their time changing out of the wetsuits and back into their usual clothes. They used the time to orientate themselves with their surroundings. Beyond the exit of the tunnel was a broad stretch of water with the sprawling outskirts of the city of Kiel beyond it. There was plenty of room for maneuvering the submarine, if they could find a way to get it out. The German engineers who built this base had chosen their location well.

They climbed into the bed of the pickup then Smith drove them back along the country lane, and up onto the hill top.

Chapter 12

Once inside the base they examined the rubble obstructing the tunnel again. With large crowbars and the application of some well-considered physical effort, they toppled one of the smaller boulders from the top of the wall down into the maneuvering dock. Beneath it they found the top of the outer steel wall that was holding back the water of the Baltic.

"Well," said Ivan, "now we know all we have to do is lift that huge heavy door out of there and we have cracked it. It should only weigh a few tons. You want to take one end, Geordie and I'll grab the other?"

Jim looked around, appraising the options, "Geordie, can you go back to the central area and angle a couple of those floodlights upwards."

Ten minutes later the roof of the base was illuminated by the lamps. With the lights shining up, they could see that the overhead gantry crane extended far further forward than they had anticipated. At its furthest travel it would be directly above the steel guillotine door.

Jim shook his head, "You have to give it to them. Whoever designed and built this place sure as hell knew his job and by the look of things, they intended to come back here one day to finish what they started."

Moving the curtain wall of rocks should be fairly simple with small, strategically placed explosive charges. Being inside the hill would muffle the noise, so nobody outside would hear anything untoward. The steel wall would hold the water back while they cleared the entry tunnel. The problem was going to come as they started to lift. The pressure of water through the tunnel would be intense. They would need a way to control that.

But first things first. The three engineers spread out and started to check that the valves controlling the flow of water into the three smaller dry docks, containing the submarines, were functional. They then worked together to ensure that the dry dock gates themselves actually functioned and were not going to jam halfway open. It was midnight as they climbed out of the third dry dock to make their way home for some well deserved rest.

Smith was waiting for them as they headed for the center submarine to make the climb back to the surface.

"Ah, gentlemen," he looked uncomfortable, "I really hope you don't mind but Mr. Romanov feels that we need to accelerate the work down here, to get his submarine out before the German authorities become aware of us."

"And?" said Jim.

"And so he has decided that you gentlemen and I should sleep inside the base from now forward."

"And if we do not agree?" said Ivan.

"He really was most insistent and he feels he is paying you more than enough to compensate for a little discomfort. Plus, he really is not a man you want to irritate."

He was paying them generous salaries and they had all slept in far worse places over the years, so they accepted the request without too much complaint. Apart from anything else, they were too tired to argue. Smith directed them to the Officers' Mess where camp beds had been set up for them. As they walked in they found Andrei waiting for them. His skill at fading into the background did not seem to be needed here as he wore a crisp white chef's jacket and a broad smile. He had a large hot meal simmering on the stove for them and even some of Romanov's special whisky. After dinner Jim found he was alone with Andrei while the others sorted themselves out for sleep.

"So Andrei, does Mr. Romanov know you replace his fine single malt whisky with a cheaper blended kind?" He had meant it as a gentle joke, but the terror in Andrei's face made it abundantly clear he had not taken it that way.

"*Derr Mo!* Have you anything told him?"

"No of course not. I like the joke."

"Mr. Romanov is not liking other people's jokes. He can be violent if his dignity is laughed at."

"So why do it then?"

"I did it once some years ago before I knew what Romanov was and is. Now I have to keep doing it or he will notice. I was just trying to build up my income a little. I thought it would be harmless."

Jim was thoughtful. The fear in this man was palpable.

"Don't worry, he won't hear it from me, ever."

For a moment he thought Andrei would cry. Instead he nodded and turned away, but his breathing was ragged. Now just what kind of man was Romanov to provoke such fear?

Chapter 13

The night in the base had passed quietly. No ghosts from the fourth dry dock had come to trouble them and the silence had been restful. Washing water had been lowered down in drums during the previous day, along with all the equipment to let them set up a more or less comfortable home within the base. Jim woke to find Ivan and Geordie already sitting at a table and quietly working. He struggled out of the sleeping bag, rose from his camp bed, then padded across to see what they were up to. Spread across the table were three stripped down MP40 sub-machine guns from the Second World War. They were cleaning them with the attention to detail demanded by Sergeant Majors the world over.

"Morning boss, how do you like our Schmeisers?" asked Geordie.

Jim looked the old weapons over, "So are you expecting World War 3 to break out anytime soon?"

"Not really boss, but those goons in the leather jackets are winding us up and we were a bit bored waiting for you to finish snoring."

He left them to it and went in search of breakfast. Andrei seemed pleased to see him and made him a plate of superb scrambled eggs on toast with lean bacon.

Smith joined him as the coffee arrived, "What's the plan today, Major?"

Jim looked at him over the rim of his coffee mug. "If you have got us the C4 explosives we asked for we are going to start demolishing the curtain wall in front of the exit tunnel. Once that is out of the way we are going to see if we can lift the gate out of the way and flood the maneuvering dock. Should be quite exciting, you might want to bring a camera to record the big event."

"Oh, I don't think Mr. Romanov would want cameras around."

Jim was surprised, "Why ever not? Surely the story of how we recovered the submarine would be useful for his museum of Russian triumphs?"

"Perhaps. I'll see what he says."

Smith got up and left as Ivan and Geordie came in.

"Finished playing with your antique toys, gents?"

"For now, yes," said Ivan.

"Where did you find them anyway?"

"There were some down in the pit with the bodies. It looked like the navy lads were holding them when they were gunned down, but they were rusty and pretty gummed up by the rotting bodies. But they gave us the idea so we had a look round in here and found a small armory with weapons, greased up for storage and in remarkably good condition."

They finished the coffee and set off toward the work area, to start assembling the demolition charges.

"Did you find any ammunition for them?" Jim asked as they walked.

"Not in the weapons themselves, but there were boxes of ammunition and spare magazines in a separate store room near the armory at the back of this office area. Nice and dry in there so it should all work when we get the chance to try them out. There were some other nice toys too." Ivan said.

The rest of the morning passed in carefully putting the explosive charges together and identifying the best places to lay them. Geordie used the compressed air hammer drill to create holes in the rock wall where Ivan and Jim had indicated.

"I always hated this job in the coal mines," Geordie said, wiping the dust from his forehead. "I always thought the vibration was going to bring the bloody roof down."

They decided to make the demolition progressive with the smallest charges possible to avoid a major shock to the steel water door behind the rocks. They placed a row of seven small charges to loosen and lift the top strata of rock. Once that was dealt with, they planned to move progressively downwards. Having connected the detonator box to the charges, they retired to a safe distance behind one of the larger winches.

Ivan stood and yelled in his booming Welsh baritone, "Fire in the Hole!"

He ducked down again and Geordie pushed the button. Even though the charges were small the echoing noise in the enclosed chamber made their ears ring. The dust cloud rolled over them as they heard rocks rolling and crashing on the concrete floor of the dock.

Jim looked at Ivan, "Why are you smiling?"

"Look over there, boss."

Jim looked. The two leather jacketed bodyguards had their weapons drawn and were looking about them. The panic in their faces was clear, even at this distance. Amusing and interesting. Ignoring the Russians, they climbed back down into the dock to admire their handiwork. The top row of stone had mostly toppled into the dock leaving one large stone teetering and ready to fall. The wall below the top row had gained some cracks, but the steel gate behind looked untouched.

It was the work of only a few minutes, using a pair of large crowbars, to topple the teetering rock into the maneuvering dock, so that it was safe to begin to deal with the rest. Rather than try to lift the large rocks out of the dock, they had decided to use the handling winches to haul them across the dock floor and leave them in front of the dry dock with the bodies in it. They would not be needing to open the gates to that charnel house.

The winches did their work well and the rocks were hauled out of the way. Romanov came to the top of the dock wall and stood watching for a while. The scraping of large stones on concrete made conversation impossible and he went away again, apparently satisfied that progress was being made. After another bout of drilling, the charges were laid for the second row of stones. Before blowing this row Ivan went to the back of the docks to tell the Russians they were about to hear another explosion. He came back and sat down with the others behind the winch.

"Romanov brought in some of the specialists he was talking about. There are some characters in white coats in the laboratory and I saw people with bloody big tool boxes heading into the center U-Boat."

Jim nodded, "Doesn't waste any time does he? Do your thing again, will you?"

Once again Ivan's powerful cry of "Fire in the Hole" echoed round the base.

This time people on the submarine casing stopped to watch and others in white lab coats came out of the doors at the back of the base to do the same. Geordie pressed the detonator button and they were once again rewarded with a highly satisfactory controlled explosion. When the dust settled they could see that the second row of rocks had dropped into the dock and again the water gate was undamaged.

The rest of the day passed in a routine of explosion followed by the noisy hauling of large rocks.

By the end of the day the massive rock wall was gone and the heavy steel water gate was exposed. The vibration of the series of demolitions had shaken the gate, but not damaged it. But now water was slowly seeping around it. The shaking had loosened the seal around the gate, so lifting should be a little bit easier.

Covered in dust and with the gritty feeling between their teeth that always comes with demolitions, the three engineers stopped for the day and went to clean up. There was no sign of Romanov, but they found they had company for dinner. The chemists and the people on the U-Boat were already eating as they arrived, nobody greeted them until Andrei came into the room and gave them a beaming smile.

"Your dinner will be ready as soon as you have already cleaned up, my friends," he said, laying another steaming bowl of stew in front of the chemists. "With all the extra people I now have an assistant to help with the cooking."

They were highly delighted to find that the showers were now working and despite the water being cold they could rid themselves of the dust and grit. Andrei came in and collected their clothes.

"I will deal with these for you," he said, as he whisked them away.

Geordie looked after him, "He'll make somebody a bonny wife one day."

"Cut him a little slack," said Jim, "he has his own problems and I have the feeling we may be glad of him one of these days."

They made their way back to the tables set up for dinner. The rest of the people in there had finished their stew and were wandering off to find their beds when Andrei and his new, and very attractive assistant came through carrying three large portions of steak with all the trimmings. The workers leaving were clearly not impressed.

"OK boss," said Geordie, "whatever I was thinking about this wee guy I take back. I had been dreaming about a steak after all that rock heaving."

Dinner finished, Jim went through to the small kitchen area with the plates. "Andrei that was a terrific meal, but how come we got steak and the others got stew?"

"Major, when I was in the Red Army we always said you should never be rude to the people who make your food."

"The British Army has the same saying, it must be true the world over."

"Well I have done nothing bad to those people's food, but I do not have to give them my best. The Germans working on the U-Boats I do not like. And the chemists are scum from Romanov's organization. All of them treat me like the cleaning woman. You and your men are not like that."

"Whatever your reasons, those were three great steaks, so thank you for that. Aren't you going to introduce me to your new friend?"

Andrei nodded. "Tatiana! Come here and say hello to my friend the Major. He is the one who found this place. Major, this is Tatiana; she is usually the cook on Mister Romanov's yacht on the Black Sea. She is a fine cook, but speaks only a little English although she understands a little more."

Jim looked down into the deepest, darkest brown eyes he had seen in a long time. Her lovely face was framed by long dark hair and, despite the cook's uniform, Jim could see she had a slim and graceful body.

"Well, hello Tatiana. The scenery down here is improving at last."

"Hallo Major. I am being happy to meet you."

The girl gave him a small, shy smile and bobbed her head before scurrying off to the kitchen again. Jim watched the slim form with the long shining hair move gracefully back into the kitchen area.

"A lovely assistant you have there, Andrei."

"That is true, but she is too friendly with Romanov for my taste. I would not advise you to become too close to her."

For a quiet, unassuming man, Andrei seemed to have definite opinions, Jim thought. As he got back to the room he shared with Ivan and Geordie, he found them working at the table again. This time they had found themselves a trio of Luger automatic pistols and were cleaning and oiling them carefully. They seemed to be enjoying a new hobby. He left them to it and went to bed to dream of dark brown eyes.

Chapter 14

They rose early in the morning to find that their new companions had risen even earlier and were already at work out in the base. Andrei joined them as they took their time over their second coffee after breakfast, talking and looking out of the window across the base. Andrei seemed to be more relaxed around them now, and Jim stayed seated at the table with him as the other two men went to pack up their kit from the night before.

"Andrei, I don't know much about you. For instance how long have you worked for Romanov? Where are you from? Are you married? Sorry if that seems nosey, but I do like to know about the people I am working with."

Andrei looked down into his coffee cup for a couple of seconds, then said, "I have worked personally for Romanov for a little too long, almost two years now. We of his household staff usually travel wherever he goes. I think he is a little afraid of being poisoned. Normally we travel between Moscow and down on the Black Sea to Odessa where he keeps his motor yacht. My home is in St. Petersburg and no, I am not married. This life would not be good for such things. But what about you and your men?"

"Not much to tell," said Jim looking out of the window again. "We were all in the Army and were all thrown on the scrapheap when the size of the Army was reduced. We took this job because it's better than sitting on our backsides doing nothing. Our personal lives are complicated. I am divorced, Geordie has a stunning girlfriend who is an actress, she's rehearsing for a play off-Broadway in New York at the moment, and Ivan is a widower.'

Andrei nodded, "How did his wife die? I would not want to say anything that might hurt him.'

"It was a horrible accident," said Jim. "He was stationed up in the Hebridean Islands at the missile testing site the army has up there. One of the missiles went rogue and landed on his house. His wife Mary was inside. Luckily his children were at a kid's birthday party down the road. It is best not to mention it to him. He hasn't really accepted she is dead, since they never found a body or any trace of her. He is still struggling to move on."

"How is he taking care of his children when you are here?"

"They live with his wife's parents in Florida. He doesn't get to see them much. I think the parents blame him for their daughter's death. They don't make him welcome."

He stopped talking as the other two men came back into the room. They all thanked Andrei for the coffee, and then wandered down to the water gate. The water was dribbling in and there was a large wet patch across the dock floor. They found that the water gate had four heavy duty lifting eyes built into the top edge. Having cleared some stone debris from around these, they were ready for the lifting stage, if the gantry crane could be made to work. If not, they needed a new solution.

Examining the crane they found it was equipped with its own diesel engine generator that was mounted on the framework and that moved with it. This generator supplied power to run the crane unit itself and the electric motors that moved the gantry. Geordie and Ivan started to look the engine over while Jim went in search of Romanov. He found him in the missile bay examining one of the V1s in there.

He looked over his shoulder as Jim came in. "Good morning, Major, you seem to be making progress."

"We are. If we can get the equipment to work, we hope to flood the maneuvering dock today. We are going to leave the dry docks until you want to try floating your submarines."

"Good. Now tell me, Major, what do you know about flying bombs?"

"Not much about those particular ones, but I do know about the reconnaissance UAVs we used to fly in the Army's Drone Unit and these can't be that much different in principle."

"Major, I have a dream. When we get back to the Black Sea with our prize I would like to fly ten of these from the deck of the submarine as a sort of firework show to welcome us home. Can you make them fly for me?"

"I can certainly try, but they may not be very accurate after all these years and I don't think they were very precise even when they were new."

"Good, good. No need to worry about that, there is plenty of room in the Black Sea. We will talk about it after you create the underground lake for me."

Jim left him and went back toward the gantry crane. This museum was certainly going to be spectacular.

It took some time and a good deal of swearing to get the gantry engine to run. Eventually it gave in to the tender ministrations from all three engineers and coughed into life in a choking cloud of black exhaust smoke. Three or four minutes running allowed it to vent the preservative oil from the cylinders and the heavy smoke slowly dissipated. Ivan heaved the control lever across and the huge gantry juddered forward. Once the wheels were moving the wheel bearings settled and the massive gantry started to move forward slowly, but smoothly.

They moved it as far forward as they could on the rails inset into the concrete of the docks and then Geordie climbed the long ladder, up into the crane operator's cabin. He tracked the cabin and the attached crane winch across until it was lined up with the center of the massive water gate. The crane hook below him already had a heavy four-legged cable sling dangling from it. The German engineers must have left it there, ready for their return, all those years ago. By the time Geordie had it precisely positioned over the gate, Ivan and Jim were waiting for the sling to reach them.

As it lowered within reach, they pulled the heavy cables outwards until the hooks on the ends slipped around the lifting eyes. They moved well clear of the gate and waved up to Geordie. Very carefully and very slowly, he reeled in the lifting cable. The gate was heavy and it had been there a long time, so he expected some strain. The explosions had loosened the seal and shaken out any corrosion that might have stopped the lift so, with surprising ease, the huge gate started to rise. It moved a very few centimeters until it cleared the lower seal, then the water of the Baltic came blasting into the dock that had been denied to it for so long.

The low tidal wave rushed through the gap with a roar, even as Geordie stopped the lift. Anybody standing in the dock would have been picked up and smashed against the concrete walls by the powerful tsunami of water. It spread rapidly and struck the walls of the dock, causing back waves and turbulence. Even up here in the crane cabin the noise was deafening. The water boiled up the walls and filled the maneuvering dock within minutes. Geordie looked around to check that the gates of the submarine docks were holding and was pleased to see that they were. He gave a reassuring thumbs up sign to his two companions on the dock walls below.

The inrush of water slowed and the swirling turbulence in the dock calmed as the water inside the base achieved the same level as the waters outside the hill. The movement settled until Geordie was looking down on a quiet pool of dirty water with odd pieces of debris floating in it. With the inside and outside water pressure equalized, he continued the lift and brought the huge water gate clear of its mounting. With the large load swinging below him he tracked the crane across slowly and then backed it up. He laid the massive steel door down gently on the concrete between the first and second dry docks. Climbing down the ladder from the control cabin, he walked forward and joined the other two engineers on the edge of the pool.

"Anybody fancy a swim?"

"Not with all the river rubbish that has been dragged in with the water," said Jim. "Once it settles completely we may have to go in and clear that out so nothing tangles with the U-Boat's propellers as they move through."

Romanov and his bodyguards, trailed by the inevitable Mr. Smith, joined them on the dockside.

"Well done, Major. It looks as though we have one large obstacle out of the way. You and your team also seem to have a way with diesel engines."

"Most of the heavy construction equipment we have been using for years has diesel engines, so yes we know a bit."

"Then once you have finished with the dock here," said Romanov, "I would like you to give my submarine people a little help. They are having trouble with the main engines on my prizes."

He didn't wait for an answer, but turned and walked away. The three men watched him as he left, followed by his small entourage.

Ivan sniffed, "You know boss, there's something about that man that really gets up my nose. Can't put my finger on it though."

Jim nodded, "I know what you mean. But for now we have work to do."

The three ex-Royal Engineers checked that the submarine dry dock gates were holding and no water was leaking in. They then decided to reward themselves with a coffee back in the dining area. Andrei was still buzzing about tidying and preparing food for the workers' midday meal. He was happy to stop and make them a very passable coffee with some ornate sticky German cakes that had been brought in that day. They were looking out over the base from the window of the old officer's mess when Geordie spoke.

"Isn't it odd, that our British contact is John Smith, one of the commonest names in Britain, and Romanov has one of the most distinctive names in Russia? The Romanovs were the Russian Royal Family before the communists slaughtered them."

Ivan looked at him, "So what? Is there something significant about that?"

"Maybe not. It just struck me as an interesting coincidence."

Jim filed that thought away in his memory. He must ask Andrei about it later.

They finished the coffee when Smith came hurrying through the door. "What are you doing? Mr. Romanov told you to get to the submarine to fix the engine and you are idling around here drinking coffee. I only just stopped him from sending his bodyguards to get you."

Jim was surprised, but tried to remain cool. "Calm down Mr. Smith. We are taking a break after completing a bloody big job and now we are moving on to the next one."

Smith gulped visibly then turned and rapidly left the room. The three men stood up from the table and thanking Andrei, they wandered out to the submarine still brushing the cake crumbs from their black overalls.

Chapter 15

Dropping down though the conning tower hatch they made their way aft to the engine room. The six German submarine engineers, that Romanov had brought in, were working on the starboard engine, their tools scattered around them. There was not much room in any U-Boat engine room and there was certainly not room for three more big men. Rather than get in the way they decided to move across to the next boat where work had not yet started and agreed they would work on these engines to see if there was more chance of getting these ones ready to run. The thought of beating the experts to getting an ancient engine working was attractive to three competitive people.

In the end, after considerable effort and any number of skinned knuckles, both teams succeeded in getting the big diesels in both submarines to run. The dense white clouds as the preservative oil was burnt off took some time to clear, but after further adjustments all four of the engines in the two boats were running smoothly. Once the engines were closed down the German submarine specialists started crawling over both boats, checking everything they could before they dared to fill the docks with water.

The next morning, with the safety checks still in progress, the three engineers felt themselves to be at a loose end and had decided to leave the base and take themselves into town for a well-earned break. As they were heading for the boatswain's chair to lift themselves to the surface they were halted by the voice of Romanov. They hadn't seen him for a couple of days and had assumed he was away running his business interests.

"Gentlemen. I do hope you were not thinking of leaving?"

Jim turned to him "Yes, we were, but only for a few hours break from here. It's been a long couple of weeks."

"I am afraid I can't allow that, Major. We are so close now that security becomes vital. And anyway I have an interesting task for your special talents." He crooked his finger for them to follow him and set off for the rear of the base.

"Hang on Mr. Romanov, we've been working our arses off down in this base and now we want to see some sunlight."

Romanov spun round with a look of frustrated fury on his face. "You are working for me now and I expect results. I do not pay you to sunbathe. You would do well to remember that."

Jim decided that this was not the time to have an argument so shrugged his shoulders and indicated to his two men that they should follow Romanov.

Geordie was not impressed "Bloody good job he's paying us a small fortune or I could really get fed up with this guy."

They followed Romanov into the workshop area where the V1 flying bombs were stored on their trolleys. Romanov turned and waited until they were all inside the room. It was clear he had calmed down as quickly as he had flared up.

"Major I need twenty of these in flying condition."

Jim looked at him, "Why, in heaven's name, would you need so many? I understand your plan for the ten, but won't the rest just be museum exhibits?"

Romanov smiled, "Major, I am not some dusty museum keeper. I am a showman and I want to grab the attention of the world. If I can bring two working V4 submarines to the Black Sea with missiles on board, I can fire them from the deck and have the most impressive firework display. If I can demonstrate that the weapon system aimed at American cities in 1945 was truly viable, I will startle the world, especially the Americans."

Ivan and Geordie looked at each other. Ivan spoke for both of them, "It would make one hell of a show, boss. We might even make it on to a YouTube video."

Jim nodded, "OK we will give it a go, but we will need the nose cones to make sure the rockets are balanced for flight. Not the ones with the nerve agent in, if you please."

Romanov laughed "I think releasing nerve agent over the Black Sea would rather ruin the effect I am trying to achieve, don't you think?"

He seemed to find the idea funny and left the flying bomb hangar still chuckling.

The team turned to one of the missiles and decided to open it up to educate themselves on how it worked. They were surprised at how simple it was compared to a modern Unmanned Aerial Vehicle or UAV. They had to remind themselves that even though it was old technology it had actually worked and had done quite a lot of damage. It wasn't very accurate, but the Germans had been able to hit London when firing from the other side of the English Channel. Had they been closer, they could no doubt have concentrated the missiles' impact in a much smaller area.

They tested each missile, in turn. Some were still fully functional, others had minor problems that they cured by cannibalising spares from the ones that had bigger problems or from the stocks in the storage area. The empty warheads were brought round from the chemical laboratory and were fitted in place on the twenty best missiles, with sandbags fitted inside the nose cones to simulate the weight of the ancient explosives and chemicals. They had no way to test fire the pulse jet engines inside the base, but as far as they could tell, the remarkably simple motors should function once they were fueled up. They marked the serviceable missiles with green tags so they did not get confused with the ones that were not ready for use, and moved the trolleys supporting the tagged ones to the front of the hangar.

Ivan rested his forearms on one of the completed missiles. "A pretty good four days' work there, boss" said Ivan. "Do we get to see the fireworks when these go off?"

"Do you know, I have never asked? Do we want to sail on these antiques when they go round to the Black Sea? I don't even know if they have enough people to crew two boats yet."

Ivan and Geordie agreed they did want to go. If nothing else it would make a great story for the pub when they got home. Jim nodded.

"OK then, I will speak to Romanov next time we see him."

"Speak to me about what, Major?" said Romanov, as he came through the door.

Jim told him and Romanov laughed again.

"Major, these are old boats and it's a long way to their new home. I will need as much of your expertise and skill as possible to make sure we get there, so of course I need you along on the journey."

The next few days were spent in refueling the boats. Restocking them with food and water. Installing modern GPS navigation systems and making final checks of everything that might be needed to ensure a safe journey. Once that was done the V1 flying bombs were wheeled out along the docks and with Geordie operating the gantry crane very carefully; they were loaded through the forward deck hatch and lowered down on the hydraulic lifts and into the tracks inside the large missile compartments of the two boats selected to go. Once firmly settled in the steel tracks they had wedges placed under the trolley wheels and broad webbing straps over each missile unit to ensure that even if the seas were unkind they would not shift and damage themselves.

All that remained was to fill the dry docks and sail them out. To do that they would need trained submarine crews. The submarine men they had already would only be enough to man the two engine rooms. With all the preparation that had gone into this exercise there must be some crews coming or the whole thing would have been a waste of time.

Romanov gave the order to fill the two docks and with Geordie on one control and Ivan on the other, the water valves were opened as slowly as possible. Even so the water rushed in under considerable pressure and filled the docks remarkably quickly. In less than an hour the U-Boats were starting to float for the first time in over seventy years. Men stood around the dock edge and all through the boats looking for leaks and holding their breath. It became clear that the German U-Boat builders knew their business and the boats were watertight, at least when on the surface. The true test would come when they submerged to exit the base through the tunnel. Romanov seemed hardly able to contain his excitement. He gave the order to secure all the watertight doors and the deck hatches and then to retire to the mess area for a celebration dinner. He immediately had the attention of all the tired and dirty men.

"And tomorrow," he announced, "the crews who will sail them for us will arrive. After a they have a few days of orientating themselves we will be on our way into history."

The three British engineers thought that was a little over the top but, as Romanov had said, he was a showman.

The celebration dinner was subdued. The men were too tired to do more than eat and fall into their beds. Even the lovely Tatiana did not raise much more than the occasional smile.

There was no early call the next morning and most slept late, but the three British engineers were up early as usual. Force of habit from years of military life got them out of bed, shaved and dressed before anybody else was stirring. They stood in the window of the old officers' mess and looked down on the base. The first two submarines sat lifeless on their reflections in the still water of the dry docks in the huge silent base. Like all military submarines they exuded an air of menace with their black hulls and functional markings on the conning towers. It was hard to believe that these were relics of a long finished war and would soon be museum exhibits in a holiday resort on the Black Sea. There was a satisfaction in what they had achieved by finding the base and bringing these two boats back to life.

The third boat sat forlorn in the empty dry dock beyond and in the fourth dock the jumbled remains of the slaughtered Russian prisoners of war still lay with those of their *Kriegsmarine* captors.

Ivan looked across the rim of his coffee mug at Jim, "OK, Boss. What's bugging you?"

"How do you know anything is?"

"I've worked for you for a long time and I know that look. The last time I saw it was on the banks of the Weser just before that bloody Pontoon bridge failed and caused all that damage."

"You've got me. We are just about to cross a line here. Up to this point we haven't done anything wildly illegal. But once we take those boats out of here that is going to be theft of German government property at the very least."

"Well you could be right there, but the present German government people are just normal politicians. The bastards who had this base and those boats built were something special. I don't have any problem taking their stuff."

"You might be right. I'll think about it."

As they turned back to the window and stood contemplating their achievement, the roof hatch, high above, opened to a dark sky. Ropes dropped down and within seconds they saw men sliding down to the deck of the center U-Boat. They counted thirty of them as they waited for their personal belongings to be lowered. They did not seem to have brought much with them as each man walked across the gangplank with only a holdall each as they assembled on the dock. They were dressed in black coveralls with green badges on the left shoulder. There was no gawking despite being inside a massive secret base. Who could resist a look round something as amazing as this?

The men in black coveralls were split into two equal crews and one headed to V4-1 waiting patiently in the now filled dock. They were led across by one of Romanov's bodyguards. There was a slight trembling in the water as they tramped across the gangplank and disappeared down into the boat. The remaining crew returned across the walkway behind them, climbed the conning tower external ladder and entered

V4-2. The three engineers decided to wander across and say hello. Perhaps this group would be more forthcoming than the rest of the people Romanov had brought in so far.

They got as far as the first gangplank and were met by one of the Russian bodyguards who blocked their way. He didn't speak English, but placing himself on the walkway and staring at them got the message across. The second gangplank could be seen from where they were standing and it too was equipped with a large unsmiling Russian. There was no point in arguing so they took themselves back to the mess area for some of Andrei's excellent coffee and a breakfast of bread rolls with cheese and ham.

"Well boss," said Ivan as Andrei poured a second mug of steaming coffee and Tatiana cleared away the plates, "it looks like the sailing crews have arrived. We must be getting ready to move out soon."

"Can't be too soon," said Geordie with a small smile, "I think Tatiana is feeling the pressure of being underground."

"What makes you say that?"

"Well I've been watching her and with two perfect specimens of masculine beauty sitting right here she still keeps smiling at the boss and those early morning assignations for a quiet coffee are getting more frequent."

Jim felt himself flush a little as he changed the subject. "Very funny, you two. I wonder how we find out who our new crewmates are?"

"Arabs!" said Andrei. "Only Romanov would hire Arabs to sail these ships."

"I wonder where he got Arabs with submarine training?" said Geordie.

"Not difficult" Jim said. "A number of the Middle Eastern nations have small submarines for use in protecting their oil rigs in the Gulf. As far as I recall they are all diesel electric boats so a U-Boat should be quite familiar to them. I guess they are going through familiarization drills now to get ready for sea."

As they were finishing, Smith appeared. He had been absent for some days now that they came to think about it. "Hello Mr. Smith and where have you been hiding?" said Jim.

"Hello Major, gentlemen, not hiding I have been doing some different work for Mr. Romanov, making further arrangements for other parts of this expedition. We seem to be ready for the adventure to begin.

Mr. Romanov would like to hold a briefing this afternoon to make sure everything is prepared."

"Can I have a word with you in private, Mr. Smith?"

"Of course, Major."

They walked out onto the dock and Jim leaned against one of the large crates in the storage area. "I'm getting concerned about the legality of taking these boats out of here. It smells like theft of German government property. You said that you and some lawyers were going to fix that ... have you?"

"Not your problem, Major. You just do your job and we will worry about the legality."

"It is my problem if my men and I end up in a German prison for our trouble."

"Oh dear. I had hoped to avoid having to say this to you, but Mr. Romanov anticipated your attack of morals."

"Saying what?"

"Our observers report that you seem very fond of your nephew. Joking with him as you two ran through the fens. Mr. Romanov feels you would be very sad if the boy was to be found face down in one of the waterways."

"You cannot be serious. You're threatening me?"

Smith looked down at his feet then up at the angry Englishman. "Did you think those bodyguards were just for show? I think you should consider your position very carefully and don't tell your men. We don't want any trouble from them, do we?"

Jim seriously considered grabbing Smith and pounding his smug face to a bloody pulp. But he had to consider David and he had no way to warn him. He swallowed his anger and turned back toward the mess area.

"Just call us when you want us," said Jim, "it seems we aren't going anywhere. Tell me something though, how come Romanov has hired Arab crews for his boats? I would have thought he would want Russians to sail them into Odessa as part of his publicity stunt?"

Smith paused and looked at Jim. "I'm sure he has a very good reason for the people he has chosen. If he feels you need to know he will tell you, but maybe you should just do your part?"

Chapter 16

At the briefing Romanov stood at the front of the mess hall with a large map behind him and looking very pleased with himself. Jim looked around the room while people were taking their places. The German submarine engineers were there, as were the two chemists. The bodyguards stood at the back of the room, unsmiling as usual. It must be difficult to be so stone faced all the time, he thought. Smith entered leading four of the black suited Arab sailors. He guessed these must be the skippers and first officers. No reason to bring in the whole of the boat's crew. Romanov cleared his throat and the low murmuring stopped. Everyone turned to their employer.

"Gentlemen," he said, "the time has almost come for our voyage to begin. We will warp the boats out into the maneuvering dock one at a time as soon as the crews are ready and loading is complete. Once the first boat is out we will move the second. The first boat will wait outside the base and then we will head out into the Baltic together. It will be dark when the first boat leaves and we will show no lights."

He went on to describe the route they would take. Having entered the Baltic they would head north into Danish waters and pass through the *Storebælt* channel. Coming out of that they would enter the *Kattegat* and then turn west into the *Skagerrak*. Sailing through there would bring them to the North Sea.

"There is to be no delay, once we are under way," Romanov said. "We must be into the North Sea before dawn. We have to be away from German and Danish waters before we run any risk of being seen."

To the south of England is the English Channel, one of the busiest, most congested and closely controlled shipping lanes in the world. They would avoid this by sailing around the north of Scotland and out into the Atlantic. Once they were well to the west of Ireland they would turn south, keeping well away from the coasts, and head for the Straits of Gibraltar.

"Now," he said, "let me introduce our two Captains for this adventure. Captain Ibrahim, late of the navy of Saudi Arabia and Captain Ahmad late of the Egyptian navy. Captain Ibrahim will command V4-1 and Captain Ahmad will take V4-2. If you check the list on the wall at the back of the room you will find which boat you have been allocated to serve on."

The two captains had not stood up, but had sat stony faced when introduced. They had not even acknowledged their names. No doubt it would become clear which was which when they got aboard.

Romanov was about to finish when he said, "Oh Major. This afternoon I would like you and your men to ensure the boat's crews are familiar with the maneuvering winches ready for lining the boats up with the tunnel. You will not be able to handle them as you three will be on the first boat with me."

At least they would be kept together as a team, which was comforting, Jim thought. He nodded and walked toward the two Captains to make arrangements for instructing their crews. They saw him coming and pointedly turned and walked out of the room.

The two first officers remained. "You are the Major?" one of them said.

"I am and I was going to speak to your skippers about training your men."

"Ah yes. They are both busy so have left us to make the arrangements. Can you start now?"

Jim showed no sign of the annoyance he felt. He had bottled up his feelings before when senior officers had been as rude as this. Now he was a civilian he had not expected that to continue. This was becoming a little too pointed. He was about to react when he felt Ivan's hand on his arm. He turned toward the Welshman.

"Let it go, boss. We'll see about this crap later."

Jim nodded and swallowing his pride turned back to the two first officers.

"Very well gentlemen, can you have your handling crews on the dockside in ten minutes and please ensure they have someone with them who speaks English. I am afraid I am no linguist."

The crewmen in their black coveralls proved to be intelligent and quick learners. Despite being surly, they asked all the right questions and were very soon handling the winches competently. As the lessons on the handling equipment finished Jim and his two men began to return to the mess area for lunch. They stopped and looked across the base.

By both of the two submarines that were scheduled to leave, the Arab crews were pushing trolley mounted torpedoes along the dockside. They found a large crate to sit on and watched as heavy webbing slings were put around the underwater missiles and the crane was started and used to lift them through the submarine deck hatches.

"They must have been stored in amongst those piles of crates near the headquarters, boss," said Ivan. "This museum is going to be pretty authentic if those are live."

Jim nodded slowly. "I had been wondering what the German engineers had been doing for the last couple of days. My guess is they have been working on those beasties and they are fully ready to go. But what the hell are they going to do with live torpedoes? They can't be used for this firework show that Romanov wants. Something doesn't feel right about all this."

After lunch they waited until the loading of the last torpedoes had been completed and then Geordie and Ivan returned to the dry dock gate controls. On a signal from Jim they swung the winch handles that ground the gates slowly open. The submarines were now fully in touch with the waters of the open ocean. All that prevented them from sailing away was the hillside around them and the tunnel they had to maneuver through.

Fuel lines were slung across from the docksides and the diesel tanks were topped up on the two U-Boats from the large fuel bunkers within the base. Batteries had already been checked and recharged by the German specialists and any found to be suspect had been replaced from the stores on the dockside.

The next evening the crews and specialist teams boarded their allocated boats. The three ex-Royal Engineers were the last to board V4-1. As they did so the gangplank was swung back and the mooring lines were loosened. The twin diesel engines started with a throaty roar that echoed around the base. The cables were passed across from the winch and secured to the rings in the foredeck and gently, ever so gently, the boat was pulled forward into the maneuvering dock. As she moved, the cables from the winches that controlled the aft end of the boat were passed across and secured to the afterdeck rings. Once clear of the dry dock that she had sat in for the last seventy years the four winches pulled until the boat was precisely aligned with the exit tunnel. Captain Ibrahim checked that all periscopes and antennae were fully stowed, diving planes in the fully retracted position, and batteries on line ready to take the boat out of the base. Once satisfied he ordered all the crew and passengers to go below before securing the deck hatches.

Jim looked across at the other boat in time to see Tatiana's long dark hair disappearing down into the hull of the submarine. He turned and climbed down through the hatch and descended the ladder.

All watertight doors were shut and the diesel engines were shut down. The cables to the deck rings were released by crewmen who were the last to enter the ship and close the final deck hatch. The order was given and the boat slowly submerged in a welter of swirling water as the roaring air vented from the ballast tanks.

The three Englishmen were standing by their allocated bunks in the old Chiefs' Mess aft of the control room, fingers crossed and staring around looking for leaks. Their large holdalls were stowed in the two spare top bunks. They listened as the submarine settled gently onto the concrete floor of the dock. They heard and felt the propellers start to spin as the electric motors turned the drive shafts.

As the propellers started to bite they pushed the water backwards and the boat started to move slowly forward, scraping along the concrete dock floor. The noise inside the submarine was loud and unpleasant, although they knew it should damage nothing but the paint work. As they left the dock and entered the tunnel the noise level dropped as the boat slid along a layer of slimy river mud. The sides of the tunnel took up the challenge and the scraping of metal along the stone walls was as loud as the dock floor had been. Then the noise was gone. They were out.

The Captain took the boat to a point around five hundred meters from the shore line and ordered the periscope raised and the diving planes deployed. He tracked the scope around slowly. They were alone in the darkness. The boat surfaced and the watertight doors were opened. The Captain and Romanov climbed up into the conning tower and turned to await the arrival of V4-2. Romanov looked down the conning tower ladder and saw Jim in the control room below.

"Major!" he called, "Come up and watch this!" Jim climbed the ladder and stood beside Romanov in the cool dark night. "Major, without you this would never have happened. You should be here to share in this historic moment. Hitler's *Kriegsmarine* is going back to sea!"

Jim stared into the darkness toward where he knew the tunnel entrance to be. The water was smooth and untroubled. There was no moon and the stars reflected off the surface of the still water. Then the water boiled and the reflections vanished as the second U-Boat slid up from the bottom. There was no cheering or exchange of witty light signals; this was to be a stealthy journey. Jim looked at Romanov. The Russian's face was impassive. Unusual for a showman who had just had a major success, but maybe Romanov was so much more.

The two boats turned north and headed away from Kiel. While close to the city they used only the electric motors and traveled slowly to avoid drawing attention. It was a cold, clear night with no traffic and only the reflections from the lights of the city to keep them company. As the boats entered the Baltic the large diesel engines coughed into life and the two boats accelerated to their maximum speed of twenty-five knots. The boats slipped between the Danish islands without attracting attention. The channel widened out into the *Kattegat* and despite the increased traffic, the submarines, with their low profile and black hulls passed unnoticed. Even if they had been seen by any merchantman in this area they would have assumed them to be part of the modern German navy exercising in their usual training waters.

In the early hours of the morning the boats turned west into the *Skagerrak*, heading for the North Sea. Lying in the cramped bunk Jim could feel the boat make the turn and then feel the increased wave motion as they cleared the shelter of the headland. Once into the North Sea the boats turned North West to pass around the top of Scotland, keeping well clear of the Danish coast. With the wind and the waves no longer directly on the bow there was an uncomfortable twisting movement added to the fore and aft rocking motion of the long sleek boat.

Andrei, who now shared the fourth bunk in the Chiefs' Mess was clearly no sailor and lay in the enclosed space of his sleeping pallet and groaned. He had yet to be sick, but had the plastic bag ready for the inevitable moment.

After a few hours of pounding Jim decided against staying in the enclosed space. Waiting for Andrei to reexamine his dinner was not his idea of fun. He climbed out of his bunk and headed into the control room. The Arabic crew noticed him and pointedly looked back to their instruments. He made it to the base of the conning tower ladder and called to the Officer of the Deck for permission to come up. The first officer he had spoken to at the briefing looked down at him and after a moment's consideration gestured for him to climb up. Jim climbed the vertical ladder and entered the conning tower bridge. Two lookouts monitored the horizon left and right, the deck officer and a third lookout tracked their binoculars forward. Spray was breaking over the forward deck and the occasional wind driven wave covered it and ran toward the conning tower as a gray-green mound before striking the metal wall and breaking.

"Looks like we could be in for some lumpy weather," Jim said to the conning tower crew.

He might have saved his breath for all the reaction. After a few moments silence the officer turned and handed him a pair of binoculars. Without a word he pointed over the port side of the boat. Jim looked where he was pointing. Through the binoculars and the mist he could see forbidding gray cliffs with the sea breaking at their base.

He looked at the Arabic officer who said, "Cape Wrath. The most northerly point of mainland Britain." He pointed out into the mist to starboard. "Somewhere over there are the outer islands. It is difficult to believe that people would choose to live in such a terrible place as this."

He turned away, the conversation was over. Jim took a few more breaths of the cold refreshing air, then took another look round at the angry sea before he climbed down into the muggy air of the boat.

He stood in the control room below the conning tower and looked around. The air smelled of diesel oil. Their clothes and bedding already stank of it and their food, such as it was, tasted of the stuff. The pipework around the boat dripped condensation constantly and even their bedding felt wet. He could not imagine how the U-Boat crews had stood this for weeks with the added threat of being hunted by the two most powerful navies in the world. They must have been remarkable men.

He kept looking around the control room as he passed through and again was studiously ignored by the operators at their wheels and instruments. The navigator pointedly turned his chart over as Jim passed, making sure it covered the screen of the newly installed satellite navigation system.

A little redundant since Jim knew exactly where they were. He had stood on those rugged cliffs looking out at these storm tossed waters with his wife, during their honeymoon, with just the melancholy cry of the seabirds to distract them. Those had been very different days; just married and just promoted to Captain, his life had seemed golden. When he got back to barracks his orders to move to Iraq had been waiting for him and the separations had begun. His marriage had started to go downhill from that point though he had taken years to realize it.

He passed through to the chiefs' mess and found his two colleagues and Andrei lying in their bunks, keeping out of the narrow passageway that crewmen passed through to get to the engine room and the heads. Geordie and Ivan were reading while Andrei was clutching his improvised sick bag. His color was a little better; maybe he was getting used to the motion at last. Jim announced that he had seen the top of mainland Scotland through the mist, but was greeted with indifference.

"I'll be happier when we see Gibraltar through the sunshine," said Ivan. "Once we get to the Mediterranean I wonder if we can get dropped off somewhere warm with a large supply of icy cold beer that doesn't smell of diesel."

Jim shook his head. "I think Romanov wants us along until he gets to his museum so that we can help fix anything that goes wrong."

Andrei looked up from his bunk, but said nothing and turned his face to the back of his bunk. Jim filed that one away for later; he had been managing men for many years and could see that this one knew something he wasn't telling.

The tedium of life on board the U-Boat continued. The Arabic crew would have nothing to do with them and after a meal or two they became unhappy with the standard of the food coming from the galley. Andrei took over cooking for the four of them, more for something to do than anything else. The small German engine room crew asked if he would help them as well, so he was now cooking for seven. He was happier now that his mind and hands were occupied.

Romanov stayed in the old Captain's accommodation and avoided them all; if the present skipper resented that they saw no sign of it. Visits to the conning tower were rare since they were clearly not welcome. On the odd occasion one of them went up for a breath of fresh air, the heavy Atlantic swells were sweeping across the casings and when they looked across at the second boat they could see it lifting and crashing in the waves. Communication between the two vessels was by hand held VHF sets with a range of no more than five miles. The stealthy cruise away from Germany was still in motion. Presumably Romanov wanted his prizes safely installed in his museum before the Germans found out they had lost these two spectacular pieces of their history.

The monotony was slightly relieved by patrolling the boat looking for leaks from the old pipework. Even when they found and fixed one there was no acknowledgement from the Arabic crew, even those who had been getting dripped on refused to notice the help they had received.

Every twelve hours they took turns to inspect the lower deck areas. Lowering themselves through the hatch between the electric motors then working forward through the machinery spaces, battery and air system compartments. Checking the batteries for signs of leakage to ensure no deadly chlorine gas was produced by contact with sea water was essential. With his marked dislike of dark enclosed spaces, this task was a trial for Jim but he steeled himself and took his turn, even though he returned each time in a cold sweat with trembling fingers and panicked breathing.

After the first two nights in his shallow bunk Jim started to experience the Coffin Dreams well known to submariners. He would wake suddenly in the middle of the night watch, with the surface of the upper bunk just in front of his face. Sweating and trembling, he would slide out of the bunk and prowl the control and missile compartments until he calmed.

When Geordie came back from one of his crawls and walks around the boat, he tapped Ivan and Jim on the shoulder and hunkered down between their bunks. "Just been through the control room," he said quietly, "something isn't right. I managed to get a look at the satnav screen as I passed and it's showing our course as 278 degrees. That's almost due west."

Jim nodded. "According to Romanov's plan we should have turned south a few days ago to travel down past Ireland toward Gibraltar. Maybe we were just turning to avoid some ship?"

Geordie shook his head. "I've been awake for the last couple of hours. If we had made a turn like that I would have felt the motion of the boat change. But the pounding from the waves had been constant."

Jim looked across at Andrei who was lying quietly watching them.

"Time for you to tell us what you know, Andrei. You have been working for Romanov for a while. What is going on and what haven't we been told?"

Andrei leaned out of his bunk and looked nervously up and down the passageway.

He swallowed, then whispered, "I do not know why we are doing this. I do know there is no museum on the Black Sea. Romanov is not the rich business man he claims to be. He is rich, that is true, but he makes his money from crime. He is Russian Mafia."

The three engineers absorbed that for a few seconds.

Ivan broke the silence, "What the hell does a Mafioso want with a couple of old submarines and where is he taking them?"

Andrei shook his head. "I do not know. It is not wise to question him too closely. He can be quite ruthless if he is annoyed."

"For the time being I think we will keep what we know to ourselves," Jim said. "But anytime you are moving through the boat try to get a look at the charts or the satnav. It might give us a clue about just what the hell is going on."

Chapter 17

Although they kept an eye on the control room they did not manage to check the charts or get another look at the satnav screen. The navigator was not careless again when they were around. Jim tried to go forward to speak to Romanov, but was told quite forcefully that he could not see him. The leather-jacketed bodyguards were quite adamant and even in Russian it was clear what they meant.

The heaving of the boat became more pronounced as the waves built up around them, and the crew was clearly getting nervous. Their experience of submarine work in the Middle Eastern waters had not prepared them for a storm in the cold, angry waters of the North Atlantic. Geordie stood in the hatchway that led to the control room watching quietly. After a while he came back and squatted between the bunks.

"They're scared," he said, "not scared of dying, but scared they will sink the boat before they achieve their aim. They are pleading with the skipper to take the boat down away from the storm."

Andrei looked puzzled. "How do you know these things? They speak only in Arabic."

Ivan laughed, "I don't know how the Russian Army works, but in the British Army we train people to do all sorts of strange things just in case we ever need them. Geordie understands Arabic. He can't speak it worth a damn, but he can understand what they are saying."

Jim looked at Geordie, "Any clue about what the crew's aim might be?"

"Nothing, boss. I'll keep an ear out, but they are being careful. Every time I go near them they clam up. If I didn't know better I'd say they didn't like me and by the way, I speak Arabic perfectly well." Geordie smiled. "It's not my fault if Arabs don't understand their own language."

"Well, Andrei," said Jim, "from what you know of Romanov and where we are do you have any guesses about what we are doing?"

"Major, if I knew I would tell you, but I have heard nothing. I am sure it will be about money or power or both. They are the only things that matter to Romanov. He will do anything to acquire more of both."

Jim sat back into his bunk and looked across at Ivan. "Any guesses?"

"Not a clue. How he can make money in the middle of the Atlantic with two old U- Boats escapes me." Then he looked up. "Unless he is going to sell them to one of the South American navies or to one of the South American drug cartels? They have been smuggling cocaine into the U.S. using small improvised submarines for years now. These two could carry tons of the damned stuff. The Argentinians could use them to replace that one they lost in South Georgia back in the eighties."

"Possible, but if that is true we seem to be going the long way, judging by the course setting that Geordie saw. I wonder if those Germans in the engine room know anything?"

Ivan nodded at Andrei, "They might not speak to us, but they might speak to the cook when he next feeds them."

Andrei looked surprised, but nodded, "I will try. Their leader, Hans, might know something."

The next meal was yet another canned stew that came with dark, diesel tasting bread. The three engineers ate in silence and waited for the Russian to come back. Eventually Andrei reappeared and sat on the edge of his bunk.

"They know less than we do," he said, "but Hans says they are uncomfortable with the Arab crew as much as we are. Nobody has told them anything except to keep the engines running at high cruising speed. The boat has been making fifteen to twenty knots for days now."

As he finished speaking they heard the sound of a klaxon siren through the ship. Arabic crewmen dashed through the passageway and secured the watertight doors before heading forward again and securing the door between the Chiefs' Mess and the control room. The sound of the big diesel engine died and the compartment tilted as the sound of high pressure vents came through the hull. Jim noticed Andrei clutching the edge of his bunk with white knuckles. Despite the sweat he could feel prickling between his own shoulder blades, he patted the Russian on the shoulder and winked to reassure him. The motion of the boat eased almost immediately. They had submerged.

"I wonder what finally convinced the skipper to take her down?" said Ivan. "Maybe they want to use the best china for lunch?"

They felt the floor come level again as the boat ceased its dive.

"Not very deep," said Jim, "I thought they would go further down than that to avoid the weather and if it was just for an easier ride they wouldn't have made it a crash dive."

They could still feel the motion of the waves above them.

"Listen to that," said Ivan.

They sat still and through the hull, they heard the swishing and heavy rumbling sound of propellers in the water.

"That must be something big to make that much noise underwater," Jim said. "It seems we dived to avoid being seen. If that's true we will be heaving about again shortly."

Geordie smiled "That's true, boss, but don't call me shorty."

It was an old joke and had never been that funny, but it eased the tension in the small compartment as they sat and waited for the next development. It wasn't long in coming as the watertight door was opened and they were summoned into the control room. A number of seals had failed under the increased pressure and jets of icy cold water were shooting across the command compartment. They worked rapidly to stop them. Eventually the leaks were under control and they turned to look at the Captain who studiously ignored them.

"Don't mention it. You're welcome," said Ivan, as they headed back to their bunk area.

No more than ten minutes later they heard the klaxons again and felt the deck tilt upwards. The motion of the waves increased and the heaving deck that they had become used to was back.

"My guess would be that its dark or the weather is really bad with low visibility."

"OK, I'll bite, how do you work that one out?" said Ivan.

"We were only down for a matter of minutes. If the visibility was good we would have stayed down for longer to avoid being seen. As it is we must be in reduced visibility so the skipper feels safe to come up quickly."

As he was speaking they heard the first diesel rumble into life. They waited for the second, but no sound came. The wheel in the watertight door to the control room spun round and the hatch was swung open to let the Captain pass through. He ignored them as usual and went aft, opening the other watertight door as he went. They could hear the shouting from the engine room, most of it from the skipper. He stormed back through to the control room and the watertight door swung shut again. The dirty face and oil stained coveralls of one of the German engine room team appeared in their compartment.

"Forgive my English," he said, "but problems we are having some with the engine. Hans asks is it possible for you to help?"

By way of an answer the three engineers swung out of their bunks and headed aft. As they came into the engine room the stench of diesel oil was even stronger and the decks were slippery with the stuff. They set to work with the German engineers, checking through the engine systems. Having worked on the old diesels in the underground base they knew their way around and within an hour they had identified the problem as a blockage in the fuel feed pipes caused by a failure in the filtration system. It took time to remove the affected pipes and to flush them clean. Finding the spare filter in the jumble of spares they had taken aboard took just as long, but once that was fitted and the pipes back in place and resting in their mountings, they tried the engine again. It coughed and wheezed as the air in the fuel pipes worked its way through, but then the satisfying roar of the cylinders firing almost deafened them. The engine room staff were grateful, but returned to nursing their charges after a few shouted words of thanks.

When they got back to their own compartment, Jim said, "Better get changed. The clothes you have on must be soaked in diesel."

Ivan and Geordie exchanged a knowing look. Ivan said, "In a bit boss. I'm OK for now."

Jim knew enough not to question his old Sergeant Major. Something was going on that he was not aware of, but since he trusted his two companions implicitly he let it slide. With the boat back at cruising speed they could feel the waves pounding over the bow again.

"We seem to be heading into the weather," said Jim, "and as far as I know the prevailing wind in the Atlantic blows from west to east so chances are we are still heading west. Might be nice if we could confirm that."

Ivan looked thoughtful. "What time is it?"

Jim checked his watch, "Just before dawn, that engine took a while."

"Thought so. Be back in a bit. Geordie, your turn to check the lower decks, might be an idea to have a look in the bilges this time, after that dive."

Ivan rolled out of his bunk and went forward into the control room. He got to the bottom of the conning tower ladder and called up for permission to come on deck. The first officer was up there and after a second or two's hesitation, he gestured for Ivan to come out onto the conning tower deck. Ivan climbed up and thanked the officer. He explained about the diesel soaking his coveralls and his wish to dry them out in the wind. He chatted about the weather and the sea, getting nothing but grunts from the officer next to him. He stopped talking and as dawn broke he stared along the narrow foredeck to the sharp black bows that were piercing the waves.

"Nice to get some sun on your back for a change," he said. "Well thanks for the fresh air. I can't stay gossiping with you all day."

He dropped back down the ladder and made his way into the compartment in time to be handed a mug of diesel-smelling coffee.

"Well, it looks like the weather is starting to clear up a little, the waves are a lot smaller," he said. "And we are heading directly away from the sunrise. Not very precise, but as near as damn it, we are still heading due west."

Jim looked around at them all. "If we have been heading west consistently since we left Cape Wrath we must be almost at the East Coast of the US. So selling the boats to South Americans seems to be out. Maybe he has found an American collector?"

Andrei made breakfast and passed it to them. He took three bowls back into the engine room for the Germans who were tending the diesels. He rejoined them and they sat and ate in silence. Breakfast over, they were settling in for yet another boring day when Romanov appeared in their compartment for the first time since they had left Kiel.

"Gentlemen, forgive my absence, but I have been a little busy with some details of my museum projects. However, would you pack up your belongings and come forward into the control room. This is as far as we go. We are transferring to another ship."

With no more explanation, he carried on aft into the engine room. Moments later he was back heading forward.

"Come on gentlemen, no time to lose."

The three engineers grabbed their bulky ex-Army haversacks and Andrei took his garish *Spartak Moscow* sports bag and they headed forward to make a queue behind the Russian bodyguards at the foot of the conning tower ladder. The three engine room Germans joined them, also carrying their bags over their shoulders. Romanov had a few quiet words with the Captain and then led the way up the ladder. As they climbed out of the hatch one of the bodyguards was standing on the bridge deck watching them. Romanov shouted up to him from the aft deck and he shrugged and preceded them down the outside ladder.

Ivan waited till he was clear, then whispered to the others, "I don't like this. Romanov said something about the Arabs would take care of us. Best we get ready as soon as we are down on the gratings."

Geordie nodded and climbed over the edge of the conning tower and down the ladder. As soon as he was down he started to rummage in his haversack. Ivan joined him and started to do the same in his bag. Jim wondered what they were planning, but years in the Army had taught him when to let his NCOs get on with things. Moving along the deck was easier than Jim had anticipated. The waves had moderated considerably and the movement of the U-Boat was much more comfortable. They moved further back toward the stern and gravitated into three groups, Romanov and his heavies furthest aft and the engine room men closest to the conning tower.

As they watched, a sleek modern luxury yacht appeared out of the slowly clearing mist and stopped about two hundred meters from them. A large hatch swung up at the stern of the yacht and a Rigid Inflatable Powerboat was quickly launched across the swimming platform. A crewman jumped in, started the engines and the boat slid rapidly across the intervening sea to come alongside the submarine.

"Say what you like about Romanov he has good taste in equipment."

"Why's that boss?"

"Unless I am reading the markings wrongly that's a Ribcraft with twin Mariner outboards. Probably the best sea boat for rescues you could wish for."

Romanov and his bodyguards jumped the gap into the boat and as Jim stepped toward it, the driver pushed the throttle levers forward and the boat roared off. Romanov waved as he headed for his yacht, then turned to stare ahead.

"Oh shit! Here we go!" said Geordie.

Jim spun round in time to see two of the Arab crew appear at the rear of the conning tower carrying AK-47 assault rifles. They leaned over the edge of the tower and opened fire on the nearest group. The three Germans were ripped by the 7.62 mm bullets and crashed to the deck. One slid slowly over the edge of the casing into the water, dragging his bag with him.

The two gunmen had emptied their magazines in the first attack and were down behind the bridge coaming reloading when Geordie shouted

"Boss! Think fast! Catch!"

Jim turned to see a black MP-40 submachine gun in the air heading his way. He snatched it to him and pulled the cocking lever. Geordie stepped up beside him with another weapon ready in his hands and waited until the two Arabs stood back up to kill them. As they appeared he opened fire. The short burst from the old weapon struck the first killer in the forehead and he went down in a spray of blood. The second ducked out of sight. The two ex-soldiers knelt on one knee with the weapons at the ready.

Jim looked around. The yacht was leaving, foam churning at its stern as it moved back into the mist. Apparently Romanov did not need to stay for the amusement. There was shouting from the conning tower though they could see nobody.

"What are they saying Geordie?"

"They are clearing the deck and getting ready to submerge. Apparently they see no need to lose another man to finish us off."

Ivan's voice came from behind them, "OK guys! Time to leave!"

Jim turned to find Ivan kneeling on the deck with an inflatable dinghy rolled out in front of him. Now he knew why he had not changed clothes. His haversack had been full of other things.

"I'll buy it. Where the devil did you get that?"

Ivan turned the stop cock on the small inflation cylinder and as the boat inflated said, "Remember asking for a dinghy so we could look for the outside of the tunnel entrance? We didn't need it then, but I brought it along anyway."

The vents around them started to blow and the U-Boat started to dive under them.

"Let's go! Andrei come on!"

Geordie grabbed the Russian who was standing in shock at the speed his world had changed and pushed him toward the dinghy. Ivan threw the boat over the side into the foaming water and held on to the mooring line. Geordie practically threw the dazed Russian into the dinghy, his submachine gun falling from his hand as he did so and disappearing under the churning surface of the water. Jim and Geordie piled in on top of the Russian and Ivan jumped in last as the U-Boat slid beneath the water. The small, overloaded dinghy rocked dangerously, but stayed upright.

The water calmed and they found themselves alone on a very large gray ocean apart from one of the bags belonging to the engine room men that slipped out of sight as they watched. The yacht was gone and the two U-Boats were now beneath the water, heading away from them.

Jim looked at his two companions, who were grinning from ear to ear. "Nice job guys. I don't suppose you packed a helicopter in there as well?"

"No, boss, sorry. But it looks like we have been luckier than some."

Jim looked over his shoulder to see what Ivan was looking at. There was a body, floating face down, close to them. The long dark hair spread out on the water made it clear who it was. The bloody mess at the back of her head told her story.

Geordie stared then shouted. "Bloody hell! Her fingers are moving she's alive!"

The four men paddled madly with their hands the few yards to Tatiana. Ivan leaned over the front of the boat and his massive strength made lifting her out of the water child's play. She was unconscious, but still breathing. They moved around in the small boat as best they could to try and make her comfortable.

Jim examined the back of her head, the bullets had done a lot of damage, but as far as he could see had not penetrated the skull. The blood spattered across her chest was more of a worry. As he cradled her head, her eyes fluttered open and looked into his.

"Hello beautiful. Nice of you to join us."

Chapter 18

An hour later the inside of the U-Boat was all quiet efficiency. The dead man had been brought down into the boat and was stretched out on what had been Andrei's bunk with the curtain pulled across to shield him from his shipmates. The skipper took the boat to periscope depth and watched intently as the outer marks for the shipping channel slid past them. The sonar operator listened for other traffic coming their way. Not an easy task in the large, busy river, using outdated equipment. The skipper gave a running commentary of everything he was seeing to his navigating officer who identified each landmark and buoy on the detailed chart spread in front of him.

Forward, in the missile bay, the securing straps were being removed from the V1 missiles and stowed out of the way, then the compressed air tanks were checked for sufficient pressure. The wedges under the wheels of the trollies would stay in place until the last minute. Two hours and ten minutes after shooting the Germans and drowning the other four Europeans, the Captain heard his navigator tell him there was five minutes to run until they were in position. He ordered the electric motors to slow speed and as they reached the planned spot, he stopped the boat and then let her gently settle to the bottom of the estuary, seventy feet below, to await the appointed time. The sonar man reported the second submarine moving toward them and stopping. He heard the sound of ballast tanks filling as the other boat also settled into the river mud to wait. The crew were quiet, feeling their own thoughts. The hour of prayer came and every man aboard faced Mecca to make his peace before they visited vengeance on the enemy.

The clocks in the control room ticked around to 10:00 a.m. Eastern Standard Time with every man checking his own watch. The two submarines rose slowly to periscope depth. The radio antennae on both boats were deployed. For the first time they would use their full power radios. Even if they were detected, it was now too late to stop them.

The two U-Boats in turn transmitted confirmation that they were ready. The luxury motor yacht heading out into the Atlantic confirmed receipt of the readiness signal and gave the order to start the attack. V4-1 acknowledged, then V4-2, and then a third voice agreed that he was ready too. Both of the submarine skippers were surprised. Was this another attacker they did not know about? Perhaps another brother was bringing an airliner to join the attack? That had terrified the enemy before and would cause even more confusion.

At 10:06 the two old, but still deadly, U-Boats rose from the murky depths of the Hudson River into the misty gray morning. It was good that the waters had calmed as the wind dropped. It would make their task much easier with a stable launch platform.

The large hatches on the foredeck of each boat swung open as crewmen ran forward to handle the V-1 Flying Bombs that rose on the hydraulic lifts from the missile compartments of the two boats. They pushed the trolleys forward to the back of the deck ramps and gently, but firmly, slid the V-1s forward into launching position. They connected the launch control cables and ensured the missiles were linked to the catapult slugs between the launch rails. The handling trolleys were heaved over the side and out of the way as the deck hatch closed behind them. The crewmen ran behind the conning towers for shelter from the exhaust of the Pulse Jets and the two Captains in the conning towers saluted each other, then ducked for cover and gave the order to launch. The crewman at the small launch station beside the radio operated his controls. The pulse jet engines burst into throbbing life, the compressed air forced the catapult system to drag the weapons up to flight speed and the two missiles pounded the length of the launch ramps and leapt into the air, heading for Manhattan Island. Before the exhaust smoke had fully cleared, the deck hatches reopened and the second missile on each boat rose into the misty morning light.

Loading and launching took eight minutes. They needed a mere seventy-two minutes without detection to complete the attack and to bring New York to its knees. At its normal speed of three hundred and fifty knots each flying bomb would reach lower Manhattan in just over two minutes. As soon as it did, the timer would operate and the crude guillotine device inside would sever the control cables sending it into a power dive. As the dive commenced the warhead mechanism would also operate and mix the two chemicals into a deadly nerve agent that would spread as a gas on impact. Even after all these years, this predecessor of all the cruise missiles that followed, would be unstoppable and deadly. New York lay unprepared for the assault winging toward it.

Chapter 19

In Central Park the TV cameras rolled, beaming images of the Mayor of the city presenting awards for valor to men and women from the Fire and Police Departments. The Mayor thought it the perfect day to showcase the city and improve its image for tourists.

The chiefs and senior officers of those departments stood by in their finest uniforms to honor their people. The Mayor looked up toward the buzzing, pounding noise of the pulse jet engine approaching him. Others looked in the same direction. One camera swung round and was the first to pick up the small aircraft as it approached and then suddenly dived into the park. It struck the ground a little over three hundred meters from the ceremony. As usual with first-responders, and despite being dressed in their best uniforms, the police and fire officers ran toward the crash site to render assistance, to what they assumed was a light aircraft with a crew. It was their last, selfless act.

The cloud of nerve agent released by the missile blew toward them on the gentle breeze. The cameras recorded the running men and women suddenly stopping and starting to choke. In seconds the manicured grass of the park was littered with writhing bodies that shook and went rigid. The camera crews and news reporters continued recording the scene and commenting on it without understanding what was happening, until a few seconds later when the cloud reached them as well. The cameras continued to roll and to transmit the scene even while their operators lay dead behind them. In the studios the anchor people tried to raise the outside broadcast crews to ask for a better understanding of what they were seeing. There could be no response.

In the park the small crowd of spectators, realizing that something deadly was happening, panicked and ran screaming away from the scene. Some, the fastest, who ran to the sides of the park, survived. Those who ran away downwind did not. The terrorist crews could not have asked for a better start to their attack.

The second missile skimmed over the park and crashed into Harlem to unleash its silent cargo. People in the streets and shops who came into contact with the deadly airborne droplets were killed where they stood. Drivers in their vehicles lost control as their lives were snatched from them by the invisible killer. The trucks and cars careered across roads into shops or buildings. Fires started as the fuel tanks of some of the older vehicles exploded.

New Yorkers watching their televisions reeled in shock. The nightmare of the World Trade Center was back. They could not imagine that in eight minutes more would come.

The two subsequent missiles launched almost simultaneously. The first crashed to earth in Church Street on the edge of the Tribeca district, the second came down in the Lower East Side. The nerve agent spewed into the streets and took the lives of all it touched. The screams, as people saw others dropping and ran, echoed through the canyons of the city. The screaming and running, terrified people spread the panic. Nobody knew what was happening.

Most New Yorkers had been nervous of another terrorist attack for years and with good reason. The attack on the World Trade Center was seared into their memories along with recollections of friends, relatives and neighbors who had not come home that day. Now there were small aircraft landing all over the city and they had nowhere to run. Police officers had no direction and no clue as to what was happening, but they did their best to calm people and to start an orderly evacuation. They had little chance of success and were overwhelmed. Sadly, courage is no defense against nerve gas. Office buildings and banks emptied as people tried to avoid the horror by running away from a terror they could not see. Some ran to the river, others ran away from it. Nowhere was safe.

Every eight minutes with mechanical precision two more missiles appeared with their ancient jet engines buzzing and pounding over the city. As they reached it the internal guillotines operated and the power dive started until the missiles smashed into the ground. The flying bombs were affected by the breezes that swirled around the tall buildings and through the broad streets. Each was affected in different ways and so the nerve gas was dropped indiscriminately over the city, but with a concentration around the Financial District at the southern end of Manhattan. The seventh missile from V4-2 smashed through the front display window of a large department store filling the space with the vapor that would not be dispersed quickly by the wind. The sixth, from V4-1, fell harmlessly into the river as its old engine exploded a minute after take-off. The eighth swung east in a gust of wind and crashed to earth on the Brooklyn end of the Williamsburg Bridge.

Many of the panicked thousands fleeing across the bridge were caught by the gas from this explosion. The rest turned and ran back toward Manhattan, trampling over those still trying to cross the bridge and adding to the panic and fear. Military and law enforcement authorities could gain no clear picture of what was happening in the city, although it was evident that a devastating attack was in progress. Calls to the Mayor's office and to the headquarters of the police and fire departments added to the confusion as shocked officials tried to make sense of what was happening around them. The Homeland Security plans put in place after the strike on the World Trade Center swung into action, but the confusion and hysteria in the streets slowed down the practiced reaction.

Twenty minutes into the attack, a fast pass over the city by two F-16 fighter aircraft caused further panic as the sound of the jets above were assumed, by already scared people, to be another part of the attack. The two jets flew the length of Manhattan, then down the Hudson toward the sea. They failed to spot the two submarines in the mist on the water below them and would probably have assumed them to be part of the US military, never dreaming that these could be the source of the terror. The crews on the decks of the submarines heard the jets pass over them, but did not pause their deadly work.

At the docks around the river, some merchant ships were launching their boats to use the river to get away from the horror. Others, whose engines were already prepared for sea, slipped their mooring lines and left the dockside. But one old and battered cargo ship moved quietly amid the carnage. There were no boats leaving it and no rush on the decks. It slid slowly into an empty dock on Manhattan Island and dropped the mooring lines. Crewmen ran down the boarding ladder and secured the lines to steel bollards on the dock.

Had anybody had the time to look, they would have seen the freighter's Captain on his bridge watching the arrival of the slow flying missiles through his binoculars. Beside him stood the man known as Smith, also watching and smiling with satisfaction as the plan unfolded. Both men wore full, military issue, chemical warfare protective equipment. The powerful lenses swept across the city looking up the streets and seeing the bodies lying still and stiff. The Captain stepped to his left and picked up the microphone from the wall unit. His voice was muffled by the charcoal filled filter of his mask, but it was still understandable as he spoke.

"This is the captain. Open the door and send the vehicles."

At his command, a large section of the ship's side opened out to form a large hatch. The hatch fell to the dockside, anchored to the ship at what had been the bottom to form a steep ramp. The rumble of engines starting came from deep inside the vessel. Then one after another, ten military Humvees drove out of the ship and down the ramp. The vehicles were painted in U.S. Army camouflage and the crews were also wearing full military chemical warfare protective equipment. Each vehicle carried a prominent sign back and front that read "Chemical Decontamination Unit." They drove at speed out of the dock area and spread out as they went, mounting the sidewalks where they needed to get around the snarled up and abandoned traffic. They drove past bodies and frightened survivors without paying them any attention.

The first person in any sort of authority to see them was a Police Patrol Man who stepped out from behind a Yellow Cab to stop and warn them of what lay ahead. His arm was still outstretched as he hit the road surface an instant before the Humvee drove over him without slowing. The second and third vehicles drove over him too before they peeled off, away from the leading truck. The lead Humvee, still sporting the patrolman's blood across the fender, screeched to a sliding halt outside a bank. As it stopped, four men exited the vehicle. All wore the chemical protection suits and masks, and all carried M-4 assault rifles plus a holstered pistol on their belts. Without a word being spoken and without a glance toward the civilians scattered around they trotted up the wide stairs into the bank entrance, avoiding the wreckage of the V1 that had landed in the once elegant plaza.

Customers lay unmoving across the marble floor, the security guards among them. Nothing moved. Behind the high glass screen, clerks were face down on their desks or sprawled beside them. The first of the men approached the door beside the glass screened area and smashed the lock with the large sledgehammer he carried. It took a few blows to open the security door, but nobody was coming to stop him and he could take his time. The door rocked back on its hinges and the team entered and split up. One man turned left and started to empty the cash drawers throughout the customer service area. The other three hurried through to the back of the bank and down the stairs.

As expected at this time of day, the main vault had been opened. A bank employee lay face down across the threshold. The body was dragged unceremoniously to one side of the corridor and dropped to the marble floor. They stepped inside the vault. Sitting trembling in the corner of the large vault was a survivor. A young woman sat on the floor shaking and crying with shock. She reached a trembling hand toward them in hysterical supplication. She was cured by a single round between the eyes from the rifle of the first man into the vault. The others made no comment and began to collect the cash stacked on the shelves in the middle of the room. The safety deposit boxes were next. Smashed out of the wall by the heavy sledgehammer and the large crowbars they had also brought.

As two men continued to work their way through the boxes, one went back up the stairs carrying two full sacks. As he exited the front door of the bank, the fourth team member was already standing on top of the Humvee with his rifle at the ready, watching for any movement in the street. The two sacks were thrown into the back of the truck on top of the one that already lay there. Without a word to his colleague the man from the vault returned there, to continue collecting whatever the team could find of value. Cash, jewelery, deeds and share certificates were now stacked on the metal shelves in the middle of the vault. The third man started to sweep these into the heavy duty sacks he carried back to the waiting Humvee.

As the fast, efficient search ended there were now six remaining sacks at the door of the vault. The three men stepped out into the corridor and started to move the sacks up the stairs. The leader stopped, turned back to the vault to a place the security cameras could not see and just inside the door dropped a set of Muslim prayer beads.

They loaded the sacks onto the cargo bed of the Humvee and all climbed in. As they drove slowly to their rendezvous point they scanned the silent streets. They had one more stop to make before they were finished. The vehicle pulled up outside a catholic church and three of them got out and headed for the steps up to the entrance. The fourth man resumed his station on top of the vehicle, scanning for any interference from survivors. The streets were still. Nothing moved except the trees in a small park, waving in the gentle breeze.

The man keeping over watch turned to see his team leaving the church. One carried an ornate crucifix and the other a set of large antique candlesticks that looked valuable. The third man carried nothing from the church, but stopped to press the button of a radio detonator in his left hand. The stained glass windows of the church erupted with the blast, scattering fragments in all directions. Smoke billowed out of the door and the sound of falling masonry and splintering wood came with it. They paused and looked back to make sure that the fire had started, then returned to their seats in the truck.

Moving on slowly they continued to watch for survivors or other interference. There were very few and fewer still who approached them. Those that did were dispatched with one or two accurately placed rounds from an M-4. There was no sound from the men. They coldly took lives, but seemed to generate no emotion in themselves as they did. This had clearly been planned in great detail as hardly a word passed between them.

Only once did they show any sign of twisted humanity. The driver stopped the Humvee next to a roadside stall selling tourist trinkets. He climbed out and went across to the deserted stall, returning bearing four tee-shirts emblazoned with the logo that proclaimed "I Love New York." They drove on.

Ninety minutes had passed since the launch of the first flying bomb from V4-1. The U-Boats may have been dimly seen on the misty river, but had not been identified as the attackers. They continued to the next phase of their part of the plan.

Meanwhile in the stricken city the other Humvee teams were rummaging through the bank vaults that were their allocated targets. In only two banks did they find the vaults closed. One had not been opened yet and in the other they found the body of the dedicated employee who had given his life to safeguard his employer's business. These two teams wasted no time trying to crack open these massive doors and moved on quickly to their secondary targets where they found the vaults open. The haul of booty from these vaults was probably not as large as the primaries would have been, but speed was now essential. As each team finished their allocated task they moved rapidly to the rendezvous point, outside Our Lady of Victories Church on William Street.

In one of the banks an Arab *Ghutra* headdress had been caught on a splintered door frame, artfully placed out of sight of the cameras to suggest it had been wrenched off accidentally. No other clues had been deliberately left. More would have made the trail too obvious.

As the last of the Chemical Decontamination trucks pulled up to the back of the line the sound of sirens could be heard heading toward them. The New York authorities had recovered amazingly quickly and were trying to regain control of their city to help their stricken and traumatised people, using plans they developed after the attacks on the World Trade Center.

The leader of the attackers, standing by the front vehicle, waved his arm and climbed back into his seat. The convoy moved off, traveling quickly and staying close together. They turned away from the sound of sirens and headed back toward the port, turning into the dock they had left not long before, and without hesitation drove up the ramp in the side of the cargo ship. Cables from the deck cranes were now attached to the dockside end of the ramp and as soon as the last vehicle had mounted it, the ramp was hauled back up to once again become the side of the ship. Sparks flew from the edges of the improvised hatch as waiting welders secured it back in place with spot welds.

Mooring lines were cast off from the dock and the ship slowly edged back from the quay.

Chapter 20

Unknown to the crew of the slowly moving cargo ship, as they moved down the river toward the sea, they passed directly over the top of one of the submerged submarines waiting until the appointed time before executing the next phase of their mission.

Inside the submarine, the control room clock moved incredibly slowly for the crews waiting on the bottom of the river. Eventually it reached two o'clock in the afternoon. Both submarines drifted up to periscope depth and the captains took a careful look around. Fire, police and Coast Guard boats and ships scurried around them helping to find survivors and searching for the madmen who had carried out the attack. These vessels were not the targets the attackers were waiting for. They must wait until the targets they had been told to expect appeared. They settled down to the muddy bottom again, as they had been instructed and waited, listening to the sounds of the traffic in the river above them.

The man at the sound station of V4-1 strained his ears to identify the sounds he had been trained to recognize, over the last four months. Nothing but small boats racing past in the confusion of the surface and slower heavier merchant ships trying to leave the area. He stiffened in his seat and the captain and first officer, who had been watching him, stepped closer. There it was, the deeper sound of a warship or a large sized commercial ship entering the area. Then another. Their targets were here. He turned to his captain and nodded, holding up three fingers. Three targets; better than they had hoped.

The captain returned to his control room and ordered periscope depth and waited as the greased tube hissed upwards. As the water cleared from the lens he could see the gray bulk of the US Navy warship, that had been visiting the city as part of Fleet Week. He did not care what type it was. Soon it would be making a nice new reef for the fishes to hide in, if there were any fish in this cold, dark, polluted water. He ordered the forward torpedo room to make all four tubes ready for firing and maneuvered his boat slowly to bring the bow round toward the warship. They were making no effort to avoid him. They did not even suspect his presence. Fools. They would pay dearly for this arrogance. He called out the range and direction to his tactical officer who made the calculations and passed instructions to the torpedo room.

The Captain took his eye from the periscope and looked at the tactical officer.

"Ready?"

"Ready sir!"

"Fire two. Fire three."

The order was passed and the U-Boat juddered slightly along its length as it fired its first ever torpedo attack and the weapons, made for a very different war, surged through the water.

The number two torpedo failed after running half the distance to the target. It nosed down and plunged to the bottom of the river. It had run just long enough to arm itself and as it struck the bottom of the harbor the contact detonator operated and the warhead exploded, sending a tower of white water boiling up from the surface of the river. The bridge crew of the warship heard the explosion and saw the tumbling water rise from the river. Then they saw the track of torpedo three aiming straight for them. They were moving too slowly to maneuver out of the way and the first officer had just time to sound the collision alarm before the torpedo struck the ship four seconds later.

In a war zone, with all the crew on high alert, those four seconds might have been time enough to close at least some of the watertight doors, but this was New York and most of the crew was on deck wearing clumsy chemical warfare equipment and staring at the city they had come to try and help. The massive explosion amidships punched a huge hole in the side of the ship and sent tons of filthy river water flooding through the hull. The damage control parties were helpless and the pumps had no chance to save the ship as she filled with the water of their own river. The radio officer tried desperately to get a message sent but the rapid list of the ship to port gave him little time.

Out of the mist still hanging over the river came a larger gray US Navy ship this one marked with the large red crosses on a white background that signified an unarmed hospital ship. With not a care for their own safety this unarmed vessel pulled alongside the stricken warship to rescue her crew. The recovery nets were thrown over the side nearest to the men in the water and the hospital ship's boats were being lowered when she was seen through the periscope of V4-1.

The submarine skipper could not believe his luck. The large navy ship had stopped exactly where he had just fired his torpedoes. With no need to move the boat to achieve a firing solution he ordered the immediate firing of tubes one and four. Again the boat shuddered as the torpedoes accelerated away. This time there was no failure and both the underwater missiles struck the hospital ship on the port side and exploded, ripping huge holes below the water line. Despite the warning from the previous torpedo attack the rescuers had not secured the watertight doors. They had made the sad mistake of relying on their hospital ship markings and had concentrated on saving the men in the water. Their undoubted courage contributed to the rising death toll on the river.

Having launched her four forward torpedoes, V4-1 settled back gently into the river mud in the deepest part of the shallow water to reload the tubes. Due to the specialized design of these boats, only enough extra torpedoes for one more load were carried in the forward torpedo room. While this reload was going on it was the turn of V4-2 to cause mayhem and confusion in another part of the river.

Her captain decided to make his attack on the largest ships he could find rather than wait for navy targets. He brought the boat to periscope depth as soon as large propellers were identified by his sound man. The water cleared from the periscope lens and presented him with a view of a huge, laden, container ship. Her decks were piled high with the large metal container boxes holding the consumer goods that this decadent society craved. As soon as he had a firing solution, tubes one, two and four were flooded and their torpedoes launched. A ship of this size would need more torpedoes to sink than the navy ships. He kept one torpedo in reserve in case another target swam into his path.

The three torpedoes ran hot, straight and normal. At this range he could hardly miss a target of this size and all three underwater missiles struck the ship along the starboard side. The impact shook the huge vessel, dislodging a number of containers from her decks into the river where they settled to float with their tops at water level.

The merchant navy captain was on his bridge and wide awake after the attacks on the two navy vessels. To save his ship he ordered her turned toward the Brooklyn shore. With huge torrents of water pouring into his ship his only chance to prevent a complete loss was to beach her as soon as possible. It takes a long time to turn a ship of this size, but as she settled down into the water he managed to find an open area of shoreline and drove his ship onto it.

He had been lucky. The design of his ship put most of his crew above the waterline and the torpedoes had hit away from the engine room. He had lost no people, but the massive containers floating awash in the harbor could cause serious problems to other shipping until they were recovered.

Chapter 21

Captain Ahmad, skipper of V4-2, lost interest in the container ship once his weapons had impacted her. He scanned for further targets. He could hardly believe what he was seeing when through the mist he spotted the greatest prize of all, an aircraft carrier, moored and vulnerable. He swung his boat around to bring his stern tubes to bear and sent his few torpedo men racing aft through the boat to get ready to fire. As soon as his firing solution was confirmed the two aft torpedoes were fired. They ran true and struck the massive ship in the stern ripping, off a propeller and tearing open the hull.

The USS Intrepid has been a floating museum in New York for years and the river has filled the dock she sits in with silt so that, as the ship settled, she only sank four feet before coming to rest. The ship was empty of tourists and staff who had already fled the chemical attack. Still unaware of his mistake, the skipper swung his boat around to bring his single loaded forward torpedo tube to bear and fired again at the retired carrier. Again he scored a hit, but since the ship was already on the bottom he could sink her no further.

In the excitement and confusion of the wasted attack the understrength crew had lost control of the buoyancy of the U-Boat and before the skipper realized the error, she had partially surfaced and was wallowing in the dirty river water.

HMS Huntingdon, a frigate of the Royal Navy, had been on a goodwill visit to New York as part of Fleet Week and, having stayed on for a few extra days, had been leaving harbor as the attack began. She was now returning to render whatever assistance she could to the most important ally Britain has. She cruised up the river with all hands at battle stations following the torpedo attacks on the US Navy vessels. The ship's company was keyed up and ready for anything. The port bridge lookout was the first to see the attacking submarine wallowing in the water. A Royal Navy officer is not trained to hesitate and Nick Evans, the commander, seized his golden opportunity with both hands and started issuing rapid orders.

Within seconds the semi-automatic 4.5 inch naval gun on the foredeck had slewed round and aimed at the conning tower. Checking that there was no chance of overshooting and damaging New York even further, the captain gave the order to open fire. With a firing rate of twenty-five rounds per minute and a reputation for accuracy the modern 4.5 inch naval gun is a formidable weapon, particularly at close range. The first two rounds missed, but the third smashed into the conning tower and the fourth and fifth struck the pressure hull below it.

Inside the submarine's control room the crew were unaware of the British warship until the first round penetrated the conning tower above them and exploded. Whether they had time to wonder what it was in the two and a half seconds before the next round crashed in amongst them was doubtful. Most of them were slaughtered by the flying shrapnel of the exploding shell and the submarines own casing. Those that were wounded had only to suffer for a further two and a half seconds before the next round entered the compartment and snuffed out their lives.

The U-Boat was finished as an effective weapon from that instant on, but the captain of the Huntingdon was taking no chances and a further four rounds struck the submarine along her aft casing. The Chiefs' Mess was pulverized, the engine room penetrated and the huge diesel engines dismounted. The final round smashed into the aft torpedo room and ripped a massive hole in the stern. The crew in the forward sections may have survived for a few seconds or minutes, but the boat sank fast with such damage and nobody got out.

By this time the US Navy had realized they were dealing with two attacking boats loose in the river. One was now no longer a threat, but the other must be found before more lives were lost. The US Navy had suffered badly in the attacks that had cost them two ships within minutes of each other, but the crews of her warships are highly trained and accomplished professionals. They would mourn later, but first an enemy had to be dealt with. It had been a mistake to initiate the attack as Fleet Week ended with so many warships available close by.

An underwater search in such enclosed and shallow waters with so many obstructions was difficult and the number of false echoes from debris and numerous sunken ships on the bottom of the river was confusing. As long as the last submarine sat silent on the bottom it would be difficult to find and destroy.

The Captain of V4-1 was in no hurry to conclude his attack. His crew were still engaged in the slow and awkward process of reloading the forward tubes. Once that was complete he would have six torpedoes left to strike at the Americans, four in the forward tubes and two aft. His sound man was reporting large numbers of high speed screws passing up and down the river. The sounds were becoming more regular, so the enemy was probably settling into a search pattern. They had heard the multiple rapid explosions through the water as the shells had ripped their brothers to pieces and they had heard the structure of the other U-Boat cracking and tearing as she sank.

They were now the last element of the attack and the captain had to make sure that it was effective. If he succeeded this was to be a day the Americans would never forget. It would make the attack on the World Trade Center pale by comparison.

He checked his watch. The night would be coming on now. The short days at this time of year would work to his advantage. He could surface in the night and make his attack; he might even be able to make an escape if he was lucky. His first officer came to him and calmly reported that the forward tubes were loaded and ready for use. He was tired, the loading had not been easy in the reduced space available for the task in this boat.

It was too risky to make the attack now with the Americans scouring the river. He would wait. Maybe they would think that Ahmad had been alone? Perhaps they would think that this boat had already escaped to the open sea? He left a skeleton watch in the control room and ordered the rest of the crew to their bunks. They deserved rest and soon they would need their energy to continue striking at the Americans. He went to his small cabin. The extra privacy was welcome now that Romanov had left. A strange man, that Romanov, he never said why he had set up this attack at such expense to himself. Perhaps he, too, had a grudge against the Americans? Whatever the Russian's reasons, the money he had paid would compensate their families well.

Chapter 22

Unaware of the greater tragedy unfolding in the city Jim lay quietly in the rubber dinghy with Tatiana in his arms. She was awake and in pain, but the sound of his voice seemed to help a little.

He told her where he was going to take her when they made it back to shore. He described the misty wetlands of the Fens of East Anglia and made them sound mysterious and welcoming. He described the English pubs scattered alongside the waterways, where they would call in to get warm during their walks together.

She spoke very little and never complained about the pain. She looked into his eyes and searched his face as she gripped his hand weakly. Jim felt the despair of being unable to help this lovely, brave woman.

He promised that help was coming and that everything would be alright. She smiled weakly and then her eyes closed as she drifted away again. Ivan and Jim kept her lying down between them to try and give her some of their body warmth. Jim whispered to her whenever her eyes opened and she looked around.

♦ ♦ ♦ ♦

It was early morning when Ivan spoke. "It's over, boss. She's gone."

Jim looked up at him in disbelief then gently pressed her neck to feel for the pulse that was no longer there.

"But I was just talking to her. She can't be gone."

"And the last thing she heard was the sound of your voice. That will have been a comfort to her. We have to let her go now."

Andrei said a short prayer in Russian and crossed himself in the fashion of the Orthodox Church before they gently eased her limp body back into the water.

As they watched in silence she slipped below the surface and vanished from view. As Tatiana slowly sank, Jim felt the gratitude for her survival leave him, to be replaced by a cold hard ball in his stomach. The need for revenge. He made himself a promise, somewhere, somehow Romanov would answer for that girl.

Chapter 23

Captain Ibrahim slept well. Above him the search went on, but his silent, unmoving craft avoided detection. After four hours the sound man could hear through his headset that the search was running down. The US Navy had scoured the river intensively. They had investigated anomalous readings and found small wrecks from New York's turbulent history. They had even found a steam locomotive lying on its side in the mud. How that had got there was anybody's guess and would be worth investigating on a more peaceful day.

The Navy had sent divers down to V4-2 and despite the poor visibility they had identified it as a World War Two U-Boat, of a type never seen before. They had even managed to retrieve the bodies of two of the crew from the engine room. Torn and battered as they were, there was enough left of them and their uniforms to allow them to be identified as Arabic. One even had a small Quran in the pocket over his heart.

The bodies lay on the cold, steel floor plates of the deck hangar on a Navy destroyer; the helicopter it usually housed was flying a pattern search, looking for any trace of another attacker. Investigators examined the bodies to try and give them an identity or a nation of origin. Their uniforms were not of a type known to be used by any navy, but the label left in one of the suits of coveralls was in Russian. That didn't help much; the Russians had supplied many Middle Eastern governments with equipment for their armed forces.

Across the world, US forces had gone to a heightened alert status. They had a justifiable anger, that could unleash awesome military power as soon as the target was identified.

The sweeping of the river area was wound down and the focus of the search moved toward the open sea where it was assumed the second boat would be heading. Already ships were converging on the area and the sea was saturated with sonar searches. If fish and whales were affected by such sonar searches they would be having a miserable time. The river became quieter as the navy moved downstream. The sound operator in V4-1 listened carefully before reporting to his captain;

if he was right this was the time to return to their task. He walked the few steps to the captain's small cabin area. He pulled the curtain back gently. The captain lay on his back with the framed picture of his wife and children on his chest.

The picture was famous among the crew. The captain's family had been wiped out when a US Air Force practice bomb had gone astray and hit their house. They had no terrorist connections and lived in a quiet village away from the trouble spots. All they had wanted was to bring up their children in peace until an American bomb had slaughtered them. It was an accident of course and as a military man he had accepted that in training for war such things happen. He grieved for his family, but did not blame the pilot for an equipment malfunction. But then he had seen a photograph of the aircraft that had dropped the bomb. Someone had painted a little house and three small people on the nose of the aircraft to indicate a kill. For a while the Captain had gone a little insane with grief and anger. He was no longer fit to command a submarine and had been discharged from his navy. Now it was time to complete his personal revenge.

The sound man touched his captain's shoulder. He was instantly awake. He looked at his sound man who nodded, "It is time."

The captain placed his photograph carefully on the shelf above his bunk and swung his legs to the floor.

"Pass the word to the cook to make strong coffee for everyone, then wake the crew."

The captain paused to organize his thoughts. Then he walked back through the boat talking to the crew as they stirred back to life. He picked up his coffee from the galley and went back into the control room. He stood sipping the thick, black, aromatic liquid, trying to ignore the faint tinge of diesel oil while staring at the detailed chart of New York harbor. He knew exactly where he was and where the currents ran. If he kept the boat quiet he could let the current take him to a new area where he could surprise his enemy once again.

The men of the control room took their places. The torpedo men went through to their positions cradling their coffee. Nobody spoke, they were all prepared to die for their mission but, no matter what the reason, contemplating one's own death is a sobering thought for all men. The captain drained his cup and carefully set it down at the back of the navigator's table. He looked around the control room. They were all looking at him expectantly.

"Are we ready?" They all nodded, some smiled.

"Very well. Up periscope and then slowly raise the boat. I want the periscope to break the surface slowly so it is not seen."

The scope rose silently and he stepped to it. The wheels were spun and valves opened, the boat slowly and quietly rose out of the clinging river mud and started for the surface. There was a loud thump and a heavy grinding noise from above them as the boat shook along its length. The periscope wrenched violently in the skipper's hands and water gushed in under pressure as the periscope distorted.

"Take her down! Quickly! Quickly!"

The boat sank back to the bottom of the river. Although only just submerged, in this shallow part of the river, the flow of cold, dirty water into the control room was intense. In minutes it would start to affect the electrics and they would be in real trouble. If the batteries in the lower compartments were submerged it would create the deadly chlorine gas that would kill them all. The Captain considered for a second. No time for clever solutions, he needed to act now.

"Surface! Surface!"

The crew responded rapidly and the boat rose again from the bottom. He watched the depth gauge drop until he knew the conning tower was breaking the surface. He climbed the ladder, followed by his bridge crew, opened the hatch and climbed out onto the bridge deck of the conning tower. The wreckage of the periscope hung across their heads.

The lookouts took station and one called, "Captain!"

He looked where the man was pointing. Wallowing alongside them was one of the containers from the cargo ship that had been torpedoed earlier. They had tried to surface under it and destroyed the periscope. Foul luck, but an attack on the surface should present no problems in the misty, moonless night.

The four men on the conning tower bridge scanned the harbor. They had not been seen and the oily water was calm and silky. There were still ships in the area though none close to them.

The captain called down the hatchway "Electric Motors only." The deck officer looked at him quizzically. "It is quiet. We do not want anyone to hear those diesels start and then look this way."

The officer nodded and spoke into the voice pipe to relay the order, then returned to scanning ahead through his binoculars.

"Slow ahead. Come right ten degrees."

The long sleek boat slid forward in the night, parting the water to either side of its sharp bow. With hardly any bow wave and little or no wake behind them they moved slowly down river, heading toward the sea. The illuminated figure of the Statue of Liberty came into view.

The officer of the deck said, "A shame the Germans did not fit deck guns to this boat. We could have made quite a mess of the green lady."

The Captain snorted, "A useless gesture. I am here to take revenge not make political statements. Find me a meaningful target for the rest of our torpedoes."

Even so, all four of the men on the deck looked up as the imposing statue came closer to them. Illuminated by the floodlights and rising out of the river mist it was an impressive sight.

The US Coast Guard cutter rapidly overtaking them went undetected as the U-Boat crew looked forward and sideways. The skeleton crew meant that the bridge deck was not fully manned. The submarine had appeared on the cutter's radar as soon as it surfaced and the night vision systems had identified it as soon as it started to move. The cutter crew could hardly believe the situation. The enemy was in front of them and they had yet to be seen. This submarine could not be allowed to escape. The crew had been warned to be ready for a collision as soon as the U-Boat had been seen. No loudspeaker announcements were made and no klaxons were sounded. The U-Boat was not to be given any extra chance to spot them.

Down below in the U-Boat, the exhausted sound man returned to his station, sipping his coffee He put on his headset. For two, then three, then four seconds his tired mind refused to process what he was hearing. Then it made sense. He leapt from his seat, knocking the coffee over the plotting table, the old fashioned headphones wrenched from his ears jerking his head back. He ran into the control room, pushing startled men out of the way. Reaching the conning tower ladder he started to climb rapidly.

"Behind us! Behind us!"

The bridge crew spun round to look behind. They did not need binoculars. As he reached the deck the sound man looked back and saw to his horror the creamy white bow wave of a ship at speed and above it the bow of the cutter with the familiar red and blue hull markings of the Coast Guard. There was no time for anything and no point in screaming.

They stood paralyzed and watched their end unfold.

The cutter was slightly out to one side and approaching fast. They saw it heel outwards in the turn. A few seconds more and the bow sliced into the pressure hull behind the conning tower. The casing of the U-Boat was strong, but it had been built for pressure and not this sort of impact. The metal tore as the bow of the cutter penetrated the pressure hull. The momentum of the Coast Guard ship continued, the U-Boat was forced sideways and started to roll. As the cutter mounted the aft end of the submarine the conning tower rolled down into the polluted water. The hatch was still open and the cold water cascaded in as the weight of the cutter pressed the U-Boat down. With such a rush of water there was no chance for anyone to climb the ladder and escape. The control room flooded, smashing men against the bulkheads and controls. With the pressure hull ruptured the integrity of the boat was gone and the compartments aft of the conning tower filled. The air in the sealed forward torpedo room held the bow above water for a short time, but then the weight of the water in the rest of the boat dragged her back down into the dark river mud.

The cutter was now resting in the disturbed water above her victim. The rescue lights came on and the search for survivors started, more in following standard operating procedures than in any hope of actually finding anyone. The impact had been so violent that there had been little time for any escapes. The Petty Officer on the port wing of the bridge swung his searchlight around again, this time there was something there. A man in the water and he was still moving. The crew flung the scrambling net over the port side and some climbed down to grab the survivor. As they watched he slipped beneath the water. He may be an enemy, but he was still a sailor in need and two of the Coast Guard crew dived into the cold water after him. They swam down into the dark and found him by touch. Striking back for the surface they brought him back into the air. He was still alive, though in poor shape. They swam him to the side of the cutter and strong hands pulled him out of the water and into the ship.

In minutes they had him into their small sick bay doing everything they could to save the man they had tried to kill minutes earlier.

Chapter 24

New York is a city well used to sirens as emergency vehicles try to make progress through the crowded streets. But these sirens were different and the vehicles were moving slowly to weave through the mess of abandoned cars and taxis. Often they had to mount the sidewalk to get around the solid mass of abandoned vehicles. The vehicles were different as well. These were specialist military armored vehicles adapted for chemical and biological warfare. They moved slowly through the deserted streets of the city using their complex array of sensors to sniff the air. Searching for answers to determine what lethal substance had been used to cripple the most famous city on Earth, to determine what countermeasures were needed.

The hatches and viewing ports of these camouflaged vehicles were sealed tight as the crews moved them slowly forward and tried to interpret what their instruments were telling them. Their computerized systems had been programed with every known toxin that the US Military was aware of. In the early days of development the nerve agents developed by the German Army in the mid-1940s had been used as test chemicals and these were still in the databanks. As the leading vehicle reached the financial district the first traces of the droplets were picked up and analyzed. The results were sent back to a command vehicle well north of Central Park where specialists analyzed the findings.

They had to dig deeply into their records to find these long disused chemicals but eventually it became clear that amongst the horror and killing there was one small glimmer of light; this was a non-persistent agent, originally designed to disperse rapidly so that German troops could advance through the area without harm, after the ancient gas shells had done their deadly work on their enemies.

The breeze from the river and the light mist that still stirred through the streets was having its effect and the fatal droplets were being blown away and evaporating. Within an hour of starting the search for answers the chemical detection vehicles were able to report the city clear of nerve agent so that the emergency services and the investigators could enter the stricken streets to bring help to the survivors. Scattered through the city were people who had been injured in the panic, trampled by running crowds or crushed against walls and buildings by mobs of severely frightened people. Broken bones, crushing injuries and severe abrasions could be helped and most would heal. For those who had been touched by the deadly chemicals there was no help. Ambulances from all over the state came into Manhattan escorted by police cars and fire trucks. Their crews searched the streets for survivors and using handheld loudspeakers they urged people who had shut themselves away to come out and be helped. The number of bodies lying in the street or inside buildings that had been contaminated was truly awful. The department store that had been hit was particularly difficult for the rescue teams as most of the shoppers at that time of day had been women and children. In the enclosed space the gas had been horrendously effective.

In City Hall the casualty count kept growing as the reports came in. City morgues were swamped and the Army brought in casualty clearing specialists to deal with the overflow. Hospitals too were augmented by mobile military facilities that had been identified and prepared after the 9/11 attacks. Slowly the situation started to come under control. The mental trauma would take many more years to heal.

While the injured and the dead were being cleared from the city and dealt with according to their needs, other vehicles entered the area without fanfare. These were the forensic examiners made famous by TV shows that trivialized the complexity and thoroughness of their work. The scientists and their assistants combed through the debris of the banks, looking for indications of who had perpetrated this horror. They crawled the floors, examined locks, dusted for fingerprints and swabbed for DNA. The results were pitifully thin. The attackers had taken sound precautions to avoid leaving any trace. The prayer beads were found in one vault and the Arabic headdress hanging from a splintered doorway outside another.

The burnt out church was examined and the explosive residue sent for analysis. As they stood in what had once been the main aisle of the church the local police lieutenant looked around at what had been his spiritual home since boyhood.

He sighed deeply and turned to the investigators, "Where has the crucifix been moved to?"

"We haven't moved anything out," the technician told him, "this is just as we found it."

The lieutenant grabbed a couple of his police officers and started a rapid search around the altar. With the permission of the forensic team, they moved ashes and debris aside and checked wherever the artifacts from the altar could have fallen. The stunning altar furniture that had been there throughout his childhood was gone.

He called the lead investigator across to him. "There is something odd going on here. This altar had two huge candle sticks and a wonderful crucifix. They were old and famous and now they are gone. This is something more than just an attack on a church."

The investigator looked around. "That adds to what we are finding. This is far too professional for a random church attack by religious nuts. I'll pass it up the chain."

Chapter 25

In Washington there was less confusion than there might have been. The terrorist attacks on the World Trade Center and the Pentagon had identified some weaknesses in response to assaults on the US mainland. Without fanfare, the military and other agencies had studied the actions taken after those attacks; they had found the errors and carefully put these to rights. Now a well-oiled machine swung into action to identify the source of the attack and to plan a response. There was to be no knee jerk reaction until all the facts were known. This attack had come from nowhere. None of the normal intelligence indicators had shown any increase in activity in the past few months. It was unlikely to be one of the groups who had been penetrated by US Intelligence or one that was under close surveillance. This in itself was a worry. Intelligence operators always worry about what they do not know. These attackers must be a sophisticated group with access to weapons of mass destruction. How then had they been missed by the best intelligence service in the world?

New York police and the FBI combing through the banks that had been looted were passing their findings, no matter how small, to join with other information being sifted and processed. Army Intelligence was trying to identify which military unit had been seen with Chemical Decontamination vehicles in the city. The Navy had divers down in the dark river water examining the wrecked submarines. The Coast Guard was patrolling with the Navy off the coast looking for anything that might give further clues, such as a support or command ship. The Navy was sweeping the Eastern Seaboard to ensure that there were no more submarines lurking. The Air Force had standing air patrols and AWACS aircraft, with their slowly spinning radar domes, watching over the city to ensure all civilian air traffic stayed well within the designated air lanes. Across the world US Intelligence agencies were calling all their informers and agents to try and identify the source of the attack. Allied governments, and even those less friendly to the USA, were hurriedly trying to find out if any of their nationals had been involved.

In the studied quiet of the Intensive Care Unit of a city hospital, doctors worked hard to save the life of the single unconscious survivor of the attackers who had been rescued from the water. He had been transferred off the Coast Guard cutter as soon as possible and moved to one of the best medical facilities in the city. FBI agents stood guard at the door waiting for a chance to speak to him and to make sure that none of the victims from the city made an unofficial visit.

The evidence accumulated slowly and was collated carefully. There was to be no jumping to conclusions this time. The *Ghutra* headdress that had been found was a typical Arabic head dress used all over the Middle East. This seemed to indicate an Arabic connection until one of the analysts pointed out that in recent years they had become a fashion item among young people. His daughter wore one when she cycled to school.

Likewise the Muslim Prayer Beads, sometimes known as a *tasbih*, that were found in the vault. Although an indicator, this was not allowed to be conclusive evidence, especially as the string of beads bore no signs of wear.

The fire bomb attack on the church seemed to indicate a group intent on destroying a Christian place of worship. But there was a growing feeling that something was wrong. The destruction of the church could be by religious extremists, but the theft of Christian artifacts did not seem to fit the pattern expected of such people.

Intelligence officers were only too aware that the default blame setting in the US had become Al Qaeda, ISIL, or some other allied Muslim group, but the clues seemed just a little too obvious. They needed to make sure that the Arabs had not been set up as decoys, to focus retaliation on Al Qaeda, to allow the real culprits to escape.

The survivor in his hospital bed had been stripped of his clothing. His meagre belongings lay on an analyst's table. The coveralls were of Russian manufacture. The green badge sewn to the sleeve was in Arabic but, crucially, when examined by an expert, the embroidered text was found to have been misspelled. His boots were German. He carried a *Tasbih* in his pocket, but one that was considerably more worn through use than the one found in the vault. His physical appearance had been assessed and he was thought to be of Middle Eastern origin. The abrasion to the front of both of his ears was unexplained. He had no tattoos and no more than superficial scars on his hands.

The most intriguing part of the puzzle was the wreckage of the missiles. The explosives that distributed the nerve agent had not been powerful enough to destroy all the delivery vehicles themselves. The twisted and damaged metal bodies were examined and puzzled over. They were not of any type known to modern US military authorities. Then one of the staff from the Harbor Defense Museum in Brooklyn spotted the wreckage in Central Park as he was trying to make his way home, from a visit to his daughter in Manhattan and identified the missiles as the V1 Flying Bomb from the Second World War. The intelligence team knew that close to twenty of these weapons had been used, but had no idea where so many of them could have come from.

The body of the NYC policeman who had been run down was recovered after a shocked witness reported him being deliberately killed by the US Army. His clothing was examined and traces of army issue camouflage paint were found. After analysis they were determined to be an exact match for the paint used by the army on its vehicles.

The bullet that had killed the young woman inside the vault was recovered and found to be a match for those fired from the US Army's M-4 rifle. With the same bullet being widely available in gun shops across the USA, the discovery did not help much.

The Military Police started an intensive search to identify the military unit that had been in New York during the chemical attack. The local units had all been checked and ruled out of the search. After mobilizing Military Police units across the nation and widening the search considerably, the source of the vehicles was identified as a National Guard unit outside Baltimore in Maryland. When the commander was interviewed it was found that an official notification had been received that their Humvees were to be withdrawn temporarily for modifications and upgrades. This was to be carried out in batches of ten so as not to reduce the effectiveness of the unit. Three days later a group of fully accredited US Army drivers had arrived to collect the first ten trucks. Paperwork had been checked and was all in order.

Police reports were checked and the convoy had been seen heading into the Baltimore dock area, but no suspicions had been aroused so no action had been taken. They had not been seen to leave the docks and a rapid search was carried out to confirm they were not there now. It took time to search every part of the sprawling dock area of Baltimore, but no trace of the ten vehicles was found so it was a reasonable assumption that they were on a ship.

The records in both Baltimore and the massive ports of New York were gathered and checked for any vessels that were common to both at the right times. There were a number that matched, but either they were too small, or of the wrong type, to be carrying Humvees, or the time scales did not fit. A junior analysis clerk was given the task of a more detailed and laborious check, although nothing was expected. It had become clear that this had not been a real US military unit and that considerable organization had gone into the planning of this operation. It was also clear by now that this was something different to just a politically motivated terrorist attack.

The Navy examination of the two wrecked submarines was inconclusive to begin with. Visibility was poor and the currents in the shallow river are fierce. A massive recovery ship was brought up from the Norfolk naval base to raise the U-Boats from the bottom. V4-1 was the first to be raised as its position was closer to the dockside. Cables were passed around it, no mean feat in itself, requiring considerable skill from the US Navy divers. Huge flotation bags were attached and as the lift commenced, these were inflated to assist. Searchlights picked out the crippled black hull as it broke through the surface of the river. A submersible barge slipped beneath it and then, pumping out its tanks, raised the U-Boat clear of the water. The water gushed violently out of the gashed and twisted hull bringing two bodies with it and leaving another wedged in the tear in the hull with one arm hanging loose in some sort of supplication. The bodies were removed carefully so as not to destroy evidence. The presence of TV cameras ensured that due reverence was paid to the dead. Despite feelings running high, the US military are sensitive to claims of their callousness toward enemies and ensured there would be none of that this time.

Naval officers climbed warily inside the U-Boat. They made their way slowly forward and aft in two parties, stepping over twisted bodies and debris as they went. Follow-up parties of naval investigators collected documents and charts carefully, trying to ensure the waterlogged paper did not tear. The navigator's GPS unit was removed to be tested to see if a record of the boat's course could be found.

As the forward party moved on they came to the large missile compartment. Now empty, except for two battered bodies and the pathetic personal items in the water swilling around them. There was little to indicate what had been stored here. They moved through to the watertight door at the forward end of the compartment. Turning the door clamps they swung the hatch open to find four unconscious and injured crewmen lying against the bulkhead. They had been thrown violently around in the forward torpedo room and the oxygen was nearly gone when their saviors arrived, but beyond hope they were alive. That gave the Intelligence team four more sources of information and was seen as a gift.

Chapter 26

The Press, as usual, were baying for instant answers and White House press conferences were descending into a farce as the Administration tried to keep the situation under control. At the end of the day President Barker demanded a report from his National Security Advisor who was forced to admit that they still did not know who was responsible. There were clues that men from the Middle East had been crewing the submarines, but there were anomalies that pointed elsewhere. The Pentagon, FBI, CIA and all other agencies were being extremely careful to ensure that, when the retaliatory strike came, it was aimed at precisely the right spot this time. In the interim, US Forces across the world remained at a high state of readiness. Allied nations were pledging support by the hour. The scale of the attack had yet to be fully assessed, but it was clear at the outset that when the numbers came in they would be bad. Perhaps even worse than the 9/11 attacks.

The American public was at first stunned, but was now becoming angry and the fury of a powerful nation must be channeled if it is not to do more harm than good. The President phoned the British Prime Minister to thank him for the prompt action of HMS Huntingdon and learned that the British Armed Forces were mobilizing. Reserves were being called up, "Called back to the Colors" as the Prime Minister termed it, an expression he had just learned from his military advisors and was ridiculously pleased with.

The President then called the Russian President to keep him up to date. The Russians were by no means the enemies of the past and the relationship between the two countries was improving rapidly, but they still had formidable forces and still became nervous when the US increased its military alert state. Sitting in the Oval Office, the President was pleasantly surprised to hear an unconditional pledge of support from Russia. He had not expected that. The numbers of civilians killed had appalled people across the world, even old adversaries. The Russian accepted a personal invitation to come to the White House urgently and join with the British Prime Minister to discuss a coordinated way forward. Other heads of government could be invited later.

In her own office, the Vice President was calling all heads of government of the allied nations who could be relied upon for support. The President was taking the difficult ones. His next call was to China and again he was surprised at the full and open offer of support from Beijing. It began to appear that this tragedy might have a positive outcome after all, if managed carefully.

Chapter 27

In the dark of the Atlantic night, the cargo ship carrying the ten Humvees and their crews plowed eastwards at full speed without lights. They did not know it but during the night they passed within a mile of a small rubber dinghy with four lost, cold men huddled in it. The men in the dinghy did not see them either. Given the recent performance of the people aboard the freighter, it was a blessing in disguise.

The speed of the cargo vessel was not impressive by modern standards but every hour they were another eleven nautical miles from their victims and more importantly, their avengers. Aboard the ship, the bags from the ten Humvees had been unloaded and taken aft to the crew's mess. Now it was a counting house for cataloguing the spoils of the raid. Money was piled on one set of tables being sorted into piles by currency and denomination. Those piles were impressive. Another set of tables held jewelery which was being expertly appraised and sorted. Artwork was stacked against a bulkhead to be dealt with later. The largest table was the one dealing with Bearer Bonds, the untraceable documents that allowed large sums of money to be moved around without coming to the attention of the tax authorities. Since these documents are not registered, whoever holds them can claim to be the legitimate owner, making them highly attractive for money laundering and tax evasion. Safety Deposit Boxes in reputable and secure banks are usually the safest way to keep these valuable assets secure, at least they were until the assault teams had visited. Walking between the groups of tables was a tall, thin, studious looking man with a calculator that he continually keyed numbers into, until he gave up trying to follow the enormous value of the haul.

Every now and then, men who had been the raiders on the ground would stick their heads around the door to observe what was going on with the accounting. He, or they, would then wander back to the area allocated to them to report to the rest.

Aristotle Christophides, the Captain of the freighter, a suitably scruffy looking Greek, went to the leader of the assault group to pass on the instructions he had been given. The men were to change out of uniform and into civilian clothes. The uniforms and weapons were to be loaded into the Humvees and these were then to be pushed over the side of the vessel to sink to the bottom of the Atlantic. It was a shame they were not going to pass over the final resting place of the Titanic; it would have been amusing to read about a convoy of trucks being found alongside the great ship next time it was visited by scientists.

The assault teams objected. They had no problem with dumping the vehicles or the uniforms, but were vehemently opposed to dumping their weapons before they were safely away. The Captain shrugged and turned on his heel, it made no difference to him whether they kept the weapons or not. As he left, the assault team leader galvanized his men. They changed and took the uniforms and chemical protective equipment down to the hold where the ten vehicles stood in darkness. The spot welds holding the side hatch in place had been cracked open. They could hear the deck cranes moving above their heads and then the side of the hold opened as the large hatch was lowered to below the horizontal by the cables that had raised it in the dock. It took a few men to push each of the heavy four wheel drive vehicles on to the ramp formed by the ship's open side. Once on the ramp, they rolled slowly and then faster over the end and somersaulted into the water. The job was quickly done and the hatch was closed. The welder who had unsealed it for this task set about re-welding it, more permanently this time. The men returned to their quarters to finish watching the recorded film on the TV in the corner of the room.

The counting continued through the night and well into the next day. The numbers were higher than even the highest estimates. The number and value of Bearer Bonds in particular had been wildly underestimated. Americans appeared to be very keen to keep large amounts of money away from the attention of the Internal Revenue Service. Estimating the value of the art would take weeks, but it was obvious that there were some startling pieces in the haul. Disposing of these would need to be managed carefully with discrete approaches to selected private collectors, who could be trusted to enjoy secret ownership.

The freighter continued on its way, untroubled by the P3 Orion aircraft that flew over them from time to time. After a low pass they always flew on, satisfied that this was just a harmless cargo ship. The name of the ship had changed since she left New York as it had when she left Baltimore. The false deck fittings that gave her a distinctive shape had been collapsed and the company colors on the funnel had changed. They had changed the tattered flag that flew at her stern. She was of no interest to the US Navy now. The real ship that bore this name and registration had sunk in Malaysian waters well over a year ago, but no insurance claim had been submitted, so she still plowed the seven seas as far as Lloyds of London was concerned, and through them the authorities now searching.

The ship's Captain and Smith stood in the radio shack surrounded by an extremely high tech array of equipment for a rusty old freighter, listening to the sounds of the search coming across the airwaves. They would know as soon as there was any hint that they were suspected. The captain waited until the scheduled time for the call to come in. Every day at this time he was contacted to be given his instructions and to report his progress over the secure channel. Yesterday he was told to dump the vehicles and weapons. Today he would report his position, course and speed as well as the fact that his passengers were clinging to their weapons. He wondered how his employer would react to that.

He made his report and was greeted with a silence from the other end of the call. His employer was used to being obeyed absolutely, that had been made painfully clear to him over the last few years. Then he was told that, should a US Navy or Coast Guard ship appear, the weapons were to go over the side immediately. There was to be no evidence that could connect the ship to the assault. He was told to check that the hidden storage was ready to take the haul presently being counted. The Captain agreed, but knew it was in perfect condition. He had been smuggling drugs and weapons in there for years and he had lost count of the Customs searches in various ports that had been unable to find anything of interest.

It was unusual for his employer not to react with fury at being disobeyed. Maybe he was mellowing with age? He chuckled at the thought, Romanov would never mellow. In his business any sign of weakness could be fatal. It could also be fatal to ignore his orders. His first mate had found that out, two years ago in Singapore. A shame about that, he had been a good mate, but headstrong and he had been warned. The body had not been a pretty sight when the police had fished it out of the harbor.

He was surprised not to have been given a destination by now. He was plowing toward the distant coast of France, but was pretty sure that would not be their objective. The French police and customs were way too efficient and would be cooperating with their friends, the Americans, on a job of this seriousness. Still, he knew enough not to ask. He would be told when the time came.

Chapter 28

In Washington the intelligence continued to flow into the command center. There had been no further clues from the banks; no fingerprints, no DNA and no descriptions worth a damn, the chemical protection suits and masks had seen to that. The five surviving crewmen from the submarines were still unconscious and the doctors were being difficult about waking them prematurely. The President had issued instructions that they were to be treated humanely in view of the worldwide media scrutiny and the medical staff were taking his orders seriously.

Laboring forgotten at a small desk pushed against the wall of the situation room, the junior analysis clerk read and re-read the lists of shipping spread in front of him. He had called up the Lloyds Register of Shipping on his computer and was comparing everything he could find about every ship on the list. It was tedious and time consuming, but the clerk chosen was ideal for the job. He had a high threshold of boredom and found puzzle solving fascinating. He worked long hours and had been all but forgotten by the rest of the analysis team. They even forgot to include him when they went to collect coffee. He did not mind. While working he had no need for human interaction and he was uncomfortable among the smart uniforms anyway.

He found nothing in common between Baltimore and New York that could help the search, so started to check the previous ports of call logged for each ship by Lloyds. It was fascinating to see where they had come from and the range of cargoes they carried. Then he saw it. One cargo freighter had come to Baltimore from Palermo in Sicily. Nothing unusual in that, but something was wrong in the figures he was seeing. He pushed his glasses up onto the bridge of his nose and concentrated on the data. He stared until it became clear. The time taken to sail from Palermo to Baltimore was too short. He called up the distances and using the high school math that Mrs. Brindle had taught him all those years ago, he found that to reach Baltimore in that time the ship would have been traveling at 57.6 miles an hour. Not even the Queen Mary, with her powerful modern engines, sailed at that speed or even close to it. He raised his head and looked across at the big conference table in the middle of the room. His analysis training had emphasized the need to share information to ensure every snippet was brought together. So why was he the one not at the table? No matter.

"Got something," he said.

His words fell into the gloomy silence around the big table. Every head turned to him. Very gratifying. He explained his findings. A ship had traveled across the Atlantic at impossible speed to Baltimore, it had rested there for three days and left again, it had collected no cargo and delivered none according to the port records. The next entry had it entering harbor in Walvis Bay, Namibia. The speed required to travel from Baltimore to the African city was again excessive. But the dates to travel from Palermo to Walvis Bay gave a perfectly reasonable speed for a ship of that type. The ship that entered Baltimore harbor could not have been the one it claimed to be.

The junior clerk found all his papers lifted and taken to the central table where senior analysts pored over them until they declared that there was nothing else to find. He had found an anomaly, but it led nowhere. He was then allowed to return to his quiet, cluttered desk to continue his painstaking search. The senior analysts might be right, but he had been given a puzzle to solve and nobody had told him to stop yet.

The ship that left Baltimore could possibly have been employed to deliver the stolen Humvees to New York. But if he took an average speed of a freighter and calculated a time to sail to New York no similar ships had entered the harbor at a suitable time. There had been a delay of some two and a half weeks between the ship leaving Baltimore and the attack in New York. That ship had to have been somewhere during that time. Normally, with his clearance level, he would have had no access to high grade satellite imagery, but the senior analysts at the big table did. He went across during a lunch break and asked the two investigators still sitting there if he could use their access codes to check something. They were about to be dismissive, but he had found something earlier so they agreed.

Once he had entered the correct codes into his computer, the junior analyst turned down the lighting over his desk and watched as the images passed across the computer screen before him. The clarity of pictures taken from space was impressive. He had never had the leisure to admire

the results before now. Maybe he should ask for a transfer to photo inter-
pretation after this was over?

There was a lot of empty ocean on the pictures he scanned. There was
an occasional iceberg and just once he saw a whale breaching over the
Stellwagen Bank, just off Boston. There were numbers of nondescript
freighters working up and down the coasts and across the Atlantic. None
stood out until he saw one turning sharply out at sea. Now why would
a freighter need to turn like that? Surely the Captain was not changing
his mind about where he was going? He filed that image and then looked
in that area again and again. The freighter reappeared in a number of
images all in the same area spread over a period of days. He logged all
the images of the ship and saved them to be examined later. He zoomed
in as closely as he could on his desktop screen. There was something
going on, on the deck of the freighter, but he could not make out the detail. With a few keystrokes he managed to put the image up on the large
plasma screen above the conference table. The analysts, now back from
lunch and clustered around the big table, looked up.

"What's that about?" the team leader asked.

The junior analyst didn't answer, but walked over and stood before the
screen staring hard. He brushed his dark hair back from his forehead
and stared up at the big screen. The clarity was stunning and the level of
detail hard to believe. He walked back to his desk and called up another
image of the ship on a second plasma screen. He walked back and looked
between the two images.

"I said, what's that about?" said the senior analyst again, coming to
stand next to his junior.

"That, sir, is a pair of pictures of the ship that took the stolen Humvees
out of Baltimore. And if you look at the funnel and the after deck you
will see why we couldn't find her."

The senior analyst looked, as did all the others, who had come to stand
behind them. Structures on the deck that would have changed the ship's
profile were being moved and it looked like there was a boatswain's chair
at the side of the funnel with a man in it painting.

"Damn me, you did it again!"

He turned to the rest of the analysts, "OK people, we now know how
they did it, but I want to know what that ship looked like when it came
into New York and more importantly I want to know what it looks like
now. Get on it!"

He turned to the junior clerk who had found what the rest had missed.

"This is embarrassing," he said, "but I don't know your name"

"It's Malcolm, sir, David Malcolm."

"Well David, it looks like we need to take a little more interest in your skills. Ignore what the rest are doing and tell me what you would do next."

"Well sir, the appearance of the ship in New York does not matter much until after we catch them and get them into court. What matters is where that ship is now and probably where it's going."

"So if it has changed its appearance again how do we find it?"

"The satellite images are clear and we know how high above the earth the satellite is. So the math to work out the size of the ship should be simple enough. Mrs. Brindle taught me that back in High School in Cedar Rapids. We have lots of ships and planes out there so if we give them the ship's dimensions they should be able to round up any likely targets."

"Get on it and if you get this right we send Mrs. Brindle a 'thank you' note from the President. How long will you need?"

Chapter 29

Cruising at eleven knots the freighter had now reached some seven hundred nautical miles out into the Atlantic in the three days since leaving New York. Her engines were now still as a second ship came alongside them. This one was considerably smaller, but had the look of a deep sea trawler.

In fact it had been converted to be an underwater research vessel with accommodation for a large number of scientists and crew, though not in any great comfort. It had been retired from research duties when the cost of an upgrade to more modern technology exceeded the value of the ship itself. It had then been sold for conversion to a private cruising yacht but that conversion had never taken place.

The deck cranes on the larger ship lifted large crates across and dropped them directly into the laboratory of the smaller vessel through what had once been the fish hatch when she had served as a trawler. The crew and passengers climbed down the accommodation ladder that had been lowered down the side of the freighter and stepped across onto the deck of the smaller ship. The uncommonly calm weather in the North Atlantic made this exercise easy and quick. Normal weather would have made it considerably more difficult and risky. Within a half hour the transfer was complete and Christophides, the Greek skipper of the freighter, was standing on the bridge of the research vessel with his colleague and Smith. The research vessel's crew cast off the lines and the ships pulled slowly apart.

As the gap between them grew to five hundred meters the freighter skipper produced a gray plastic box from his jacket pocket. He flipped a switch and a red light illuminated above a row of four buttons.

"Ready?" he said to the other captain.

Without waiting for a reply he pressed the first button. The rumble of the explosion rolled across the water, a moment later smoke issued from the open doorway beneath the bridge. A second push and a further explosion resulted in smoke boiling out of the second deck hatch.

The third button push brought smoke from the forward hatch after the customary rumble from deep inside the ship.

He turned to the bridge crew "You might want to see this one."

The bridge crewmen walked to the starboard side of the bridge. As he pressed the last button the explosion was followed by a loud roar and a huge gout of flame as the fuel bunkers ignited. The ship was already settling into the sea before the last explosion and fire so the smoke and flames were soon wiped out by the inrushing water. The freighter slipped beneath the gentle waves and left hardly a trace except for some burning fuel oil.

"Ah well," her captain said, "that will have killed an awful lot of rats and cockroaches. A shame we had to sink her. She was a fine ship for the smuggling."

The vibration through the deck plates increased as the retired trawler accelerated away from the area and turned south west.

The Skipper and crew of the freighter were accommodated in one mess with the bank raiders in another on the opposite side of the laboratory area. The full-time crew of the trawler had a set of small cabins in the after part of their ship. The haul from the bank raids was still being processed and counted, but now with particular attention being paid to the art and antique treasures that had been scooped up with everything else.

The trawler skipper went to his radio room with its equally dazzling array of communication equipment as that to be found on the cargo ship, now resting deep below the surface. He called Romanov to report the successful transfer of the cargo and people from the freighter. He gave his position and course, as was the usual procedure for Romanov's fleet.

Behind his ship the small amount of oil spilled from the freighter, after the fuel bunkers had been incinerated, was being dispersed by the waves and the breeze. It was another twenty-seven minutes before the American spy satellite was due to pass overhead, they were well within the allocated time for the transfer and he was leaving the area at a speed that would have surprised the previous owners of the ship, who were unaware of the two new diesel engines that only just fitted into the engine room. They slowed to a more reasonable speed once well-clear of the changeover point. The reduction in the vibration through the hull was welcome to everyone on board and they settled down to enjoy the cruise into warmer waters.

Chapter 30

David Malcolm, in the intelligence center in Washington, had completed his calculations. The dimension of the ship plus any appearance points, such as bow shape, that could not be changed had been passed to all Coast Guard and US Navy vessels with orders to stop and search any ship that fitted, or came close to fitting, the description.

Some of the captains queried the legality of an order to stop and search civilian vessels on the high seas, but were given a Presidential directive to comply. The information was also passed to the navies of all allied countries and any of those that had pledged support. The first report to come in was from a Russian submarine operating south of Greenland that called in the coordinates of a ship that fitted the description. The Russians would not board the ship, but shadowed it until the US Navy arrived in a fast frigate to carry out their search.

The search was thorough and at times impolite. The Swedish captain protested, but understood and became cooperative when the reasons were explained to him. There were seven ships found that fitted the description and were within range of New York in the time allowed to get to their present positions. They were all stopped and searched.

Nothing concerning the attack was found, although one ship was found to be carrying a significant cargo of smuggled drugs. The US Navy had more important things to be concerned about so dropped the drugs into the sea and allowed the ship to go on its way.

The freighter sinking had created another blind alley and had served to divert attention away from the large trawler that now cruised calmly through the edge of the search area, carrying the culprits away from the clutches of their avengers.

Chapter 34

In the hospital in New York the surviving crewmen from the U-Boats were slowly gaining consciousness. As soon as they were able to make sense, the specialist Arabic speaking interrogators began interviewing them. There were no bullying techniques used as the medical staff would not allow it, although the questioning was intense.

The crew were from a number of Middle Eastern nations and had been recruited over a period of time. They had been briefed in general on the type of submarine they were to crew and had practiced the necessary skills before the boats left the base in Kiel.

The most useful information started to come when the youngest of the FBI agents said in frustration, "But why did you do this? What did you hope to achieve?"

The crewman he was speaking to turned his head slowly and said, "Money, just money. I have a disease that will kill me within a year. With the money I have been paid for this task my family will be secure once I am gone."

The lead interrogator looked up from his notes. "Is that the same for all of your crew?"

"No. There are some few like me who have a terminal illness. That is why we were discharged from the navies we served in. Others like the captains had a burning hatred for Americans for things they have done. Did you know your bombs wiped out my Captain's family? Just a mistake but it burned him up inside when he saw the lack of respect your people have for any of our families who die. There were many reasons, but for all of us the pay was good and will help the families of those who do not go home."

"Did you expect to die? Did you expect to be a martyr?"

The crewman laughed quietly, shaking his head, "Oh you Americans have such a simple view of the world. If you are attacked by a Muslim it must of course be *Jihad*. No. We knew it was dangerous, but we hoped to escape and we had a plan to do so. Sadly that is not to be."

The news that the attackers were mercenaries and not holy warriors was passed to Washington. The convenient clues pointing to Muslim extremists now fitted into place. That had all been a smokescreen to divert attention. Had the US authorities not analyzed the information carefully, before acting, there could have been a blood bath in some innocent nation. This would have provided a wonderful diversion and focused the attention of the most powerful military force in the world on the wrong target. It would also have alienated a number of nations who had now pledged their support.

Clever but not quite clever enough.

Chapter 32

Far away to the west of the fleeing trawler the small rubber dinghy floated on the wide uncaring ocean. After days and nights on the water the four men were bitterly cold, wet and exhausted, but the weather had been surprisingly kind to them for this time of year in the North Atlantic. They huddled together for what warmth they could gather from each other and watched for any ship or aircraft that might come near them. Aircraft had passed over repeatedly, but the tiny gray dinghy on a wide, gray ocean had not been seen.

On the first day their survival training had kicked in and they had established the routine that would give them the best chance of getting out of the dinghy alive. They could live without food for a few days, but drinking water was a more immediate problem. The first order of business was to bail out the sea water that had slopped into the small boat as they left the submarine. They were all cold and wet, but sitting in pools of water would only make that worse and would probably cause weeping sores they could do without. They had used their cupped hands to dump water over the side and then a tee shirt from Geordie's haversack had done duty as a sponge to get out the remainder. The activity had warmed them slightly.

After Tatiana was gone they settled down in the small boat and Jim turned to Ivan, "So what made you bring this dinghy along with you in the first place?"

Ivan smiled and nodded his head toward Geordie, "We both started to get an uncomfortable feeling about Romanov and his heavies. Nothing we could put a finger on, but just a niggling at the back of the mind. His attitude was all wrong for the person he claimed to be. So we grabbed anything we thought might be useful and when this dinghy fitted perfectly in my backpack it seemed like a sign, I couldn't resist it. Same reason Geordie packed the weapons."

Jim smiled, "Well you keep in touch with your feelings, guys, they paid off in spades this time."

After the first day thirst had started to become a problem and the ex-soldiers knew that drinking the sea water around them would probably kill them and would, at best, have a seriously negative effect. Andrei had to have the dehydrating effect of salt water explained to him and the others watched him carefully. Geordie had eventually produced a small plastic bottle of mineral water from his pack.

"I thought we had better save this until we really needed it."

They shared it out, each of them careful not to take more than his fair share. Once it was empty Jim slipped the empty bottle into his pocket.

"Any more of those in there, Geordie?"

"Sorry boss, I didn't anticipate this part of the cruise being so poorly catered."

An hour or so later Andrei struggled to his knees and faced outwards.

"What are you doing, Andrei?" said Jim.

Andrei looked over his shoulder, "I have waited as long as I can," he said, "but the urge to urinate is too strong."

"Wait one second," Jim said and fished into his pocket. He brought out the plastic bottle. "Do it into that."

Andrei looked at him incredulously, "You cannot mean to drink it? That is disgusting!"

"Disgusting it may be, but it could keep us alive just that little bit longer. We waste nothing."

Andrei was revolted at the prospect, but did as he was asked. Their only clean drinking water came from the occasional showers that passed over them and made them colder. But at least it delayed the need to revisit the plastic bottle.

Conversation in the dinghy was desultory at best, but they had agreed that once an hour they had to sit up and talk. They also sang children's songs with exaggerated hand and arm motions to try to generate a little warmth. Ivan taught them all the ribald Welsh Rugby songs he knew and insisted they add expressive arm movements during the rudest parts.

This time it was Jim's turn to start the conversation. "OK, folks, for this evening's entertainment we have to decide what we want for Christmas. Ivan, you start."

Ivan thought about it. "Well, I've already got a train set and a big red fire engine so there's not much else in life to wish for. Maybe in my stocking I could find a voucher for a nice holiday in the sun, all expenses paid."

Andrei looked puzzled, as usual the gallows humor of the British Army was a complete mystery to him, and he was not to know it had been keeping men like this going through adversity for hundreds of years.

"Geordie, how about you?"

Geordie grinned. "Well boss, I don't know if that guy who runs Playboy has a yacht but if he has I'd like to borrow it, full of bunnies. At least if I cover myself in naked women I'll be warm."

Jim looked across at Andrei. "Come on," he said, giving him a gentle nudge with his foot, "your turn. What do Russians get for Christmas?"

The Russian was not faring well; he had not been as fit as the three ex-Army men and the cold and damp were not making him feel any better.

He shrugged and sighed, "In Russia we often give special cakes or sweetmeats at Christmas. I think I would like something sweet to eat."

"Sorry my friend," said Jim, "not much we can do about that one."

Geordie perked up, "Don't be too sure about that, boss."

"How do you mean?"

"Come on, boss. What are the three rules of military success?"

Jim sighed, "I'm sure I should know this one," he said "but go on."

"Ivan?"

Ivan sighed too, "OK I'll play along. The three rules of military success are: One, never get separated from your weapon. Two, always keep something to eat later. And three, never march on Moscow."

Geordie shuffled round and reached into the haversack he was leaning on. His hand came out holding four chocolate bars.

"Rule two applies here. Merry Christmas, Andrei, now where's my Playboy yacht?"

The small battered chocolate bars helped and when Geordie pulled out a small bag of raisins and passed that round too the atmosphere in the dinghy was noticeably lighter.

Ivan looked across at his ex-company commander, "What about you, boss? What would you like for Christmas?"

Jim thought about it, staring out onto the limitless ocean. As the dinghy rose on a swell he said, "I'd really like that ship over there to see us."

Ivan and Geordie laughed then Jim said, "I'm serious. There is a ship over there but he is unlikely to see us at this distance."

Andrei looked at the ship mournfully, "We are too small to be seen. They would only see us if we fired a flare and we do not have one."

He slumped back down into the dinghy. Ivan and Geordie looked at each other.

Ivan spoke first, "I think rule one applies this time."

Geordie went back into his haversack and this time he produced the last of the MP-40 sub-machine guns that had saved their lives on the submarine.

He loaded it and said, "Help me up guys," as he stood up very carefully with Jim and Ivan bracing his legs as best they could in the rocking dinghy.

He waited until he could see the ship clearly then cocked the weapon and fired off a full magazine into the sky. They watched the ship to see if they had been seen. There was no reaction and no change of speed.

"Pass me another magazine, I'm going to try something."

Jim fished the next magazine out of the haversack and passed it to the still standing man. Geordie loaded and cocked the weapon. He then looked at the ship and aimed just in front and above it. He opened fire and let off a second full magazine of thirty rounds.

Andrei could not believe his eyes, "What are you doing? You are shooting at our only hope of survival. Are you mad?"

Jim looked at him, "It's worth a try, Andrei and no we aren't quite that mad. The bullets in that weapon are 9 mm, like pistol bullets. They do not have a lot of power after about four hundred meters. So at this distance they might just draw attention if they fell on the deck and were seen."

The ship did not slow and they were now out of ammunition. "Nice try Geordie. Never mind."

Geordie slumped back into the dinghy and for the first time, looked truly dispirited.

Chapter 33

On board the Coast Guard cutter the lookouts were searching for anything that might give them a clue to the whereabouts of the freighter they were seeking. The sea was cold, gray and empty, not even a seagull out this far from shore. The officers on the bridge also stared out at the unending sea. Nothing. The might of the United States had been mobilized to find one rusty freighter and nothing had been seen of her.

The First Officer, Karen Martin, was tired and becoming frustrated. She knew she would end up shouting at some poor crewman shortly. Very unprofessional. She turned to stare out of the side bridge window, to take a deep breath and control her emotions. She brushed her blonde hair back from her forehead and stared at the gray empty ocean. As she stood, two hard objects struck the glass in front of her. What the hell was that? She stepped outside the bridge and looked down. On the deck at her feet were two distorted pieces of metal and by the way the water on the deck was hissing, they were still hot. What in the name of all that was holy was going on? She stepped back into the bridge carrying the two bullets.

She moved across to her captain, "Sir, I have no idea what this means, but these two just struck the bridge window."

"Any damage?"

"No, sir, I just heard the tap as they struck and saw them fall."

The captain sat in his bridge chair and looked down at the bullets, turning them over in his hand. These were the size of pistol bullets. How had they struck his ship way out here on the ocean? He leapt from his chair, thinking as he did so that it was very unbecoming for a captain to show such excitement.

"Stop engines!"

The helmsman leaned forward and sent the command down to the engine room.

"All lookouts stand by!" The ship slowed. He gave the command "Slow ahead and hard a starboard."

The bow of the ship came round and they moved slowly back the way they had come, but further out toward the direction the bullets must have come from.

"Rudder amidships." The captain turned to his first officer. "Prepare to launch boats."

"Certainly sir. But why?"

"Because, Karen, somewhere out here is somebody firing a pistol at us. That means they have to be close by."

"Sir!" the first officer left the bridge in a hurry and gave the orders for the boats to be ready to launch.

Staring ahead, the helmsman was the first to see the dinghy with the four bedraggled men waving weakly. One of them seemed to have some sort of small flag. The cutter stopped close to them and lowered the boat from the port side. The four survivors were hauled in and the dinghy dragged aboard. The boat returned to the ships side, hooked on to the dangling cables and was hauled up to the davits. As she came level with the deck the four survivors were lifted out and taken carefully, but quickly, into the small sick bay.

The Coast Guard crew were puzzled when one of them, clutching a pair of Union Jack underpants, said in a strange accent, "Any bunnies?" before passing out.

The relief at being rescued had affected all four of the men. In the dinghy they had kept themselves wound up tightly, refusing to show any personal weakness that might discourage the others. Once they were in the warm, dry sick bay they could let it all go. Geordie and Andrei passed out completely, Ivan and Jim were in a drowsy half-sleep and making little sense. The medical orderly with the help of a couple of crewmen got them out of their soaking wet clothes and into warm, dry bunks. The hot sweet cocoa helped a lot. They were all dehydrated. After an hour Ivan's fitness and strength were starting to tell and he was the first to begin to make sense of his surroundings and the First Officer was called down to speak to him.

She stood by his bunk, "Better now?"

He nodded, "Yes thanks, Ma'am. Your timing was good, we didn't have a lot of life left in us."

She looked him over, "You're welcome. Now then, we looked at some of the stuff you had with you. A World War Two sub machine gun and three Luger pistols in the bottom of the haversack. You were wearing

Russian coveralls and you were in a German made dinghy of a type that is not normally used for emergencies. Plus, your friend was waving underpants decorated with the British flag. Could you tell me what it means and what all that was doing less than fifty miles off the coast of the USA?"

"I could, but it's probably better if we wait until the Major wakes up and we can tell you the whole story just once. I promise it will be worth the wait"

"Major? He's in the Army?"

"He is Major James Wilson, retired. I am Company Sergeant Major Ivan Thomas and that sleeping beauty over there is Sergeant Martin Peters, known as Geordie, also both recently retired from the Royal Engineers. The other fellah is Andrei, he's Russian and I don't know his full name."

The first officer wrinkled her brow; this was getting stranger by the minute. She made a note of the names.

She said, "You sound British, is that right?"

"Correct ma'am."

"Well, while your Major is recovering I will call in your details to our Headquarters. I will be back soon." She left the sick bay and Ivan settled back on his pillows.

"Thanks for that," said Jim from his bunk. "I could do with a bit more time to get my breath back. How's Geordie doing?"

"Sleeping like a baby and no doubt dreaming of nice warm bunnies."

Forty minutes later the First Officer was back. She found the three ex-army men sitting up and taking notice. Andrei was still fast asleep.

"Well gentlemen, would you like to accompany me to the wardroom where the Captain and I can listen to your story. I think we can let your Russian friend sleep a little longer."

It was not a request. They followed her along the companionway to the wardroom, wearing their borrowed Coast Guard coveralls, and were introduced to the skipper.

Jim stepped forward and shook his hand, "Captain, thank you for picking us up. I am pretty sure you saved our lives. We all owe you and your crew a debt we can never pay."

"Glad to be of service. Now would you like to sit down and tell us how you found yourselves out here?"

They settled around the wardroom table and Jim told the story from the day he was called to London. The two Coast Guard officers were silent, letting the story run its course.

As Jim finished he said, "Once they submerged and left us for dead we still do not know where they were taking those two U-Boats. You might want to have your people keep an eye out for them."

The Captain looked at his First Officer, "Oh, we know where they were going and we know what they did when they got there."

He proceeded to tell them what had happened in New York and what had happened to the two submarines. The three British men were stunned and horrified. They had never imagined an attack like this in their worst nightmares and they were the ones who had made it possible.

Geordie leaned forward and in a quiet voice said, "Do they have any casualty lists yet? A good friend of mine is in New York."

The Captain shook his head. "New York is still in a mess, casualties are still being assessed. Now tell us what you know of this Romanov. He seems to have been the driving force behind the attack. Did you see the name of his yacht and do you know where he was going after he left you?"

Jim and the others shook their heads. "We didn't get the boat's name and we were a little too busy to watch what direction he left in. But the Russian in your sick bay, Andrei, worked for him before we came on the scene. He might know more."

The Captain nodded to the First Officer. "Get him."

The first officer rose and left the wardroom without a word. The skipper then turned and ordered coffee from a hovering steward.

"I suggest you enjoy this coffee, when it comes, gentlemen. You have been involved in what is starting to look like the worst terrorist attack ever on American soil and I think the FBI and many others from the Alphabet Agencies will be keen to speak to you. You may find them a little less welcoming than us."

They drank the coffee lost in their own thoughts; this adventure could be about to turn even more sour, if that was possible. A message arrived for the captain while they were waiting for Andrei.

He read it and looked at the three men. "I am not quite sure what this means but it is from your Embassy in Washington. It lists your names and says that due to the mobilization of British Armed Forces you have been 'recalled to the colors.' What the hell does that mean?"

"It's an old term meaning we have been taken back into the Army. When we were forcibly retired we were put onto the reserve list and now we have been recalled. Not what I expected, I have to confess."

Andrei appeared in the wardroom shepherded by the First Officer. He was still bemused at being woken and walked along from the sick bay. The coveralls he had been given were way too big for him and he had been obliged to turn up the cuffs of the pants legs. Jim guided him to a chair and poured him a coffee. As he did so a crewman entered with another message for the Captain.

"It seems we will not be having any more of this conversation," he said, obviously not pleased. "Washington has instructed me to stop any questioning and to put you on board the helicopter that will be here very shortly."

He turned to the First Officer "Pass the word to prepare the helideck for a short notice landing. You four had better get down to the hangar deck and get into immersion suits, the helicopter is not going to wait."

Andrei gulped a mouthful of coffee and the four of them were guided down to the hangar and issued with the brightly colored one-piece cold weather immersion suits and life jackets. They were stiff and awkward to put on but should the aircraft have to ditch they would at least have some chance of survival in the cold water. The helicopter became visible, flying in from the west fast and low over the water. It swooped in at high speed and slammed down onto the helideck of the cutter. The four men were hustled across the deck and into the aircraft. The door slid shut and before they were strapped in, the helicopter lifted and turned toward the west.

Jim lifted an eyebrow at Ivan. "Somebody seems keen to see us."

The ride was as smooth as it ever is in a helicopter at full speed. Jim noticed that the unsmiling crewman sat watching them the whole time without attempting to speak to them. Unusually he was wearing a holstered pistol. It would appear the authorities were not inviting them to a social gathering.

After making landfall the aircraft flew low up the Potomac River and then swung sharply to the left to land on the helicopter pad outside the Pentagon. The four survivors looked through the window at the iconic building with some surprise. They were escorted to the main building by a team of six heavily armed soldiers. Given no time to remove their bulky immersion suits they looked and felt incongruous when entering a building full of busy people in smart uniforms. They passed through security and were walking along the wide, long corridor when one of the escorts made the mistake of nudging Ivan along.

He stopped and turned to the soldier very slowly.

"Corporal, do you make a habit of pushing Warrant Officers in your Army? Just because I am wearing this ridiculous suit does not give you any authority to push me."

The young corporal did not deserve that, Jim knew, but it had been a long and difficult few days. He stepped in front of Ivan to ensure his temper did not get the better of him.

"This seems as good a place as any to lose these suits," he said.

Without more ado he started to struggle out of his Immersion Suit in the middle of the broad corridor. The other three followed his example and were suitably cheered up by the nonplussed expressions worn by their escorts. Now dressed in just their borrowed Coast Guard coveralls, they left the immersion suits lying where they were.

Jim turned to the corporal, "That's better. Shall we move on?"

Chapter 34

The four were eventually ushered into a large impressive conference room. Their armed escort stayed outside the door. As they walked in they found that the spectacular, highly polished oval table was already occupied by a mixed group of civilians and senior military officers. There were four empty chairs at the end nearest to the door.

A four star Admiral at the far end of the table did not introduce himself, but pointed to the chairs, "Make yourselves comfortable, we may be here some time."

Jim led the way to the table and sat down with Ivan and Geordie to his right and Andrei in the left hand seat. They looked around the room and as they did so, the questions started to come from all sides.

Jim stood. "I understand that a horror has been visited on this country and that unwittingly we were a part of that. May I suggest that it would save a lot of your valuable time if we told you what we know and then invited questions afterwards for detail and clarification?"

One of the civilians to the right was obviously incensed by this. "How dare you? Do you think you are running this investigation? You sit down and we will run it our way!"

Jim sat. The Admiral tapped the table, his physical presence had an effect and the people around the room immediately calmed and waited for him to speak.

"The President's representative is quite correct to remind us that Major Wilson is not running this meeting. I think you will all notice that I am, and I do not need people shouting at these witnesses. The Major's suggestion is a sound one and may well save us time." He looked around the room for objections and found none. "Major, would you care to introduce your people and then tell us your story. I realize that it is not long since you were rescued from a dinghy in the North Atlantic, so if you find you need a break or anything else please say so."

The President's man was moving to object again when he caught the Admiral's look and subsided into his chair. Jim looked at the Admiral for a second or two. This was clearly an impressive man and not one to be trifled with.

Jim introduced himself and the two soldiers to his right. He turned and indicating Andrei said, "And this is Andrei, he used to work for the cause of this entire problem but I am afraid I do not know much else about him. Andrei?"

Andrei stood and looked around the room slowly.

He bowed slightly and cleared his throat. "I am Special Investigator Andrei Alexandrov Popov of the Moscow City Police. I am a part of a special organized crime unit and I and one of my colleagues have been working undercover in Romanov's organization for a little over three years now."

The Army General at the left of the table said, "I'm sorry, who the hell is Romanov and where is your colleague now?"

From the head of the table the Admiral said, "I think we are going to find that out when the Major tells his story. Thank you, Mr. Popov, from the looks on the faces of your companions your real identity has been a well-kept secret. Major will you begin please?"

Jim noticed the courtesy. Even at a time of huge stress the Admiral remained polite, so he was a gentleman as well as a commanding presence. *Worth remembering.* Jim started from the beginning when he had received the first message from his sister. He explained the steps that had occurred and why he had taken them. The room was silent as he spoke, with no fidgeting or interruptions. In a room full of large egos like this he was surprised. He turned to Ivan a couple of times for confirmation of detail, but did most of the speaking himself. As he reached the part of the story where the submarine dived beneath them he noticed that the naval officers in the room paid particular attention. He described their time in the dinghy briefly and ended by praising the swift action of the Coast Guard. As he finished he had expected a barrage of questions, but his words seemed to hang in the air.

The Admiral broke the silence. "A remarkable adventure, up to the point when you were dumped in the Atlantic. Tell me something. You say there were twenty of these V1 missiles on the two boats and we are painfully aware of where they were used. So how many more were left at the base? And could you estimate how many of the chemical warheads there might be as well?"

Jim cast his mind back. "There would be at least twelve missiles left, but I am unsure if all of them could be made to fly, unless Romanov's people found some more spare parts, which is perfectly possible given the size of the base. There were many more warheads. It looked like the Germans were awaiting a delivery of more V1 Flying Bombs when they were closed down back in 1945. There were certainly handling cradles for more. I would guess there were in excess of fifty warheads though I can't give you an exact count."

The Admiral nodded and turn toward Andrei, "Mr. Popov, it seems it is time for you to enlighten us about your employer. Maybe you could also tell us about the colleague you mentioned. Are they in a position to help us? I think your three companions are going to be interested too."

Andrei looked around the table.

"Sadly, my colleague Tatiana was aboard the other U-Boat and was murdered at the same time as the attempt was made on our lives. She is now at the bottom of the ocean." He sighed. "It has been a long day. Would it be possible to order some of your fine American coffee?"

The Admiral beckoned the Lieutenant who sat against the wall behind him and spoke to him quietly. He left the room with a rapid stride.

The Admiral turned back to Andrei. "Do go on, Mr. Popov."

Andrei started with a brief history of the rise of the Russian Mafia at the end of the Soviet era. The confusion and collapse of many communist-era institutions had allowed organized crime to blossom and it was soon out of control. Vicious gangs were controlling all sorts of criminal activity and were starting to take over legitimate businesses to launder their money. The Russian government, realizing that they were on the slippery slope to anarchy, had to try to do something about it. The police across the country were revamped and money was found to improve equipment and increase manpower. People were transferred into the police from the Armed Forces and action was started to combat the gangs. Many policemen were killed trying to re-establish the control of law and there were many setbacks, but slowly the police began to gather momentum. They thought they were closing down gangs little by little, and in fact that was true, but what started to emerge were super gangs that took over the smaller ones that could not survive.

Attempts had been made to penetrate the major gangs and get people on the inside to gather information. Within weeks or sometimes days these people would be found dead in the street with horrific injuries. The police realized that they had been penetrated and every mole that got into the Mafia was being betrayed from inside police headquarters.

Senior police officers met in secret and agreed to form a new police command unknown to the rest of the police service. They were also to be unknown to the rest of the senior policemen at the meeting once a commander for the force had been decided. Secrecy was to be their only defense.

Andrei had been recruited secretly from his job as the foreman in a failing metal working plant. He had no family left and no close ties. He had a military background having served in the Army, as a conscript, a few years before. It took him over a year to establish himself as an unemployed waster and petty thief in Moscow before he managed to get himself given small jobs by the Mafia. Once trusted, he let it be known he was a good cook and eventually that got him taken into Romanov's personal staff. He had been Romanov's personal cook and valet for almost two years. In that time Romanov had risen from number three in the organization to take over the top slot.

Number two had been involved in a bizarre road accident with a petrol tanker. Oddly, the truck driver had managed to escape the huge fireball that destroyed the bulletproof limousine containing the Mafia leader and his three bodyguards. In the world of the Mafia, that had been seen as a legitimate way of earning promotion and Romanov moved up.

Romanov's next promotion took place in a large country Dacha outside Moscow where the various Mafia groups were having a conference to divide up territories and spheres of influence, to avoid conflict between them. At dinner, Romanov had stood up to make a toast to the assembled group and as they stood to drink the toast, he had produced a pistol and put a bullet between the eyes of his now former boss. The others at the meeting came from violent gangs and murder concerned them not at all, but even they were taken by surprise.

As the body fell back into its chair and slid to the floor Romanov had apologised for the noise and carried on making the toast. The Mafia men around the table admired his style as he sat down and carried on eating his dinner.

The gang accepted the change in leadership without question. There had been concerns about the old leader going soft. He had spared the life of one of their pimps who had not been passing on all the tribute that he should. Romanov had the pimp killed the next morning and left at the edge of Red Square to be found and so consolidated his position. His management style from then on had been to richly reward success and to visit fast and vicious retribution on anyone who displeased him.

Andrei had not known about the submarine plot. It must have been developed during the secret meetings that Romanov had been having for the last ten months. Some of these had taken place in Moscow and some on his motor yacht in Odessa. Whenever they were to take place Andrei had been allowed to prepare the meeting rooms and then he and other staff had been taken away to await the end of the conference. He had never seen the other participants and knowing that Romanov had an electronic sweep carried out before each meeting he had never been able to plant a listening bug.

Being dumped off the back of a submerging U-Boat had been as much of a surprise to him as it had to the other three and he supposed he had been betrayed from within the police or had somehow irritated Romanov.

The room was quiet as he finished speaking.

The Admiral looked around. "At least we know who we are dealing with and what sort of people they are," he said. "Judging by Mr. Popov's description Romanov seems to be a sociopath and a very dangerous one. No wonder the Russian government is keen to support us; this could be their chance to rid themselves of a serious problem. Any questions for Mr. Popov?"

The officer in the Coast Guard uniform raised a hand slightly off the table. The Admiral nodded to him.

"Mr. Popov, you said you had prepared meeting rooms on Romanov's yacht and the Major said you had seen Romanov board a yacht just before the attempt to drown you. Was that the same boat you had been on?"

Andrei nodded. "It looked the same, but we were a little busy and I did not get the chance to read the name. Certainly it was the right size and the colors were the same. I would be fairly sure it was his as he has certain changes installed on it that pleased him a lot."

The Coast Guard officer nodded. "I do not want to slow this meeting down, but once we finish I would like to get as many details as possible from you so that we can try and find this yacht."

Another hand was raised and again the Admiral nodded, this time at a Naval officer.

"Mr. Popov, you mentioned modifications to the boat, can you tell us what they are?"

Popov smiled. "Certainly, I spent much time searching them out when on that boat. There is a bay at the rear of the boat to carry a fast motor boat, which is standard on a yacht of that type. But the bay has been expanded so there are also two Jet Skis carried there. In the middle of the boat there is a 'Moon Pool' with external underwater clam doors, this is to let divers use the boat without being seen. I think he got the idea from a James Bond movie. There is a lot of diving equipment. Concealed in metal life jacket lockers along the upper promenade deck are machine guns that can be swiveled up into position in seconds."

"How many of these guns are there?"

"Six. Three each side. May I continue?"

The Admiral said, "Please do and gentlemen, let's keep our questions to the end."

Andrei took a drink from the coffee cup that had appeared in front of him. "On the upper deck there is another locker that contains shoulder launched SAM-13 anti-aircraft missiles. Four I think. And I think there are another four Rocket Propelled Grenades. There is a helicopter deck and in front of it there is another heavy machine gun that can sweep that deck clean if anyone uninvited tries to land there. There is also a large storage bay with access from a concealed hatch on the upper deck. I also know he has an armory of small arms and hand grenades aboard. I can probably make a drawing for you if that would help?"

There was a silence until the Admiral said, "Quite an interesting design for a pleasure yacht. And its name is?"

"Mr. Romanov has a sense of humor," said Andrei, "at least he thinks he has. The boat is called 'Ivan the Terrible' after one of the Tsars."

The Coast Guard officer left the table and moved to a computer terminal against the wall. He searched through the databases that his service had access to and found nothing. He reported back to the table that he had drawn a blank. Geordie was the first to suggest that if the yacht was not new it might have had its name changed when Romanov bought it.

Andrei said, "There was a brass plate in the main deck cabin that had some details on it of tonnage, etc. I think that said something like 'Odessa Star' on it. Maybe he changed the name of the boat when he decided to change his own to become a Romanov."

The Coast Guard returned to his terminal. "Got one," he said. "Could you come and take a look to see if this is the right yacht?"

Andrei and Jim walked across.

"That seems very similar," said Andrei, "perhaps the weapon boxes that have been added have made it look a little different."

Jim agreed that it look very similar to the one they had seen when Romanov left the U-Boat. They returned to their seats.

"The next question really is where it was going," said the Admiral. He turned to a Royal Navy officer that Jim had not noticed before, "Our British friends monitor the straits of Gibraltar quite carefully so, if he is heading back to Odessa, they should have seen him pass through by now."

The officer stood up. "I'll check for you now, if I may use your terminal?" The Admiral agreed. "Perhaps you could help me?" the RN officer said to the Coast Guard. They both moved to the terminal and concentrated on getting the required image to the monitoring station on Gibraltar.

A small man in a civilian suit leaned forward. "It's a big ocean, as you know Admiral, but I wonder if we have any clues about where he was going from anything he said?"

He looked down the long polished table at the four men who had been working on the coffee they had been handed.

All shook their heads except Ivan. "There was one thing that seemed odd," he said. "Romanov was talking to one of his bodyguards who seemed to have a skin complaint on his neck. He said something about the Caribbean sun clearing it up within a week. If they were passing through the Caribbean that would take less than a week, so maybe they are stopping there somewhere?"

The President's man, from the White House staff, joined in again; he was still clearly not happy with them. "How did you hear this? Were they speaking in English or do you speak Russian?" he sneered.

He was obviously deflated when Ivan said, "Yes I speak Russian. Quite a few British soldiers are trained in languages."

The Admiral suppressed a smile.

"I think it's time we took a break. Please break into your command groups and assess what you have heard and what you can now contribute. I suggest you take the time to check back with your offices to see if we have anything new from them."

Chapter 35

The three engineers and Andrei stayed seated, watching the group break into huddles. The Royal Navy officer walked over to them and held out his hand to Jim.

"Hello, we haven't been introduced. James Delaney from the Military Attaché's office in the Embassy. You seem to have caused quite a stir. Is there anything you need?"

"Yes. We know about the attack on New York, but with no details. Do we know how many people were killed and just what happened?"

Delaney told them what had happened, in more detail than the Coast Guard had given them. "But at present we don't have casualty figures. New York is in a bit of a mess and the authorities are just now sorting out the confusion. They have been refusing to speculate until they are sure. You will have noticed that most of the people at the table are controlling their emotions and staying very calm. They want to know exactly what has gone on before they strike back, so your information has been very useful. But make no mistake, the Americans are bloody angry and somebody is going to regret this."

"And what's this about us all being back in the Army? The Skipper on the Coast Guard cutter told us he had got that from the Embassy."

"I'm sorry, I should have told you. One of the first things the British government did when this happened was to mobilize our forces ready to support the US. Not sure whether that is just an excuse to cover the fact that they have screwed up the force reductions or not. In any case the Reserves have been called back to the colors and you are back in." He looked at Geordie and Ivan. "All of you. Tell me something though, are you the Sergeant. Peters I read about in the newspapers after that bulldozer incident?"

Geordie was surprised his story had been seen in the US, but he smiled and nodded to confirm that he was the bulldozer driver.

Jim thought for a moment. "Well if we are back in the Army and we are going to be interrogated here in the Pentagon, what can you do about getting us some uniforms? It might make us look a little less like criminals and make these folk think more kindly of us. By the way, just how much trouble are we in?"

Delaney nodded. "Seeing you in uniform might make you more accepted by the Pentagon people. Trouble is the Embassy doesn't have a uniform store. Let me think about that one. As for trouble, we don't know yet. One of the people listening to you today is from the Justice Department and they are trying to decide if you are criminals or have just been duped. Whichever way that decision goes you should continue to be as helpful as you are able. Oh, looks like we are reconvening, better take your seats."

Delaney walked back to his place and the four sat down as the Admiral tapped the table for attention.

"We have just heard back from our British colleagues in Gibraltar that the yacht has not passed through there and with the clue that Sergeant Major Thomas picked up, I feel that the most likely area of search is the Caribbean. Now I want some options. What surveillance and search assets are immediately available? Navy?"

The Naval officer to his left looked at the folder in front of him and said, "We have one submarine training in the area and there are four surface ships actually in the islands. We can move assets from Florida and the Keys quickly if needed and the ships checking the Eastern Seaboard can be redeployed if we are sure there are no more of these submarines threatening our cities."

"Coast Guard?"

"Five cutters that could be immediately diverted from anti-drug patrols and more that could move there a short time later."

"Air Force?"

"We have P3 Orions that can be deployed within the hour and we could move AWACS down from Oklahoma inside six hours or we could redeploy one or more of the JSTARS aircraft."

"NSA?"

"We have the Atlantic surveillance satellite that can be diverted and could be on station in something like six hours."

"CIA?"

"We might have some people on the ground that could have a look round for us."

"Britain?"

Delaney looked a little surprised to be asked. "We have HMS Newbury, our Caribbean guard ship and HMS Huntingdon is still in the New York area, she could be moved south rapidly, plus of course we have the Governors of the Dependant Territories who can engage the various island police forces to check around."

The Admiral looked satisfied. "Unless the President's representative has any objections I want all the assets we have described deployed to search for this yacht ASAP. I also want all other assets made ready to move as soon as we have any further information."

He looked at the President's representative who said, "No objections. Plus I think this might be the time to invite the Cubans to help."

The individuals around the table were surprised and all heads turned toward the speaker. He looked around the room, "Relations need to improve between us and this human tragedy in New York could be a convenient way for both sides to achieve this without any loss of face for either of us."

The Admiral smiled. "That could be a useful extra asset. If the President agrees I think we should pursue it." He stood. "Any more points for today from anyone? Right, let's get these assets deployed now and find that yacht. I want this meeting to reconvene at 0900 tomorrow with full and up to date reports from all of you." He looked at Jim and his team and said, "If you four could wait one moment." He turned to a tall thin civilian across the table. "Can you join us please?" The two Americans walked round to the bottom of the table, followed by Delaney.

"Well gentlemen we have a problem of what to do with you. This gentleman is from our Justice Department and he has been listening to you, to try and determine what your status is under US law." He turned to the civilian. "Have you reached a decision yet?"

"No sir. Frankly they could be accessories to a major crime, however it seems as if they were unaware of Romanov's intentions and they have been very helpful here today. We also have to consider our relationship with the UK and these three are serving members of the Armed Forces that have been committed to supporting us. You see the dilemma?"

"I do and until you make your decision I have a solution."

Chapter 36

The Admiral turned to Delaney, "Lieutenant Commander, I guess we ought to arrest these people, but right now I am going to ask you to take responsibility for these three gentlemen. You will notice I did not say they were in your custody. But I am not sure what we do with Mr. Popov here?"

Jim said, "Sir, if you will permit, we came here as a group of four and we have been through a lot together. If Andrei agrees I would like us to stay together, as a team, to support you."

"Any objections Lieutenant Commander?"

"None, sir."

"Very well. I will see your team of four back here at 0900 then." He turned and walked away, quietly conferring with the civilian from the Justice Department.

Delaney stepped forward, "We will need an escort out of the building, but there are some Marines outside waiting to do just that."

They left the conference room and with the Marines in close attendance made their way to the exit. Delaney led them to a car park area where he opened up an anonymous dark blue MPV.

"In you get, guys. We'll get you settled in your hotel shortly, but first we have a few calls to make." They climbed in and he set off for the city. They entered the Georgetown area and after a few minutes Delaney pulled up outside a disreputable looking shop in one of the less-fashionable streets.

"I was thinking about your request earlier and this place could be the solution. It's an Army surplus store. If we buy you some plain green fatigues of the type the US Army has stopped using they will be recognizable as uniform even though they are not official."

They all entered the shop and in a short time had kitted themselves out with olive drab fatigues. Andrei had decided that he too needed to look like the rest for some kind of comfort in numbers. Ivan even managed to find them some black berets, similar to the ones the British Army uses, but they would have to be worn without cap badges.

Andrei had been wandering around the store looking in the dusty display cases. As they were standing at the checkout he approached and tossed a couple of Russian Army shoulder boards on the pile.

Delaney was puzzled, "What are those?"

Andrei smiled, "If I am to wear a uniform I think I should return to the rank I wore in the Army as a Junior Sergeant."

Delaney looked at Jim, who nodded, "I agree. Not sure how legal that is, but we need to remind everyone that we are on side in this."

Geordie grinned and flung an arm around Andrei's shoulder. "Well now bonny lad, there are two Sergeants to look after all these important people and keep them out of trouble."

They left the store carrying their packages and drove back south of the river. Delaney drove them into the car park of a huge shopping mall.

"This is Pentagon City Mall," he explained, "you can get the rest of what you need here, underwear, toiletries, socks etc. You may also want to get some basic civilian clothes for the hotel this evening. Don't worry, the Embassy is paying for all this."

The mall was even bigger inside than it seemed from outside. At the bottom of the numerous floors was a food court and the noise coming up from it as they entered was loud and constant. They orientated themselves and made their way to Macy's where they found everything they needed.

"If we need you to be more formally dressed later I will take you round to Nordstrom," said Delaney, "but for now I think we need to get you fed and watered and then I guess you would appreciate some sleep?"

They returned to the vehicle and he drove them to the Holiday Inn on Wisconsin Avenue.

"Quite a comfortable hotel," he said, "and they do a damn good breakfast. Plus, if you go out through the back you will find an area of scrubland and if you follow the path you end up at the back of the Embassy. At some point the Air Commodore will want a word with you but he is rushing round helping to coordinate our part of the military response at present."

Settled in their rooms, none of them was interested in the restaurant or the bar. They fell into bed and slept, trying to compensate for the days spent in the cold of the Atlantic. Only Geordie stayed awake as he settled himself in front of an Internet terminal in the lobby.

The three soldiers were up early the next morning ironing the fatigues they were going to wear to the Pentagon. All four of them met up for breakfast at 0730 and Delaney joined them a little later.

As he sat down he said, "I managed to scrounge these for you from the military staff at the Embassy. I thought they might help."

On to the breakfast table he tossed three sets of rank badges. The officer's shoulder slides bearing the crown of a Major. The three sleeve stripes for a sergeant and the large crown of a Sergeant Major to be worn on the cuff. He also dropped a sewing kit on the table for the two NCO's to use to attach their rank insignia.

"You can have a sewing circle in the car on the way to work."

Ivan and Geordie were not totally amused, but Andrei found it very funny. The distance to the Pentagon was not long, but they made slow progress through the Washington morning traffic. By the time they reached the Pentagon the rank badges were sewn on and they felt that they would look less like criminals and more like allies. At least they hoped so.

They arrived at the entrance to the huge building to find their armed escort waiting for them. Passing through security they were escorted back to the conference room. As they entered they found everyone clustered round a table getting coffee and doughnuts. Ivan and Jim were happy with just coffee but Andrei and Geordie set about their second breakfast with enthusiasm.

The Admiral entered and called everyone to the table. "Good morning, everyone. No preamble this morning, let me tell you what we have got. So far none of our assets have found the location of the yacht. However, our Cuban colleagues think they saw it from one of their observation posts on the eastern end of the country, somewhere called Punta de Maisi, a little to the north of Guantanamo. I have already given orders for the search to switch to the Caribbean south of Cuba. Does anyone have anything else to offer?"

The NSA agent cleared his throat, "It may be unrelated, sir, but the satellite did find something strange on one of the small uninhabited islands. Well, not quite uninhabited, there is a single large house and a few cabanas, with a small dock."

"So what was this anomaly you found?"

The NSA agent was flustered, "I'm sorry it was supposed to come up on the big screen. Ah! There it is now."

Everyone turned to look at the large display screen. A green island with white sand beaches sat in an azure sea. Around it were smaller islets and a few rocks breaking up the waves. The image zoomed in and then in some more. The clarity was impressive. They could see every detail of the house including the sun loungers by the kidney shaped swimming pool and the small drinks tables next to them.

"Move to the west," said the NSA agent, and the image moved left. "There it is. We have no idea what this is. It appears to be a railway line but it is only about fifty feet long and it seems to slope."

The Admiral looked around the room, "Any ideas?"

"Sadly yes," said Jim, "you are looking at a piece of ancient history coming back to life. Unless I am very much mistaken that is the launching ramp for a Second World War vintage V1 Flying Bomb. It looks to me as if Romanov has brought some more souvenirs from Kiel with him. The worst thing is that it looks to me as if that is pointing at Florida. My guess would be Miami, which would be well within range."

The silence in the room could have been cut with a knife as the assembly contemplated the picture above them.

Finally the Admiral said, "How old are these pictures?"

"They were taken yesterday evening at last light, so they are about eight hours old."

"And the Cubans saw the yacht around twelve hours ago. Assuming the missiles were being carried on that yacht they could be unloading or even getting ready to launch by now. Assume this is a missile launch platform and give me some options!"

There was a buzz around the room. The Air Force officer was the first to speak. "If we are sure it is a launching ramp we could wipe it from the face of the earth with JDAMS with little difficulty."

The Justice official coughed, "Attractive as that is, I do not think it is legal to bomb another country's island without a declaration of war. We do not want a repeat of the diplomatic difficulties we had after Grenada. Plus, we do not know where the material stolen from New York is being stored. It would be a shame to destroy all that."

The President's representative agreed. "The response to 9/11, although warranted, was a very big stick and hurt a lot of people as collateral damage. The President is keen to ensure that any response is measured and appropriate and does not sour relations with any of the governments who are supporting us. The bombing could be held in reserve in case all else fails."

A Navy officer stood. The SEAL insignia on his chest glittered under the lights. "I guess you know what I am going to recommend? A SEAL Strike Team can land from the water, infiltrate the island and destroy that facility quickly and with no collateral damage. All our people have been on standby since the New York attack. We can be on the move within the hour."

The Army General stood and said, "I could drop paratroops or Special Forces but it's a small island and there is a strong risk of losing some of our people in the sea. I think I agree that this is ideal for the SEALS."

"Admiral, if I may?" Jim found himself saying. "My team here were instrumental in making the New York attack possible. We would like to make up for that as much as we can. We would like to join the SEAL team on this mission."

"Thank you for the offer, Major, but I think the SEALS have got it covered."

Jim did not sit back but continued, "Sir, much as I admire the SEALs, I doubt very much if any of them have trained on seventy-year-old flying bombs and none of them will have any idea of the makeup of the nerve agent warheads. In fact the only people who have worked on them for the last seventy years, that are available to you, are sitting right here."

"You make a good point, Major." The Admiral turned to the SEAL officer. "Lieutenant Commander Duggan, can you use them?"

"I can sir, with one proviso. Are you parachute trained?"

Jim nodded. "Of course."

Andrei then said, "And I too have served in the Russian paratroops. I know Romanov well and if there are any Russian documents or inter-rogations needed I can be of use to you. Also, this maniac is a Russian criminal and Russian law enforcement should be there to assist in his arrest. And I owe him for the death of my friend Tatiana."

The Admiral looked along the table then looked at the SEAL, who shrugged, "OK by me, sir," he said, "and having a Russian along might help."

The Admiral stood, "That's a decision then. The SEALs and their sup-port here will assault and take out the missile threat. The President has instructed that Romanov is to be arrested and brought back to stand trial, if at all possible. NSA, I want updated pictures of that island ASAP and send them to the SEALs as soon as you get them. Detailed analysis can carry on at the same time, but will not delay the raw intel going to the assault team. SEALs to be given any and all support they ask for."

They stood and started to disperse. Jim turned to Andrei. "It's handy you were a paratrooper."

"I wasn't, but how hard can it be? Anyway, you three can tell me what to do."

Geordie laughed and Ivan said, "None of us are paratroop trained either. We can all learn together on the way down."

They stood waiting for Duggan, the SEAL officer who walked through the dispersing group toward them with Delaney at his side.

"Very well, gentlemen, it seems you are joining one of my teams. I'm not sure if we will be parachuting in or assaulting from the sea. I imagine you would prefer to be taken in by boat?"

Ivan said, "Oh and why would that be, sir?"

The SEAL looked at the four of them in turn. "Sergeant Major, I've been leading soldiers for long enough to spot a blatant lie from a hundred meters away. None of you have ever been near a parachute drop. Still, if we do drop, it will be into the sea if that's any comfort."

Delaney laughed, "I guess the US Navy can give you anything you need from here so we can leave your things in your hotel rooms till you get back. Good luck." And with that he turned and walked out of the room.

Lieutenant Commander Duggan said, "Follow me. There will be a chopper arriving to pick us up in about fifteen minutes."

The SEAL led the way out of the room and waving the Marine escort away, he led the group toward the main exit.

Jim walked alongside him. "So if you knew we were exaggerating our experience why did you agree to take us?"

The SEAL looked at him sideways as they walked. "I understand the need to get even with the man who tried to kill you and the need to compensate for what happened in New York. In any case you were right about being the only people who have worked on one of these damned rockets for the last seventy years. I'll take any advantage I can get to make a mission successful."

As they continued to walk Geordie said, "It's personal as well, sir. Somewhere in New York is Sam, the woman I love. She was performing in a play off-Broadway. Last night was the first chance I had to phone her since we sailed and she was not answering her phone, then or this morning. And she is not replying to emails either."

Delaney stopped, "The phone lines in New York are still jammed, but give me the details and I will get my people to check up on her, while we get on with this job."

They exited the building through the security gates and headed for the helipad where a US Navy helicopter was touching down.

"So where are we going first?" said Ivan.

The SEAL stopped again and turned to them, "Understand this, our operations are highly classified. You will be given no information except what you need to carry out your part of this mission. There will be no idle conversations. I don't wish to appear rude, but that is how we work."

Chapter 37

They walked across the Pentagon car park to the waiting helicopter and climbed in. There was less rush this time and they were allowed to strap in and put on headsets before take-off. The door slid shut as the aircraft lifted off and turned to fly back along the Potomac. They realized that, although they could hear each other, they could not hear the pilots so had no clue where they might be going.

They flew low and fast following the contours of the earth, giving the passengers no chance to identify landmarks that might indicate their destination. They were flying above a wooded area almost brushing the tree tops when they passed over a perimeter fence and found themselves over an airfield and approaching buildings that had that indefinable military look about them. The helicopter came to a hover and then landed in front of a large anonymous hangar. The pilot kept the engines running and the rotors turning as the crewman slid back the exit door. He indicated they should get out and head for the hangar. As they cleared the immediate area the pilot applied pitch to the rotor blades and the aircraft lifted off, heading away across the airfield.

The downdraft blew clouds of high speed dust around and they all managed to get some in their mouths and eyes. They were still spitting dust and grit when they reached the Judas gate in the hangar door. As they approached, the door opened and they were ushered inside by a tall African American man in a camouflaged uniform. The width of his shoulders and the muscle development obvious in his arms was impressive.

He looked at each of them in turn then said, "This way," turning and walking to the back of the hangar. He did not look back. He was obviously accustomed to being obeyed.

The large man led them to an area of tables each with military equipment laid out on it.

Duggan detached himself from the group and walked away to get on with other business. To the left, as they walked, they had seen twelve sets of equipment packed and laid out in a neat line, each with a weapon laid on the top. Now it appeared to be their turn to kit themselves out.

The soldier in the camouflaged uniform, without rank badges, turned and waited until they joined him.

"On these tables you will find the equipment you will be taking with you. Check it and make sure you know how to use it. Anything you do not understand, ask now, there will be no time later. You will be given the minimum equipment you need to do your job. You will not take part in the assault, but will follow my people in. One of my team will be assigned to you and you will do what he says at all times. You will be issued uniforms in thirty minutes so start checking this equipment now. Any questions?"

There were none, so he turned and waved forward a man who had been standing unobtrusively at the back of the tables. "This is Martinez. It may not be his real name because you do not need to know that. His rank, his history and his real name are of no interest to you. Is that clear? He is assigned to keep you alive, so do as he tells you."

As he stalked away Martinez stepped forward.

"Don't mind Wallace. He is probably the best in the business, but he sees taking untrained people on a mission as an increased risk to his team, so he is not a happy camper."

He turned to the nearest table and started to run through the equipment laid out. "OK gentlemen, listen up; we are short of time so pay attention. You have a minimal webbing harness for your material, adjust it to fit you tightly; once you have it on make sure nothing rattles and makes a noise that might give us away. This is your pistol, a standard issue 9 mm Beretta, accurate and reliable; there is one spare magazine in the small pocket on the outside of the holster. This is your first aid kit in case of injury; there is one over there opened up so you can see what is in it. Familiarize yourselves with it after this. I assume you all have first aid training? You have a small flashlight to be used only if you have to, it can be clipped under the barrel of the submachine gun you will be issued. This is your personal radio, it has a range of about 200 meters and is used to communicate between squad members only. It is voice activated so no unnecessary switches, just the one on/off switch here. Each group leader carries a longer range radio for communication between the groups when they are separated. Each of you will carry a small toolkit for dealing with the missiles and the warheads. That is in this pouch here, please check this and if there are any extra tools you need tell me in the next ten minutes. Your main weapon will be this;" he held up the black submachine gun, "this is the Heckler and Koch MP5. At short range out to about one hundred meters it is highly effective, at fifty meters even more so. You will use it only to defend yourselves and even then only in an emergency. As a matter of course all of these are fitted with silencers. All this equipment has been adapted for use after being immersed in the sea so there is no need to immediately stop and clean it after we land. But try and avoid dropping things in the sea anyway. These are your spare magazines. You have one for the pistol that I told you about and three for the MP5 that need to be stowed in the pouch on your belt. You should not need to use them. All clear?"

Ivan was starting to bristle at the brusque manner of these men. "You are aware that we are all military, are you?"

Martinez looked at him, "Yes and I also know you are not special forces trained and we don't have time to bring you up to that standard."

Jim put a hand on Ivan's arm. "He's right. Let it go."

They adjusted their webbing harnesses and loaded the equipment into the pouches, then jumped up and down to ensure nothing rattled. They familiarized themselves with the two weapons and checked the ammunition in the spare magazines. Martinez then led them to the back of the hangar where they were equipped with black uniforms and boots. Worryingly, they were also handed an emergency life jacket each, also colored black. The last two items were black balaclavas and helmets with fittings for attaching the personal radios. Already attached to the front of the helmets were night vision goggles allowing them to make their way around the island in pitch darkness, if necessary.

They assembled all their equipment back at the tables under the direction of Martinez who then said, "Right. We have fifteen minutes before briefing. Leave all your equipment here and come with me."

He led them to a door in the rear of the hangar and as they stepped through, they found themselves in an indoor firing range. Martinez lined them up and shut the door.

"As you all have military training I have to assume you have fired a sub-machine gun before. However, you may not be familiar with the firing characteristics of this particular model, the MP5. I am therefore going to give you a quick run through of how this operates and you will get one magazine each to practice with. If all goes to plan that is the last time you will fire during this mission."

He talked them through the operation of the weapon and they then stepped up to the firing point one at a time to use their magazine of ammunition. The weapon was accurate and even this unsuppressed practice weapon was fairly quiet, certainly it was a major improvement on the old German MP-40 that had saved their lives twice. The firing practice over, Martinez returned the weapon to the armorer and led them out of the range.

As they walked he said "I'm sorry this is all so rushed, but we have very little time before we have to leave. We are on the way to the final briefing now and as soon as that is finished we will be moving down to the jump off point."

Chapter 38

Martinez showed them through another anonymous door and they entered the back of a small lecture theatre. The rest of the twelve man team was already seated and they did not turn around. Duggan, the SEAL officer from Washington and the large man, Wallace, who had met them at the hangar door, were on the small raised dais with a large plasma screen behind them. It became clear that Wallace commanded this team. Projected on the screen was a map they recognized as the target island. Martinez placed them at the back of the group and then sat with them.

Wallace stood forward. "Now we are all assembled we will begin. As you can see, this is the map of the target. Points to note are marked in red. The house, the pier, the launch ramp and these three storage sheds. Each of you will be allocated to one of these targets. As soon as they are secured you will move to the secondary target you will also be allocated. Situation is as usual. Move fast, take no chances and everybody comes home alive. All personnel presently on the island are hostile. Any hostiles offering to surrender are to be taken prisoner and immobilised. Any resistance is to be met with force. Do not take any chances with these people, they are certainly armed and probably have some military training. At least some of them carried out the attack in New York so we know they have no problems killing in cold blood. Any questions about that?"

There were none.

The SEAL officer from the Pentagon stepped forward. He was now dressed in camouflage fatigues and looked much more comfortable. He did not introduce himself. That seemed to be customary on this operation; even in the Pentagon briefing room, names had not been used much, just job titles or organizations. Presumably that was so those in the group that had been assembled knew who was speaking and with what authority, without trying to remember names. In this case it was probably that these people all knew one another already.

He started to speak, "I have here the latest intel we have on the target and an analysis of what it means. The analysis is rough and ready so expect to find surprises once you get ashore."

He turned to the plasma screen and pressed the control button held in his hand. The satellite image of the island flashed up, again an incredibly sharp picture considering it had been taken from an orbiting satellite. The pier was now occupied. The luxury yacht was alongside it, and on the other side what looked like a trawler was just coming in to dock. The wake from the slowly turning propellers could be clearly seen. He used a laser pointer to indicate the deck of the trawler.

"Look here and you will find something of particular interest." The picture zoomed in to show a large group of men standing around the deck area. "If you look carefully we are pretty sure that they have M-4 Assault Rifles on their shoulders. The best guess from the analysts is that this is the group of mercenaries who carried out the assault on the New York banks. We assume they changed ships somewhere in the Atlantic. Perhaps they sank the original ship and that is why we have been unable to find the freighter. In any case, these are the people who shot civilians without a second thought and drove over a New York police officer. They are not Boy Scouts. You should expect them to resist with deadly force, so take no chances. To the rear of the deckhouse you will also see pallets ready to be unloaded. Again it is a guess but that is probably the loot from the banks. This is a complication that we had not anticipated."

He went on to show pictures of the house, the ramp and the store buildings. "Each of you will be handed an envelope shortly containing these pictures to study while in transit. The envelope also contains your target assignments. At the back of the room there is a small team of people who will be coming with you to deal with the missiles. We believe the missiles are equipped with chemical warheads and are going to be launched at Miami. The primary objective is to disable those missiles before they can launch. Should any launch before you can stop them there are F-16s and other aircraft on standby to try and stop them, but yours is the primary mission."

As the envelopes were passed around the rapid briefing continued. "In just under an hour you will fly from here to the jump off point. From there you will join a flight of three CH47 Chinook helicopters for insertion close to the target. The helicopters are already loaded with the assault boats and the helmsman for each boat is being provided by the Marines. The helicopters will put you at the launch point at 0200 and you should be ashore by 0300. That gives you four hours of darkness to get the job done. Once you are ashore the boats will retire off shore and wait for your signal for a pick up. Now that we are pretty sure about the New York assault group being on the island we know that you will be considerably outnumbered, but we cannot afford to wait in case the missiles are launched. If the island is not subdued by first light the Marines will be landing in force to support you. They are on the way already so should not be late. I repeat your primary goal is to stop the missile launches. Secondary objective is to arrest Romanov and as many of his people as possible at no risk to yourselves. Tertiary objective is to secure the cash, bearer bonds and other material they looted from the bank vaults in New York. Any questions?"

The SEALs were silent.

Ivan leaned across to Jim, "These guys are as quiet as the Hooligans from Hereford."

Andrei looked puzzled so Jim explained, "One of the British Special Forces groups, the Special Air Service, is based in Hereford. They tend to be as undemonstrative as these people."

Andrei nodded. "The Russian *Spetsnaz* troops are similar until they have a little too much vodka inside them and then they are nothing but trouble."

Jim and Ivan were surprised when Geordie stood up. "I have a question."

The SEALs looked round and waited.

Duggan nodded and gave a small smile. "For the rest of you, this is Sergeant Peters of the British Army, something of a celebrity in military circles. He was the guy who drove that bulldozer in Helmand last year. Go on Sergeant ..."

"If this group is trying to get away with the loot from New York, then why would they draw attention to their hideout by launching another attack from there? The logic escapes me."

The two men on the platform looked at each other.

The briefing officer said, "That's a good point. I will run it past the analysts. While they are chewing on it the primary mission still stands. Any more questions? No? OK, people, there is a meal waiting for you now. Eat and then a final equipment check before boarding the aircraft in forty-five minutes."

The meeting broke up and the men filed out of the room. Duggan, the briefing officer came over to the four of them, "That was a good point you made. It doesn't make sense. Mr. Popov, any ideas what he may be up to since you know him best?"

Andrei shook his head. "He may be a psychopath, but he is never stupid. Everything he does has a reason and this operation has been planned for months. Let me think about it for a while."

They followed the rest of the group to an area at the end of the hangar where food had been laid out for them to help themselves. They filled their plates and sat at a table that had been set up nearby.

Andrei looked worried. "Geordie has spotted something wrong here and I do not understand it. This could be important. I feel I am missing something."

They ate quickly and moved to check their equipment one more time. Martinez came to find them and led them to the door of the hangar. They stepped out on to the aircraft dispersal area to find an executive jet waiting for them with a line of SEALs climbing the boarding ladder. Their equipment was taken from them as they reached the ladder and stowed in the cargo hold. They entered the aircraft cabin and found that five seats had been left for them at the back of the aircraft. The main door was slammed and locked as they walked along the aisle and the engines fired up almost immediately.

The aircraft swung out of the dispersal and onto the taxi way to the runway. There was none of the customary queuing for take-off experienced at commercial airports and they accelerated down the runway and up into the air. They still had no idea where they were going; security was taken very seriously by this group. When asked where they were going to meet the helicopters, Martinez ignored the question and looked out of the window. In front of them the assault team were studying the photographs of the island and committing to memory every detail they could. The briefing for Jim and his team was very thin, just follow Martinez to the ramp and disable the Flying Bombs. After that they were to wait until it was time to return to the boats and leave.

Chapter 39

The signs in the roof panels instructed them to fasten their seatbelts, and the cabin crewman came around the aircraft collecting the briefing envelopes. No material, that exposed just how good US Intelligence gathering was, would be lost and slipped to the media, who seemed incapable of realizing that not everything should be in the public domain.

The aircraft touched down smoothly and taxied to a hangar set well away from any others. As they deplaned they saw that three CH-47 Chinooks were waiting for them with their rear cargo doors already lowered. Personal equipment was unloaded from the cargo bay and returned to the individual team members. Martinez checked that the four men had everything and led them to the left hand helicopter. The rest had split into two teams one of five and one of six, and were heading into the remaining two aircraft. As they stepped onto the cargo ramp they were faced by a black inflatable boat with a large outboard motor. Even the motor was black with no indication of manufacturer or engine size. As they stepped past it they noticed extra piping and attachments on the engine.

Martinez saw them looking and said, "Silencer kit. Makes us a lot more stealthy."

"I see your people get the best equipment too. It's another Ribcraft. Hopefully we get to ride in this one."

Once they strapped in, the aircraft engines started and the huge rotors were engaged. The vibration was unpleasant, but the flight time was short. No more than an hour later they landed again and the cargo door dropped. They climbed out and found themselves on a small airfield with a view of the sea. They were led to a small hangar and allocated one of the camp beds already set up inside.

Martinez told them "We always try to get as much sleep as possible before this type of mission. No idea when the next chance might come."

The hangar was cooled by air conditioning which was a welcome change from the heat outside. It was much warmer than Washington had been only a few hours earlier. Like most soldiers they knew the value of sleep and had the ability to drop off when the opportunity presented itself.

Before he lay down Jim touched Andrei on the arm, "I haven't had much chance to speak to you. You said that Tatiana was a colleague, what did you mean?"

"My lovely Tatiana was a police officer. She was recruited straight out of the training school before she started her first assignment. We let it be known to others on her course that she had been sent to a distant police station so her disappearance made sense. She was working as a cook's assistant on the Yacht and slipping me any information she picked up. Romanov must have suspected her or he was just cleaning house when he had her killed."

"I really liked her, she was very pretty."

"She liked you too, Major. She told me so the night before we sailed. She didn't deserve to die that way, but at least you gave her some comfort at the end."

They were awakened later by Martinez touching them on the shoulder. He had the good sense to stay off to one side as he did so. Men who are keyed up for a mission have a nasty habit of coming up swinging punches when awakened suddenly. The rest of the SEAL team was moving around quietly getting their equipment together and rechecking their weapons. Jim watched with a practiced eye. These were professionals to a man and he was glad to be part of such a team for this operation.

They assembled inside the hangar door and Wallace, the imposing African-American team leader, who had still not mentioned his own name, said, "OK. Everyone ready? Everyone clear on their task?" He paused to check that he got the right answer from all of them. "Let's go and do business."

They trooped out through the small door in the front of the hangar and automatically moved into their groups. As Martinez was leading them toward their Chinook Jim moved alongside Andrei.

He touched him on the arm. "You're quiet. Are you certain you want to do this?"

Andrei stopped and turned toward him, waiting until the other three were a few paces off and then spoke quietly. "Major, I thank you for your concern, but you do not understand what a monster Romanov is. I have told you little of him, but there is much blood on his hands and the misery of others gives him pleasure. I have been brought along as a part of a magnanimous gesture by the Americans who will let me arrest him. But I have to tell you that, if there is a chance for me, he will not be getting arrested this night."

Jim looked at the Russian's face and saw that he was calm and quite serious. He would not want to be Romanov if this man caught up with him alone. They walked to the rear of the helicopter and found the three others in their team already buckling themselves in to the canvas seats along the side of the fuselage. They climbed past the inflated rubber boat and took their seats.

Martinez pointed to a young soldier sitting opposite him and said, "This is our boat driver. He will deliver us to the beach and then wait offshore in case it all turns bad and we need to get the hell out of there."

The man nodded to them, but did not speak.

The helicopter crewman checked that they were properly belted in and then threw the switch that closed up the rear ramp. He spoke into the boom microphone of his helmet and the engines started. The rotors engaged and spun up, rocking the aircraft to start with, then settling down to give a steady uncomfortable vibration. The crewman doused all the cabin lights, explaining that it was to allow their night vision to develop before they had to disembark. Jim checked his watch, ninety minutes until they were supposed to be at the launch point. He had no idea what speed they were traveling so could not estimate distance. He settled down into his seat and tried to relax as much as possible. He must have slept because the next thing he knew Ivan was nudging him awake.

The crewman was back and was about to climb past them to the ramp control. Martinez signaled them to put on their helmets, but to keep the night vision goggles up. The helmsman stood and gestured for them to climb into the inflatable boat, which seemed a little strange while still inside the aircraft. The Americans had been extremely efficient this far so Jim assumed he knew what he was doing and shrugging, he climbed in. Once they were aboard and hanging on to the grab handles around the inflated side tanks, the helmsman climbed in and positioned himself by the outboard motor.

They felt the aircraft hit the water remarkably gently, then the ramp was down and the boat was being propelled out of the helicopter and onto the calm surface of the sea. There was a strong downdraft as the helicopter lifted away. Jim was watching it leave when he realized that the outboard engine had been lowered into the water and started.

They were moving forward with virtually no sound. The extra sound dampening was very effective. The three black boats moved together to allow Wallace, the team leader, to see that they were all ready to go. In the starlight they could dimly see his arm wave as the signal to move toward the objective. The boats split up and moved rapidly apart.

Martinez instructed them to lower the night vision goggles into place and turn them on. The other two boats were suddenly visible again as bright green shapes moving across a pale green ocean. There was a slightly brighter shine from the outboard engine but even the heat signature had been damped. Jim could see no sign of the island they were approaching. That was good; they had been dropped far enough away so the helicopters would not have alerted anyone on shore. Within a few minutes the trees and higher ground of the island started to rise over the horizon. The helmsman slowed the boat to allow the third boat that was to come in from the far side of the island, to get ahead of them. The second boat was keeping pace with them about four hundred meters away.

The island was becoming clearer as they approached. They could see the heat signature of the main house and the outbuildings. Soon they could see the trawler. The motor yacht that Romanov had been traveling on was missing from the pier. The boat running alongside them had the task of subduing the two vessels. With one ship missing their job should be a little easier.

Jim spotted the sandy bay, which his group was supposed to land in, a little left of the pier. Above it the land rose and the launch ramp should be just over the low ridge. He heard the two quick clicks through his radio headset. Boat three was in position on the far side of the small island. The helmsman on his boat and the one on the second boat had evidently heard it as well as the two boats accelerated toward their goal. As they neared the shore they slowed to what felt like half speed and the five men gathered their legs under them ready to jump clear of the boat. The helmsman stood in order to look down through the clear water to judge the depth. When Ivan looked over the side he saw that the bottom was shelving upwards quickly as they got close to shore.

A quiet word from the back of the boat, "OK. Go now!" and they slipped over the side holding their weapons high.

The helmsman had judged well and the water came halfway up their thighs, keeping all their equipment dry. As they waded slowly ashore the boat slid back into the darkness and out to sea. As the water got shallower they spread out to make a more difficult target. They did not pause at the edge of the water, but walked forward across the sand to the tideline at the back of the white beach. The land climbed up away from the beach and was studded with a few palm trees and bushes. Fairly open going, but enough to give them cover from watching eyes if they needed it. The night vision glasses showed no sign of any guards in their area and they continued to move forwards, keeping a watch all around them as they went.

Chapter 40

The black boat with its silent warriors coasted alongside the converted trawler moored to the jetty. To reduce risk just two of these modern day Ninjas slipped over the side of the boat at the low point where the fishing nets used to be hauled in. One shadow went forward and one aft. They assumed that there would be some sort of guard or anchor watch on deck even in the safe haven of the island. They were right.

At the aft end of the trawler the guard was sitting with his chair leaned back against the deck house wall, with his M-4 rifle across his thighs. He had been staring out to sea for the last hour or so, but nothing had attracted his attention and his eyes had drooped closed as he drifted into a fantasy about how he would spend his share of the proceeds from New York. His eye shot open as the cold, hard muzzle of the silenced MP5 touched his temple. The rest of his body was frozen into immobility as he hardly dared to breathe. A hand reached to the back of his neck and slowly eased him and his chair forward so that it sat on the deck on all four legs. The hard pressure on his temple never varied. He became aware of another shadow to his left as he was lifted almost gently to his feet. The weight of his rifle disappeared from his legs and his arms were drawn behind him. His wrists were fastened with plastic restraints that bit into his skin. A gag was placed across his mouth and his ankles were secured. The barrel of the weapon left his temple and he was lowered carefully face down to the deck.

A whisper from one of the shadows said, "Do you speak English?" He nodded. "Then understand this. One sound from you, of any kind and your life ends on this deck. Do you need me to repeat that?"

He shook his head quickly. He did not know who these silent figures were, but he knew that he was not being paid enough to be a hero.

The remaining members of the team in the boat heard the two clicks in their headsets and rose from their black and silent boat, over the side of the trawler. The rigid inflatable boat slid away from the side of the larger ship and moved off into the moonless night. The six men on the trawler's deck split into two groups and each went to one of the entrances to the lower deck areas. The three who entered through the bridge came to the crew's quarters first. They worked quickly and efficiently, securing each man in his bunk without a sound. They then turned their attention forward.

The group who had entered through the forward companionway came to the two larger crew cabins. They checked both. There were too many people in an open area to risk securing them one at a time. One mistake causing a single sound, and they could have a large number of alarmed and angry, armed men on their hands. They waited for the aft group to join them, then split again to port and starboard. At the sound of the double click in their headsets, the doors to both accommodation cabins were opened slowly and a sedative gas grenade placed carefully inside. The two groups stood in the passageway outside the large cabins listening for any sound from inside. There was silence.

After a delay of two minutes for the gas to spread and take effect on the sleepers, the gas mask equipped SEALs entered the cabins cautiously and checked their targets. All were breathing deeply and not moving. The teams worked swiftly to secure the hands and feet of everyone they found. Gags were placed over their mouths and then breathing was checked to ensure no untoward casualties.

With the crew and passengers secured, the rest of the boat was searched rapidly and effectively. There was no sign of any other people aboard and no sign of any of the cash or bearer bonds. There were some antiques stored in the central laboratory area, but no paintings or jewelery. On a bench mounted to a side bulkhead they found a glorious crucifix and two beautifully detailed candle holders. The loot from the bombed church would be reconsecrated and returned after the rebuilding.

They returned to the main deck. There was no movement on the pier and no sign of the yacht that had been there in the surveillance photographs. They had completed half their mission and had no way of securing the yacht and completing the other half. They were now free to move on to their secondary objective to help to secure the buildings with the group from boat three. They left the trawler and moved along the pier onto the island. All their heads were swiveling left and right as they used the night vision devices to scan for any enemy presence.

They found nothing as they moved carefully along the track that led toward the main house. As they came within the range of their more powerful radios, the section leader started to transmit to tell the team from boat three that they were moving toward them. No point in having any blue on blue incidents on this mission.

Chapter 44

The third black boat had traveled around to the far side of the island to approach the main house from the sea. They came around the low headland and into the bay below the house as slowly as possible, so as to make no wake in the water. The troops scanned for any sign of movement in the green world that the night vision goggles fed to their eyes. The house showed up brightly both as a heat source and from the subdued lights showing through the curtained windows. There was no sound except the quiet burble of the outboard engine and the lapping of the sea on the beach. They waded ashore and the boat pulled away out of sight, to be ready if needed. They walked out of the water on to the dry sand, fanning out as they did so. They were alert for any movement, any sound. Yet still the sound when it came was a shock.

The noise of a 7.62 mm medium machine gun is loud and harsh, particularly for those it is pointing at. The gun roared its challenge from the shadows of the terrace and started to sweep the beach. There was no cover on white sands, which are more suitable for sun bathing and windsurfing. Their only hope was to move and move fast into the small cover provided by the rising land and the few palm trees at the back of the beach. The only way to get there was to run toward the machine gun, a tactic that had not worked well in the First World War and was unattractive even now.

Despite their speed and training, the SEALs could not outrun a flying bullet and the man out to the right of the group was caught and chewed by the rapid stream of copper jacketed rounds. The next SEAL in line was luckier as the high speed rounds struck his arm and shoulder. Luck is relative when dealing with bullets of this size and the two that hit him did a lot of damage as they spun him around and threw him backwards on to the sand. SEALs are nothing if not determined and despite the injuries he crawled into cover, still gripping his weapon.

The other three slithered forwards into whatever folds in the ground they could find. The operation was blown wide open so any stealthy movement from now was pointless. The next two men in the line were pinned face down in the slightest of cover and could not move forward or backward. The man out to the left was in a better position. He had found a useful depression in the earth and was worming his way along, to the left of the house. As he reached the top of the small crest he could see men issuing out from the other side of the house carrying assault rifles and fanning left and right. His team would be outflanked in minutes with nowhere to go. Five men formed an extended line on his side of the house and prepared to work their way carefully toward the beach. He had seen another six go to the other side, but he could no longer see them. He had to assume they were doing the same thing. As he waited and prepared to disrupt the advance coming toward him, he could hear one of the other members of his section broadcasting on the short range radios to try and bring aid from the rest of the assault group. He could hear no replies and had to assume he was on his own for this action.

The machine gun paused, maybe searching for targets or maybe changing ammunition belts. In either case it allowed his two colleagues to lift themselves enough to throw grenades toward the house. One was a fragmentation grenade and did little except blast in the windows on this side of the house. The second was a "Flash Bang" grenade intended to be used inside buildings to disorientate. It landed in front of the line advancing toward him and the bright flash in the darkness dazzled them for the few seconds he needed to dash further left into a covering position.

With luck he would be able to take two, maybe three, of them before his position was compromised. He waited.

Chapter 42

Martinez took point and led Jim and his party toward the launching ramp outlined against the stars. There was no movement nearby and no sign of the stubby winged missiles. They checked the ramp itself and that appeared to be complete and ready for use. They found a smooth concrete pathway that led from the rear of the ramp to a store shed some one hundred meters away. They approached it cautiously and checked around the building. There was a path beaten through the underbrush toward the main house and many footprints in the sand around the building.

Jim moved to the front door of the building near the ramp with Ivan at his shoulder while the others stood watch. He eased the door open and stepped inside. For a moment there was silence, then two men rose up from behind crates at the right side of the building. In the green light of the night vision equipment, their automatic rifles were appallingly clear and swinging toward him. Two muted cracks followed immediately by two more preceded the collapse to the ground of the two guards.

Ivan whispered, "Twenty years of Army service and that's the first time I have used the double tap I was taught in basic training for real. Works well, doesn't it?"

They checked the two guards for a pulse. They had paid dearly for sitting down to rest instead of keeping watch.

They moved further in and looked around. They found themselves inside a stone building with a hard packed dirt floor, surrounded by V1 Flying Bombs resting on handling trolleys. They closed the door to hide the light as they shone their torches first on the two gunmen who were not going to trouble anybody anymore and then on the first missile inside the main door. They checked the warhead and found that it was one of the chemical ones they had seen in the secret base in Kiel. The next two were exactly the same. The suspected attack on Miami was clearly a reality and they were just in time.

They slipped back outside and called the other team members together to report what they had encountered within the store house.

"We have about nine Flying Bombs in there all fueled and ready to go with primed chemical warheads fitted. We need the quickest way to neutralize them in case we are disturbed. Ideas?"

Ivan spoke, "Boss, the mechanism itself is fairly uncomplicated. Once the bomb has been flying for the programed time a guillotine mechanism cuts the elevator control cables and sends it into a dive. If we cut those cables now they are useless. Even if they were to launch they would fall into the sea quite close to shore."

"Good thinking. We'll do that and then deal with the warheads in slower time when we have some daylight."

They heard the machine gun open fire from the other side of the main house.

Jim stood to look toward the firing "We've got trouble by the sound of it. Geordie, Martinez, carry out a reconnaissance. Find out what's going on and report back to me."

Martinez looked as though he was going to object to Jim taking charge, but it was people from his team in trouble and he needed to know too. The two men slipped away into the darkness. The remaining three returned to the store house.

Jim called Andrei over, "I need you to watch the door. Whatever is happening over there we daren't let anyone stop this little piece of sabotage."

The smaller man nodded and tucked himself down beside the door and faded into the shadows. Ivan by now had his toolkit rolled out and had selected the screwdriver he needed to open the panel in the side of the flying bombs main body. He set to work on the nearest one as Jim stepped past him to start on the next.

With the first panel open Ivan found that the bolt cutters he was going to use to cut the cable would not fit in far enough to get the blades either side of the cable. He called Jim over and explained the problem. They worried at the problem briefly until they realized they could reach the guillotine mechanism itself. A little experimentation with a piece of wire they found on the floor and the mechanism triggered, severing the cables and allowing the elevator at the rear of the missile to sag slightly. With their new solution the work went faster than anticipated and they were back outside when Martinez reappeared. He briefed Jim and the other two remaining members of the team on what was happening. He described the two groups of the enemy about to sweep onto the beach and the position of the dominating machine gun. Geordie arrived back a few minutes later.

"Boss," he said "the team from boat two are moving up on the right. They will appear behind the group that side and I think that leaves us with the enemy team on the left to deal with. But we need to move PDQ; I think the lads on the beach are in trouble."

Jim was still, remembering the topography of the island. It was fairly flat open country but the enemy would have their attention facing the other way and darkness was still in their favor.

"Right," he said, "Martinez, we have to change the orders if we are going to help your people, and forgive me, but we don't have time to argue. We advance in line abreast keeping visual contact with the man either side. Keep spread out and call in when you make contact with the targets. Absolute quiet, but move as swiftly as we can without alerting the unfriendlies. Let's go."

Martinez nodded. "I'm going to catch hell from Wallace for this, but you're right."

They moved away from the weapon store toward the house, avoiding the trodden path. While the two teams of enemy gunmen who had tumbled out of the house were disciplined and clearly knew what they were doing, they were hampered by having no radios and were forced to coordinate their advance by shouting between the groups. This was a gift to the two groups moving up behind them.

As they closed in Jim spoke softly into his helmet mounted radio. "Team two, this is Team one. We are closing on the enemy combatants to the left of the house. Will be in position to assault in figures one minute."

A soft Texas drawl answered, "This team will be in place just before you. So you had better open the ball when you are ready."

Jim replied, "Roger that."

They moved forwards and the position of the team preparing to rush the beach showed up clearly in the night vision lenses.

"Team two, Team one is in position. All call signs fire now!"

He stood to get a clear shot over the scrubby plants in front of him and fired. He saw the others doing likewise. The suppressed MP5 kicked against his shoulder and he saw his target fall. He could hear the quiet spluttering of the suppressed weapons and knew the rest of his team were doing the same. He looked away from his target and along the line of the enemy at this side of the house, none were standing. He had heard the rapid and effective assault from the silenced weapons of Team two on the other side of the house so had no worries there.

He spoke into his radio again. "Martinez, Andrei, check the targets, secure any that are still alive. Ivan, Geordie with me to the back of the house. Move."

He did not wait to confirm they were coming to him. He knew how reliable these men were. He knew he should leave this to the SEALs, but they were still dealing with the enemy troops and the team on the beach needed help quickly. They skirted around the swimming pool, avoiding the sun loungers and reached the entrance door of the house. They flattened against the stone walls, still warm from the heat of the day. Geordie reached across and tried the door handle. The men who had boiled out of here during the attack had not thought to relock it and the door swung silently inwards.

Chapter 43

Ivan put a hand on Jim's arm as he stepped past him and took the lead into the house, Geordie too stepped in front of him. Jim smiled, even after all this they were still acting like NCOs and looking after him. To the right the passage ended in a large bedroom. It was empty. To the left the passage took them to a lounge area with a picture window looking out onto the swimming pool and terrace. They slipped between the furniture and moved carefully toward the seaward side of the house. The door at the other end of the lounge opened into an impressive dining room with a long table down the center.

As Ivan entered he saw movement at the end of the room by the window. A man was standing at the side of the window with an automatic rifle. He saw Ivan moving out of the corner of his eye and started to spin round, bringing up the weapon as he did. This time the two low cracks from the MP5 came from Jim's weapon. The man thumped back against the wall and slid to the floor. Both rounds had gone through his forehead giving him no chance to cry out. The clatter of his weapon falling from his grip was covered by the machine gun starting to fire again.

The three moved to the door leading out of the dining room and again flattened themselves against the wall, they were close. Ivan tried the handle this time and swung the door open. Geordie stepped through to find himself behind a two-man machine gun team. The gunner aiming and firing the weapon while the loader kept the belt of ammunition feeding properly and linked new belts on as the current one shortened. Geordie supposed later that he could have arrested the two, but he was no policeman and the years of Army training kicked in as he swung left to right and emptied a magazine into the two of them.

Ivan and Jim stepped into the room behind him and looked at the two men lying against the kitchen units. They would not be any trouble to anyone anymore. They swept the rest of the house as quickly as possible and reported the all clear. Team two helped by the left hand man from team three had dealt with the attackers to the right of the house. There were no prisoners to interrogate. Leaving two men to recover and pile the weapons from the downed enemy, the rest went forward to check on the remainder of team three. The two men who had been trapped in the small gulley rose up to meet them, heartily relieved. The man who had made it to the left of the firing line came back to check on his team. They found the wounded man, who had done a fair job of patching his own wounds and made sure he was in a comfortable place.

Then seven of them walked across to the body lying face down in the sand. It was Wallace, the large, impressive man who had met them when they first reached the SEAL team. Jim looked across the body at Martinez and saw a single tear roll down his cheek. The bonds of comradeship were strong in these Special Forces soldiers. Once again he could not help but be impressed.

"Let's move him somewhere more comfortable," Jim said, "he deserves that."

They bent down as a group and lifted the fallen man. Three Americans, two from the British Army and a Russian special policeman stumbled across the shifting sand with the big team leader between them, any national differences forgotten by men who had worked together and shared the same risks. He was laid below a tall palm tree with his weapons in his hands to await repatriation to the land he had died for on an island without a name.

Chapter 44

They sat above the beach and Martinez called for the three boats to come into the pier to be ready to pick them up. The shouting came from a SEAL who was running along the low ridge.

"The missiles are launching!"

He was pointing toward the launch ramp. Jim guessed that the launch crews had been in the other two store houses that had not been checked after the firing started and the mission went awry. No matter, the birds could not fly if they could not control their own tail feathers. He heard one of the SEAL group leaders on his longer range radio using the pre-arranged code words

"Boomer! Boomer! Birds are in flight!"

Now that was probably my fault, thought Jim. He must be getting old, needing to get his breath back before giving the team leaders a situation report. He stood and walked up to the house and around the corner to where he could see the launch ramp. He could see the pulsing fire of the old jet driving the missile up the ramp. He turned and watched the first missile climbing into the dark sky. The pulsing fire against the dark cloud was quite pretty, but the thundering noise of the engine was unnerving.

Something was wrong. The Flying Bomb should have plunged into the sea by now. He looked back to the second stubby winged missile in time to see it nose over and plunge into the calm water. But the first one was still flying. His heart sank.

Oh Hell! They must have missed one. If they had missed one there could be more they had missed as well.

He started running to the ramp area. He caught up with Ivan on the way, "Had the same thought then, boss, eh?"

They skidded to a halt outside the store shed with weapons raised to cover the four startled technicians pushing the next flying bomb out of the shed on its trolley.

"Where did you get the first missile from?" asked Jim, pushing the barrel of his weapon into the chest of the nearest technician.

The man shrugged and answered in Russian. Ivan stepped up and taking the man by the ear asked him again in the Russian he had learned so many years ago. It was rusty but the Russian Technician understood and replied.

Ivan turned to Jim. "The first one was being worked on in the shed they were using for maintenance so they launched that one first when they pushed it over here."

Jim looked toward Miami, there wasn't much to say.

The best he could do was, "Oh shit!"

They stood looking helplessly to the north, where the missile had disappeared from view. Two AV8B Harrier jump jets roared overhead, no more than one hundred feet up. The technicians ducked and the two soldiers were hard pressed not to flinch as well.

Martinez came running up beside them. "Those are from a USMC ship just to the south west of us, do you think they will catch it?"

Jim nodded slowly. "They might do, they may not be the fastest fighter aircraft nowadays, but they are a lot faster than the World War Two fighters that used to have to deal with the V1. Even so, that missile has a good head start. But once they lock a Sidewinder on to that big heat signature it should be game over. I hope."

Martinez said, "I sure as hell hope you're right. My sister lives in Miami."

They turned to deal with the technicians who were still standing very still and white faced next to the third flying bomb they had intended to launch. Martinez produced the plastic ties from his pack and they secured the Russians' hands behind them. Now they had a little more time, Jim and Ivan disabled the mechanism of the chemical warheads to prevent any possible leakage of the nerve gas and then joined Martinez who was guarding the technicians. They hauled the four men to their feet and escorted them down the track to the pier as the sun started to rise. As they went they saw US Marine AAV-7 amphibious vehicles coming ashore, crossing the white sand beach and mounting the low ridge toward them. The rear doors opened and the Marines fanned out rapidly and took up defensive positions.

Martinez snorted. "Jarheads! Every time they see a beach they think they're back on Iwo Jima with John Wayne."

Jim was glad to see inter-service rivalry was not just a British phenomenon. They walked the prisoners through the Marines and down the pier, on to the trawler where they were pushed into one of the large cabins to join a lot of angry men. As the gas wore off they had awakened to find themselves immobilized in their own bunks with no idea how they got that way. As the technicians joined them there was a considerable amount of shouting from those who had managed to spit out their gags, and who Jim, Martinez, and the other three men ignored.

As they stood on the deck contemplating the empty berth where the Yacht should have been, the Marines carried out a comprehensive sweep of the island. They checked every building and searched for any hiding places where a man could be concealed or where the proceeds of the robbery could be stashed for a later pick up. They found nothing. The SEALs had done their work well and cleared the island of all hostiles. The only worry now was the nerve gas warhead heading for Miami.

Chapter 45

In the cockpits of the two Harriers the pilots scanned the sky ahead as they kept the throttle pushed forward as far as possible in an attempt to catch the flying bomb before it started the dive into the city.

The Pegasus engines forced the aircraft along at the maximum speed of five hundred and fifty knots while the APG-65 radars in the nose of the two aircraft scanned the sky ahead. The V1 is a small target from astern and the first sighting was when the lead pilot spotted the distinctive pulsing tail of fire from the Argus jet engine. As dawn broke they could see the city of Miami beyond their target. They could not afford to miss. The seeker head of the Aim-9 missile locked on and launched from the starboard wing of the lead aircraft. The missile flew straight and true, but the pulsing of the ram jet on this antique flying bomb confused the sensors and it lost lock. A second missile had the same problem and it too fell away into the ocean.

The pilots realized quickly what had happened and armed their cannons. They would have to deal with this the same way they had been dealt with during the Second World War. The lead pilot thumbed the trigger on her control column and the firing of the heavy cannon caused the airframe to shudder. The cannon shells ripped into the small target and tore holes in the wings and fuselage. The engine mounts were ripped up and the engine exploded in an eruption of flame. The Flying Bomb was destroyed, setting off the remainder of the fuel in its tank in a large fireball.

The two Harrier pilots learned what the pilots of the Second World War had learned many years before. Despite looking like an aircraft the V1 was in fact a bomb and a bomb with a fuel tank of highly combustible fuel. The explosion was violent and the debris flew far and wide. Pieces of it struck the fuselage, cockpit canopy and the wing leading edges of the lead aircraft. The large engine intakes of the AV8B either side of the fuselage were also peppered with high-speed metal that entered the large apertures and began to rip the compressor blades to pieces. The vibration in the cockpit built rapidly and the engine gauges showed she was in trouble.

As the engine flamed out, the nose of the aircraft dropped toward the ever waiting sea. With no other options the pilot grabbed the ejection handle and pulled hard. Less than a second later the clear canopy above her head was shattered by the embedded explosives and she felt the punch at the base of her spine as the ejection seat powered out of the stricken aircraft.

As the parachute deployed, the seat automatically fell away, leaving the pilot shaken but safe and swinging gently to and fro as the canopy stabilized her descent. She watched as the aircraft she had just left dived, smoke trailing from its battered engine until it splashed into the blue Caribbean. The gentle breeze wafted the parachute away from the patch of burning aviation fuel and she dropped into the water.

The pilot of the second aircraft circled as slowly as possible watching the parachute deploy and his lead pilot drop into the sea. He checked to make sure the one-person dinghy mounted below the seat had functioned and the downed pilot was struggling into it, while transmitting coordinates back to the rescue helicopter that was already on the way.

People on the ground saw the fireball and the remaining Harrier as it passed by it. They knew there had been no other conventional aircraft there. Within hours, the story of the US Marines shooting down a mystery aircraft had become a tale of flying saucers and soon passed into the myth of the Bermuda Triangle, which suited the US Authorities very well.

Chapter 46

Back on the island the SEALs' inflatable boats had now pulled in to the small bay by the pier. Marines had taken over the security of the prisoners on the trawler so Jim and the rest from Boat one made their way along the pier and on to the beach. The other SEALs came down the low ridge carrying the injured man on a stretcher with a Navy Medical Corpsman walking beside him, supporting the intravenous bag that was plugged into the casualty's arm.

Behind them came six more SEALs carrying their downed leader in a black body bag, shoulder high. As they passed, the Marines removed their helmets in respect. Nobody spoke, there was no need, these were men who understood combat and the price that had sometimes to be paid. The body was laid carefully in Boat three and the injured man was taken into Boat two. The rest of the assault party climbed in and the boats moved back from the beach.

Geordie turned to Martinez. "Why not get the body flown out?"

Martinez was staring out to sea. "We came in together. We go out together. We look after our own."

Geordie nodded thoughtfully, he could see where that would work for a close knit group like this.

The three Chinook helicopters reappeared and landed on the water in front of them ready for the boats to be driven up the ramp and inside the aircraft. The boat helmsmen accelerated and slid their boats up the ramps and into the body of the helicopters. As soon as they were inside, the cargo doors closed and the aircraft lifted away. The men climbed wearily out of the boats and took their seats. The air crewman passed around plastic bottles of cold water and they all drank thirstily. It had been a long night.

Jim was surprised when they thumped down to a landing very shortly after take-off. The cargo doors opened and he found himself on the deck of what looked like an aircraft carrier. They unfastened their seat belts and climbing over the boat, walked through the rear door and on to the wide deck.

As they stepped off the ramp Martinez explained, "Marine Corps Amphibious Assault Ship. It's where the AAV-7s came from probably."

A party of Navy Corpsmen were already removing the dead SEAL from the helicopter, handling him with utmost care. The injured SEAL walked across the deck with him, determined to show no weakness in front of mere Marines. They were directed off the deck and into a debriefing room within the ship and gathered around the large map at the front of the room. The SEAL officer from the Pentagon, Duggan, stood on the raised dais looking at each man in turn. He waited until everyone from the ship's company had left the room and the doors had closed before speaking.

His words were simple as befitted the moment. "Good job, everyone. A shame we lost the Lieutenant Commander, but casualties were lighter than we had a right to expect. On first look the doctor thinks Paulson will be OK but, with that damage to his shoulder, he may never be fit enough to continue as a SEAL. Lieutenant Martinez, you now have command."

The team leader from Boat two stood. "Sir, the mission is incomplete. We don't have the yacht and we don't have Romanov."

The debriefing officer smiled. "That's true, but we are searching for him high, wide and handsome. Once we find him we may need you again. After this I want you all to get as much sleep as you can to be ready for Phase Two when it comes."

Andrei held up a hand.

"Yes Mr. Popov?"

"I have been thinking about why Romanov would draw attention to himself with this foolish second attack on a city. Knowing the man as I do, I think it is a decoy to give him time to get away in his yacht while we are focussed here. He must have known this would not take long so I think he must be hiding nearby waiting for the search to end."

Duggan looked at him. "That thought had occurred to us, but it is useful to have it confirmed by someone who knows our target. Have you any ideas where he might hide? Have you heard any mention of islands or ports?"

Andrei shook his head. "Sadly, I have nothing to give you. But it will have been well planned and prepared for sure. Romanov always prepares. There must be somewhere nearby where a yacht of that size could be hidden. It will not be easy to find, I think."

Beyond the steel sides of the assault ship the massive assets of the US and its allies scoured the Caribbean. Ships plowed search courses. Large numbers of aircraft crossed and re-crossed the area, passing in and out of other national airspaces with the ready agreement of the various governments. Radio intercept stations scanned for signals and satellites took hundreds of photographs at each pass. The intelligence coordination center in the Pentagon sifted the mass of data and came up with nothing. They were forced to report, to an increasingly irritable President Barker, that Romanov had vanished from the face of the earth and that even the huge defense budget had not provided equipment that could find his vessel.

Chapter 47

Miles away from the assault ship and light years away from the trouble around him, Winston Royale was pulling in the last fish of the night, singing an old Bob Marley song quietly to himself. A moonless night like this one was a gift. It made the light he dangled over the side of his small boat even more attractive to the reef fish that swam toward it looking for food. Around his feet he had a fine array of fish that would be in the hands of the chefs in the big hotels on the beach of his home island before the rich tourists had finished their breakfast. He pulled the wet tarpaulin over his catch to keep the fish cool and fresh and turned to start his ancient Seagull outboard motor.

He was winding the rope around the pulley ready to yank the two stroke engine into life when he heard the low rumble of another engine and saw the black shape on the water behind him. He struggled to his feet and stared over the stern of his small boat. There were no lights and only that rumbling sound, then an area of blackness that had no stars in it. He strained his eyes to see what it might be. Then the powerful floodlight came on. It was mounted near the stern of what he could now see was a large expensive motor yacht. He had seen others like it in the harbor of his home island over the years. He had even sold some fish to the cooks on such beautiful boats though they were careful never to let him on board. He watched as the lovely ship slowly reversed into Black Beard's cave.

They must have known about the sharp turn inside that cave and needed to see where they were going, he thought. It must be important for them to go into that cave and risk the jagged rocks, or maybe they were just more foolish tourists. He had seen many of those, on their expensive boats over the years. He watched for a few minutes longer until the boat vanished from view and then waited until the light went out inside the cave. Now that was a light that would bring fish from miles around, he thought.

He turned back to his own business and pulled the old motor into life. He settled himself down on the rear thwart for the trip home. He would have a good story to tell his friends this fine morning when he got back into port.

Chapter 48

The debrief was quick, effective and without any fuss. They trooped down through the ship's passages to the canteen for a very welcome American breakfast, then went to their allocated bunks. They slept like babies, but not until their weapons and equipment had been cleaned, checked and repacked. The full team, including Jim's group, were awakened and returned to the briefing room some hours later. The briefing officer from the Pentagon had news for them.

As they settled into the chairs at the front of the room he said, "Cutting to the chase, we think we have found the yacht. Mr. Popov seems to have guessed correctly about Romanov's intentions. We have a report from one of the island police forces about a fisherman who was telling a story, in which he says he saw the yacht being taken into a sea cave an hour before dawn … about the time that you were completing the clearance of the island. He only saw it because they had to turn on the lights to find their way around the bend in the cave. The intelligence analysts are in agreement with Andrei that they are waiting in the cave until the search is called off. Apart from that one old fisherman with sharp eyes they might have made it too. The local police chief for that island group tells us that the cave goes a long way back and they would not have been seen from outside."

Options were discussed and the Marine preferences for an assault were decided against. The SEAL officer stated, "The President wants Romanov alive if possible and he wants the material looted from New York intact. An assault, Marine style, would put those two things at risk. Additionally, there is not a lot of room in a cave for a full on assault without major risk of casualties to our people. Apparently the thinking is that a lot of this stuff belongs to the mob and lots of other people with something to hide. The President wants to see if he can use it to damage them. So, gentlemen, we think we are back to you. You are the nearest prepared SEAL team and you owe this guy, so I assume you are motivated."

The low growl of assent from the assembled young men made it obvious that he had that part right.

"Major Wilson," he continued, "your people of course do not need to take part in the initial attack. We can hold you back from this until this team have secured the boat."

There was a silence as Jim looked round at the other three. Each one nodded in response to his unvoiced question.

He stood to reply, but Martinez was on his feet first. "Sir, with respect. These four are part of this mission and they have proved to be effective. If they will go we would like them along to watch our backs again."

The briefing officer swiveled his gaze around to Jim who said, "Thank you for that," to Martinez. He then looked back at Duggan, "We would be honored to remain part of this team for a little longer. We want to finish this and we still have to pay back for our part in enabling the tragedy in New York."

The SEAL officer smiled. "I thought you might say that. I take it you are all accomplished SCUBA divers as well?"

The Marine Assault Ship was under way and by the feel of the vibration through the deck plates she was making best speed. The full team were called back to a second briefing two hours later. Aerial reconnaissance of the cave had revealed nothing; the yacht was too far back inside to be seen. There were no available charts of the inside of the cave, but if it was deep enough for the yacht it was deep enough for divers. The water in that area is crystal clear so moving in during daylight would be highly dangerous as the divers could be seen from the deck or from any lookout position in the rocks. That was why the ship was on the move.

The intention was to put the SEAL team as close to the target as possible before launching. The ship would therefore move to a position below the horizon from the island. Using helicopters to get closer would not be advisable as the cave itself would amplify the sound of the rotors and warn those inside. The sophisticated communications equipment on the trawler had been examined and it was assumed that something similar or better would be installed on the yacht. In which case they would have been able to monitor transmissions and would know by now that the island assault had been a success. They would know too that a major search for the yacht was underway. To make sure that there was no suspicion that they had been found, ships and aircraft were still pretending to scour the Caribbean and transmitting negative reports as they went.

Martinez took Jim and his team down to the equipment space after the briefing. "I guess you know as much about diving as you do about parachuting?"

Andrei nodded. "Nobody swims in the Moscow River by choice," he said, "and to swim under the surface makes no sense. I think I would meet too many old friends there."

Ivan spoke for the other three. "We know basic SCUBA technique, but we are not familiar with the rig you have there," he said, pointing at the contraption on the shelf.

Martinez lifted a rebreather tank onto the bench "In which case this is going to be the driest pre-combat diving lesson I ever heard of."

He explained how the equipment worked and how to put it on. He explained that the rebreather equipment did not produce bubbles like a normal SCUBA kit did, so they would not need to worry about them breaking the surface. He showed them the tiny luminous markers on the underside of the swim fins so they could follow the man in front in the dark. He produced the waterproof bag they would need for carrying weapons and showed them how to use it. He then explained exactly how to swim under water using the equipment.

He stopped. "You do know how to swim, right?"

This time they were all able to answer honestly. Martinez made it clear that since they were not up to the swimming fitness standards of a highly trained SEAL they would be at the back of the group as they moved in. To ensure they did not get lost, a very real possibility underwater in the dark, a SEAL would be swimming each side of their group to guide them.

They returned to the briefing room where the rest of the SEALs were working on the method of subduing the yacht with minimal risk of casualties. Having seen the men on the deck of the trawler in the satellite photographs and seen some of them in action on the island, they knew they had military training. They would need to assume then that they would be ready for an attack. With machine guns mounted around the main deck and covering the helideck, simply climbing over the rail was not an option. It would make sense that armed sentries would have been placed near the entrance of the cave to keep watch and they would be able to see into the water with ease. This was clearly a job for professionals and although Jim and his two men were experienced soldiers, they were engineers, not Special Forces.

Ivan whispered to Geordie, "Did you ever fancy joining the SAS when you were younger?"

"No. Never did like the beer around Hereford."

Andrei was listening intently to the discussions. When there was a pause in the conversation he stood and went forward. "All you say about the ship is correct and this will be dangerous. I think you have assumed that the doors in the bottom of the ship that lead to the moon pool will be closed and can only be operated from inside. Am I right?"

They agreed he was correct.

"Then I may be able to help. The moon pool doors will be closed almost certainly, but around the doors I have heard there is a panel where there is an external control that can open them. I do not know how the panel is opened or where it is exactly, but if you can find it that may help, I think."

This opened up new possibilities and the SEALs went back to their planning.

Twenty minutes later Martinez walked back to them. "We have a plan. We just need to refine it now and get approval. It relies on that door opening panel being there. Are you sure it exists?"

Andrei looked at him. "I am as sure as I can be. I have heard it spoken about when I was on the yacht. It was one of the special modifications Romanov had put in when he bought the boat."

Martinez said slowly, "That's about all we have that will make this work. It will have to do. If the door mechanism is not there this could get bloody, are you still sure you all want to come?"

Jim didn't even look at his team. "We're in, whatever happens."

Martinez nodded and returned to the main group.

Ivan turned to Andrei. "I hope you're right mate," he said.

"So do I, my friend. I have no wish to die in a cave of all places."

Andrei went off to a whiteboard at the front of the briefing room and busied himself by producing a more detailed diagram of the yacht's layout. There would be no time once they were on board to explain where people should go.

Chapter 49

The plan was quickly approved by higher authority and the next briefing was called in the middle of the afternoon. Jim noticed that two of the SEALs were missing.

He mentioned it to Martinez who said, "The briefing will explain it. They are getting into position now."

Jim had to be content to wait as the briefing started. The situation was as before with no direct sightings of the target motor yacht. There had been satellite passes over the island where the cave was located, looking for alternative entrances, but with no result. The simulated search was continuing with plenty of fake radio traffic for the communications people on the yacht to listen to. This included a frigate that passed by the cave side of the target island apparently on its way to search elsewhere. In fact the pass had resulted in a series of very clear photographs into the mouth of the cave. These were projected onto the screen and when blown up, two camouflaged observation positions, one on each side of the cave mouth, could just be seen. The assumption had been that these would be there, but it was good to have confirmation and an actual position for them. The cave must be deep after the bend as no portion of the boat was visible.

The team gathered at the front of the room for the briefing. This time the three Britons and the Russian sat amongst the young SEALs. They had been accepted, at least for now. The briefing repeated some of the material from previous ones and emphasized the need to take Romanov alive if at all possible, and the cash and other material stolen from the vaults was to be recovered. The maps of the island were not helpful and the aerial photographs not much better. The photographs taken by the frigate were of much more use. They knew the water was deep enough for them to enter submerged or the yacht could not have moved in there. It was to be assumed that there were no strong currents within the cave or again the yacht would have had problems. Then came details of the assault.

Duggan was there to brief them again.

Geordie leaned over to Martinez and whispered, "Duggan looks fit, so how come he is just briefing and not coming on the raid?"

"Ever since he lost his foot to an anti-personnel mine in Helmand Province, this is the closest the Navy will let him get to combat. He could take a standard Navy job but he knows our work best," Martinez whispered back.

The Englishmen looked at Duggan with new respect. It took courage of a different kind to stay in the service with an artificial foot.

The detailed briefing started. "As you know, two of our people are not here. They have been taken to be positioned for a HALO drop before you arrive. They will neutralize the cave mouth sentries, so you should not be seen swimming into the cave. They will then enter the cave and if there are guards on the deck they will attempt to take them out once your assault commences. You should not rely on this and act as though the decks are fully manned by hostiles. As you enter the cave stay as deep as possible and move slowly so you do not disturb the water. With the rebreather units there will be no air bubbles so you have a good chance of being undetected."

Duggan looked around the room for the nods. Satisfied, he carried on.

"The yacht has mounted machine guns on the main promenade deck and on the helideck. Assuming that these are manned and ready, entering the yacht over the side or over the stern would be impractical despite the inviting swimming platform at the stern." He allowed himself a small smile. "Thanks to our Russian colleague here we know that the boat has a large underwater hatch that gives access to a diver's moon pool. He believes that there is a small hatch by the access doors that give on to the external controls for these. While most of you lie quietly on the bottom below the ship, trying not to sleep, two of you," he looked up and two men raised their hands, "will search around the access doors to find the control hatch. Once you have located it things get interesting. You will need a diversion and the two men on the walls of the cave are it. You signal them and they will 'go loud.' That should bring everyone to the upper decks to defend the yacht. It should also make enough noiseso the opening of those doors will go undetected. You then enter through the moon pool and clear the boat in the standard way. You should all have familiarized yourself with Mr. Popov's diagram by now and you have been assigned to your teams. All clear?"

He looked around the room again as if imprinting every face in his memory. Then he said, "And when you are clearing the internal spaces what will you do?"

This must have been an "in" joke as the SEALs chorused, "Check the corners!" and laughed.

Andrei whispered to Jim, "They should be taking this seriously. Romanov is no laughing matter."

Jim looked at him, "Oh they are serious, believe me. The small jokes are what makes this bearable and eases the tension."

The briefing continued with timings and allocation of roles once inside the boat. The role for the four non-SEALs was to deal with any further nerve agent warheads that were found and to identify Romanov. They had an hour before they were to climb back into the stealthy boats and head toward the island which would still be invisible to the ship as they left. As usual they were taken to the mess deck to eat before they started out.

Andrei took the chance to ask, "What did he mean about a HALO drop? What is it?"

Martinez explained "It stands for High Altitude Low Opening. The parachutist is delivered to the target by a C-130 aircraft flying at very high altitude so it can hardly be heard or seen from the ground. The parachutist leaves the aircraft and free falls to a very low altitude before opening his chute. He is usually on the ground in seconds after the chute opens. It is a sneaky way of getting people into a place without detection."

Andrei had paused with a piece of steak on his fork half way to his mouth; the blood from the rare meat ran over his fingers. "That sounds incredibly dangerous. What happens if the main chute does not open?"

Martinez shrugged. "It's a risk," he conceded, "but without it the risk of being shot as you land is even greater."

"I shall pray for your two men and beg the Lord to keep them safe," said Andrei.

After eating, they went back to their equipment and checked it again. Then Martinez checked it.

Duggan came to see them. "Are you sure you want to do this?" he said. "It's risky."

Andrei answered for them all. "If your HALO men can take such a risk to take down a Russian criminal, we can go for a swim in the warm, dark sea."

Chapter 50

The SEAL team with the four extra men in support made their way down through the confusing complex of companionways inside the assault ship, until they were almost at water level. They paused alongside a passageway as sailors opened a large steel hatch at the end of a short steel lined corridor. The last light of the day flooded in as the sun dropped toward the horizon. They moved forward in turn and boarded a set of three inflatable boats from the doorway in the side of the ship. They shoved off from the ship just as dusk fell. Although they did not know it, the C-130J Hercules aircraft carrying their two HALO jumpers was passing overhead at high altitude as they climbed in.

The two HALO jumpers sat on either side of the fuselage with their oxygen masks already in place, breathing slowly and calmly. As they neared the island the aircraft crewman clipped his safety harness to the ring in the side of the fuselage and opened the rear cargo hatch. A small red light in the panel above him came on and the two SEALs stood up and walked carefully to the start of the hatch door. It was cold up here, really cold. They could feel it even through the insulated jump suits.

The green light came on and the crewman waved them out. They walked briskly to the end of the cargo door and stepped into space, immediately adopting the free-fall position to control their precipitous flight. They plunged downwards toward the thin cloud layer. Up here they were still in the sunlight, but the island below them was already dark. Both men checked their position and the altimeter on their chest constantly, this was no time for a mistake. They reached terminal velocity and the island climbed up toward them rapidly.

At the last possible second they triggered their parachutes and the violent deceleration punched the air from their bodies. By the time they took their next full breath the island was just feet below them. They adopted the landing position and rolled onto the ground. They continued to roll rapidly back into an upright position and ensured that their parachutes collapsed and did not drag them into the sea. They checked around for any sign of activity before collecting their parachutes into a ball that could be hidden away from prying eyes.

The parachutes were stuffed down into the sand and weighted down with their harnesses to avoid detection, should the target yacht crew have any patrols watching the top of the island. They then took cover to orientate themselves before moving. Once they were sure of their position they took a compass bearing and moved carefully toward where they knew the cave entrance to be. Approaching the cliff edge they went down on to their bellies and slithered forward until they could see down to the sea below.

They could see the small waves breaking against the rocks, except directly below them where the water swept smoothly into the cave. They spread out, one to each side of the cave entrance and fixed their black climbing ropes at the top of the cliff. Silently they stood with their backs to the sea and started to walk backwards down the cliff face using an abseiling technique. This was their most vulnerable time; if they were seen by the sentries the mission was finished before it started. They had taken precautions by dropping well wide of the entrance. They would work their way inwards once they were at a suitable height.

The two men continued down until they were level with the point at which the two camouflaged sentry points had been seen from the passing frigate. They unclipped the ropes and began to move slowly inwards from each side, keeping close to the cliff face.

Although the two guards were well hidden, from normal view, the night vision goggles identified their heat signatures clearly as bright green figures against the cooler rock of the cave. Using a series of code clicks, through the short range communication headsets, the two SEALs would wait until they were both in a good firing position. Even if those in the yacht's communication room heard the clicks they would have no way of knowing how far away they were or what they signified.

Out at sea the boats were traveling at speed in a close line abreast formation. They were not heading directly for the cave where their wakes might be seen approaching. They were aiming to arrive at the island out of sight of any watchers inside the cave mouth. They would then skirt slowly around the shore until they were within easy swimming distance to allow the divers to move in. They would not be in communication with the two HALO parachutists until they were almost at the entrance to the yacht's hiding place and even then there would be no radio chatter.

The night was clear and the sea was calm which made for a swift and comfortable passage, although cloud and rain would have made it safer. The island raised itself over the horizon off to starboard as they drove forward. From here they would be out of sight of the sentries, but they stayed on course for another fifteen minutes before turning in to their objective. The cliffs of the island rose before them; the only narrow beach was away to their left and shielded by a submerged reef, making a night approach highly dangerous for a rubber boat.

As they neared the island the helmsmen slowed the boats down to reduce the wake. On a flat calm night like this even the wake of small boats might be noticed by an alert sentry. They came to within a hundred meters of the craggy shore and turned to follow the towering cliffs toward the cave entrance. The boat carrying Jim and his group was at the back of the three now moving in line astern. That would put them at the back of the swimming group when they entered the water so they had less chance of getting lost. Martinez had taken over command in place of Wallace and had been replaced as their minder by another two SEALs, who had not introduced themselves. They would swim on either side of the four non-SEALs to guide them and keep them together.

As the boats crept along the shore every few minutes there were two clicks in the earpiece of Jim's short range radio. Then he heard the two clicks answered by three clicks. They were in range of the HALO drop men. The cave entrance must be close. The three helmsmen took the engines out of gear and allowed the boats to drift.

Chapter 54

Up on the cliffs the two SEALs now moved slowly and carefully into a firing position on either side of the cave entrance. To give themselves a clearer shot, the one on the left of the cave entrance would take the sentry inside on the right side of the cave, and the one on the right would take the left one. This increased the range slightly, but meant that they did not have to lean into the cave to find their targets who were set back a little, to avoid being seen from above.

The night vision goggles clearly showed the two targets sitting behind their camouflage netting watching the sea. A click in the headset and two rapid quiet cracks from each of the suppressed weapons sent the two sentries slumping against the walls of the cave. The loudest noise was the coffee flask of the left hand man being knocked over as he slid to the floor of his camouflaged hide. They waited to ensure there was no further movement, from the two downed sentries and then sent three radio clicks before moving into the cave mouth. They eased their way past the sentry posts, pausing only to check their targets for a pulse, then carried on into the cave on either side of the water channel below them.

Hearing the three clicks, outboard motors were put back into gear and the boats moved slowly to within two hundred meters of the cave entrance. They stopped again, closed up to each other, stationary in the water. The pathfinder checked yet again that all his people were ready and gave the signal to enter the water. To avoid any noise, the SEALs did not throw themselves backwards into the water, but slipped quietly over the side. Once they were all in the water, the pathfinder set out for the cave, submerging as he went. The rest of the team followed.

For the non-SEALs, swimming underwater at night was a strange new experience and for Andrei, who had never dived before, quite a frightening one. He remembered what he had been told back on the assault ship and brought his breathing back under control. He saw the small luminous markers on the fins in front of him and followed them forward and down. As he dropped lower, the SEAL to his left placed a hand on his arm and signaled that he was deep enough. Even modern rebreather equipment has a depth limit.

The light from the stars in the clear sky above was only just enough to show them the entrance to the cave as they reached it. While that starlight made life a little more difficult it did reduce their chance of being seen from the deck of the target ship. The lead swimmer turned into the cave and swam slowly, skimming the cave floor and chasing shimmering clouds of small fish back into their holes in the rocks. The other swimmers followed him slowly with spaces between them so as to reduce disturbance of the calm water in the cave.

The swim through the cave was almost a let-down after the fear of the unknown and within a few minutes they were all below the hull of the yacht that was resting on the water above them, at the rear end of the cave. Looking up through the crystal clear water they could see the mooring lines strung fore and aft that held the boat clear of the jagged coral formations around it. They were outlined by the dim light coming from the rear end of the yacht. There was a narrow gang plank rigged from the rear swimming platform to the shore, to allow the sentries to move backwards and forwards to their posts.

The team assembled on the bottom, holding on to irregularities in the cave floor to keep themselves from drifting. As they hung in the warm water, keeping as still as possible, the fish ventured back out of their hiding places and came to explore the strange new creatures. Jim watched fascinated as fish nibbled around the edge of his diving mask and peered in at him.

There was no sound from the hull above them. They should have been able to hear generators or pumps through the water, but there was nothing, just the large streamlined shape of the hull hanging above them. Two divers rose from the bottom and started very carefully to swim inverted along the hull. They could not use a light in the clear water without being seen from above so they searched through touch. A delicate operation if they were to avoid the possibility of puncturing their skin on the barnacles and other growths adhering to the hull they were skimming under. They found the edges of the large hatch leading to the moon pool and felt around it for the smaller door that would give access to the hatch control.

After ten minutes of careful searching they found the smaller access door and opened it. With a tiny laser flashlight they examined the controls inside. There were just two controls, a large, circular, ribbed button and a keyway drive with a crank handle mounted next to it. It was time for the distraction. One of the searchers rose gently to the surface until his head just slid out of the oily, smooth water without creating the slightest ripple. Once his head and waterproof radio were clear of the water he made the prearranged three clicks to indicate readiness. He waited until he heard the two-click acknowledgment and then slid slowly back down into the water. He had two minutes to wait before the noise and commotion started above him. He returned to his companion and tapped him on the shoulder, then drifted down to the waiting group to signal them to be ready to move. Then he moved gently back upwards to re-join the other searcher by the control panel. They waited.

The noise of the Flash Bang grenades in the cave was loud even underwater and the brilliant light illuminated the channel, scaring fish around them and causing them to dash for cover in the rocks. The sound of pounding feet and shouting could be heard through the hull as the crew ran to react to the above water threat.

An M-67 fragmentation grenade landed on the foredeck and the shards of metal that flew from its explosion cleared three enemy personnel from the deck before they could do any damage. One, bleeding heavily, was thrown over the side by the blast and drifted past the divers, weighted down by the assault rifle he wore across his chest and the extra ammunition in his pockets. The ripples and splash were useful further cover for their own movements below the yacht.

Pressing the ribbed button inside the control panel was having no effect, the electrical power generators must be needed to operate the door. The crank handle was fitted into the keyway. As it turned the main clam doors of the hatchway started to move slowly outwards. As soon as there was enough gap between the clamshell doors two SEALs from the main group swam through and surfaced in the moon pool, weapons at the ready. As anticipated, the diving compartment was empty with all the attention focussed on the main decks to defend against an attack.

The doors continued to open and all the divers entered the moon pool and clambered up the two ladders set in the fore and aft bulkheads. As soon as they were on the deck that ran around the pool they shed their diving equipment and swim fins. MP5 submachine guns were removed from the waterproof bags and loaded.

Chapter 52

Illuminated in the feeble light from the moon pool and the dim emergency lighting on the bulkheads they saw that, as expected, there were doorways forward and aft of the diving compartment. The attacking party split into two groups with Martinez steering Jim and his team into the one heading aft. They opened the watertight door carefully and peered inside. They were entering a workshop with benches along the walls and tool racks mounted above them. It was deserted. They went through it checking as they did that there was nobody hiding in the dark corners waiting to ambush them. At the end of the workshop they came to another watertight door, this one slightly open. A quick look inside showed no movement. The door swung open with a heavy push and they stepped through.

They were in the engine room with two large, powerful diesel engines set one to each side of the compartment and a self-contained generator mounted at the aft end. They checked around again to clear the room; it was empty of any enemies. They turned to the open tread metal steps of the catwalk that led up to the next deck and were about to mount it when a door above them crashed open and two men in dark blue coveralls ran in. They saw the black suited invaders below them and skidded to a halt. As they turned to run back out they opened their mouths to shout a warning. With speed that surprised Jim, Martinez and one of the other SEALs had raised their weapons, aimed and put two rounds into each man from their silenced MP5s. The crewmen fell to the deck like dumped sacks of potatoes. The two leading SEALs stepped forward and checked their necks for a pulse. Both men were gone beyond pain and worry. They stepped over them and headed for the upper door, with the rest of the team following.

The door at the head of the steel stairs stood open and showed a passageway, lined with doors beyond.

"Crew quarters," Martinez whispered and with hand gestures split the team into two halves, to cover each side.

The SEAL teams moved through and rapidly checked each crew cabin leapfrogging as they went. The signs of a hasty exit were obvious in each one with sheets thrown to the side of the bunks, chairs knocked to the deck and general disarray everywhere. The only exits from the crew quarters were back through the engine room or forward up a set of stairs. With the crew quarters cleared, the first four men moved carefully up the narrow staircase, weapons raised and ready.

At the top of the short flights of stair was a door into a passageway. To the right was the galley and to the left a large well-furnished dining room with glass sliding doors that let out onto a covered deck. Half the men moved to check the modern, well-equipped kitchen while the remainder, with Martinez, slipped into the dining room. This was too well furnished to be for crew use and the ornate curving staircase leading up indicated that this was intended for the owner and his guests. The team from the kitchen returned and moved to check the outside deck while the Martinez group climbed the stairs.

One of the SEALs produced a black, metal tube with an eyepiece and held it up so that it protruded slightly above the level of the deck above. The personal periscope showed the room above to be empty, so the SEALs moved on up the stairs. The first man stopped with his eyes at floor level and checked again to make sure the periscope had not missed anything. The room was still clear.

The group moved quickly and silently into the ornate cabin which was furnished as a large lounge area. The sliding glass doors at the aft end of the room let out onto the helideck which was clear at the moment. Around the side of the cabin were large picture windows that showed a promenade deck outside. They checked if this was the deck with the machine guns mounted on it, but saw nothing.

The SEALs were all business, checking to ensure they had not been detected, ensuring there were no weapons in the area and identifying the next move. Jim and his two men were standing amazed at the luxury they saw around them and this was on a boat, what must this man's house be like? Jim noticed that Andrei was standing motionless staring forward. He turned to see what he was looking at. At the forward end of the luxury cabin was a large and well-stocked bar. On the rear wall of the bar, partially hidden by bottles was a large and beautifully detailed religious painting.

"Something special?"

Andrei nodded "Oh yes, I have seen pictures of that all my life. Unless I am confused that is the triptych from the Cathedral of Christ the Savior, in Moscow. It was the center of the Russian Orthodox Church until Stalin had it destroyed to make way for a monstrosity called the 'Palace of the Soviets'. The artistic treasures like that one were removed to museums. This and others were taken to a place of safety to protect it when the Germans invaded and they were never seen again. This is one of the most precious treasures of a country with many artistic treasures. It belongs back in the Cathedral that has now been rebuilt as an exact replica of the old one. For this creature to have mounted it in a bar is a sacrilege to the Russian people."

Jim looked at Andrei's face, there was a dark fury there he had not seen before.

"I guess this was not here when you were last on board then?"

Andrei dragged his eyes away from the painting. "No it was not. It makes me wonder what else he has on here that he has looted from other thieves in New York. Major, whatever happens, this ship must not be sunk, that triptych alone is worth more to my people than anything you could imagine."

Martinez walked over to them, he glanced at the bar. "Nice painting. Time to move on."

Chapter 53

In the forward part of the ship, the other SEAL group had moved out of the diving compartment and found themselves in a well-equipped laboratory. It would have been a useful cover story should any Customs investigator have queried the use of the moon pool and extensive range of diving equipment. The team checked the room swiftly, opening cupboards and large storage bins to ensure there were no nasty surprises left behind for them.

Many of the bins contained sacks of money sorted into the different national currencies. Others held jewelry in sample trays. Paintings and icons were stacked on end inside cupboards. This one dimly lit compartment put Aladdin's fabled cave to shame. At the forward end of the laboratory, they moved through a watertight door that led into a large storage room. Diving equipment was mounted in purpose built racks around the narrowing sides with wetsuits hanging to dry from cables strung from side to side. An open tread metal stairway led upwards. The first SEAL up the stairway peeped through the small porthole set in the door at the top. This area was far more luxurious than anything they had seen before.

He saw nobody and eased the door open. He stepped through, followed by the rest of the group who fanned out along the wood paneled corridor. Paintings with special lighting above them hung on the walls and thick carpet covered the deck. The wooden doors along the passageway were a deep lustrous mahogany color with solid brass handles and fittings. This must be where the owner accommodated his important guests, when he wasn't engaged in major robberies and wholesale slaughter.

Each cabin was dealt with in a practiced routine by three men at a time. Every cabin was checked and cleared before the next door was opened. Although the cabins were large and well-furnished, none of them stood out as being special enough for a master cabin fit for the owner of a luxury yacht of this size. At the aft end of the passage a door led into the galley that had already been searched. A door on this level would allow a room service to these cabins that actually had hot food delivered before the sauces started to congeal.

Halfway along the passage there was a wide, carpeted staircase either side. These two staircases turned as they rose and combined into a single one that led into an open area forward of the lounge and bar area. Doors on either side led out to a side deck. Behind the staircase as it rose into the open area was a further door, wider than the rest with large paintings on both sides and two bronze statues of Roman soldiers as door guardians.

The SEALs positioned themselves on either side of this door and then entered rapidly. The cabin was obviously for the owner of this vessel. The room was the full width of the ship with thick carpets and a luxurious lounging area with a plasma TV screen mounted on the wall. At the forward end of the space was a very large, ornate, four poster bed, an incongruous sight on a modern yacht. His and hers bathrooms were on each side of the bed and an impressive array of wardrobes and mirrors flanked these. The art work on the walls was a strange mixture of old and modern, probably put there because of its value and not for aesthetic reasons. Curtains swooped around the forward bulkhead and when the first SEAL checked behind them cautiously he found a wide picture window that looked out across the foredeck and into the cave.

Two bodies lay on the foredeck, victims of the fragmentation grenade that had started the assault. They lay in a spreading pool of blood and were not moving. Looking over them he could see the cave walls stretching out in front of the boat, then turning right toward the sea. The moon had risen now and the silvery light reflected off the calm water inside the cave and lit up the interior in a way that might seem magical to the romantic.

The SEAL looking through the window was not a romantic. All he could see was that, with the increased level of light, the two SEALs still on the cave walls were at greater risk of detection if they exposed themselves to fire from the enemy on the yacht. As he watched, another burst of fire came from the cave entrance, to be answered by loud automatic gunfire from an upper deck. The two HALO jumpers were doing their best to keep Romanov's crew focused away from the assault team.

Having secured the lower three decks the two group leaders along with Andrei and Jim met in front of the impressive bar. A drink about this time would have been very welcome but would be even more so once the job was complete.

Martinez started the improvised council of war with, "OK, three decks clear and many of the proceeds of the robbery found. The bearer bonds that the President is so interested in are still missing. The two men rushing into the engine room were probably going to start engines so they could be ready to get the hell out of Dodge. The rest will realize soon that they have not succeeded and will investigate. Since there is nobody on these decks they must be above us manning the machine guns and preparing to defend the ship. They know there are our people in the cave, but they will not know how many yet. If they realize there are only two they may try an attack around the cave walls. What we need to know is, what is above us. Run me through the description of the boat again, Andrei."

The Russian looked thoughtful. "As I described at the briefing, there is one more full deck above. As you say, that is where the heavy weapons are mounted. There is a promenade deck on both sides and around the front. At the rear of that deck is a sunbathing deck for when Romanov is entertaining his Mafia colleagues and their lady friends. There is a covered saloon area which has a small swimming pool inside it. At the forward end is a raised area which is the bridge and at the back of that is a viewing gallery for guests so they can see what is going on when entering port or when underway. The communications room is behind the viewing gallery and above the saloon. On top of the saloon there are two inflatable speedboats and some toys for guests to play with on the water. The gun that covers the helideck is at the rear of that sunbathing deck, but behind another boat so it does not worry the guests."

"So how do we get up there without getting our heads blown off?"

"There are stairways on each side of the deck at this level that lead up on to that deck. They are fairly open and would be dangerous. The machine guns are mounted both in front and behind these staircases. Forward of this bar is an internal staircase that leads up into the saloon for use in stormy or cold weather and there is another small door near the master's cabin that leads up straight into the bridge."

Chapter 54

The attack plan was limited by the access they had to the top deck. Two men were to return to the guest dining room to ensure nobody left the ship by the rear ramp to attack the two SEALs in the cave. The rest would split up and climb all the staircases at the same time. Their arrival on the upper deck would be preceded by a shower of Flash Bang grenades to disorientate the defenders. Martinez removed a radio from a waterproof bag at his belt and warned the two men in the cave that they were about to appear on the upper deck. That would try and avoid any blue on blue casualties and, once the confusion started on the ship, they could provide over watch and selective sniper fire if a target presented itself.

The team split into smaller groups and headed for the stairways they had been allocated. Every man checked his weapon and ensured the magazine was properly in place and full. They eased the pistols in their holsters and cocked the submachine guns. All of them knew this was going to be an action carried out fast and at close quarters, any hesitation or mistake could be fatal. There was no false bravado or high fives. These men were controlled and professional, with an almost mystic trust in the comrades alongside them. The leaders of the small groups stared at their watches as they counted down the last thirty seconds before the coordinated movement began.

The figures on the watches reduced to zero and the grenades were thrown. Three landed inside the bridge, four went up each of the outer stairways, two going forward and two going aft. Another four went into the upper deck saloon. As the grenades exploded with vicious noise and incredibly bright flashes, the SEALs leapt up the stairways with their weapons at the ready, moving at a speed that startled Jim and his companions. They spread out quickly ready for any movement.

On the bridge the grenades had been extremely effective in the enclosed space. The four men in there were shocked and dazed and offered no resistance as they were grabbed, thrown to the deck and restrained with plastic wrist ties. The SEALs in the bridge then moved outside to the wings of the bridge to provide fire support onto the side decks if required.

The effect in the deck saloon had been similarly shocking and in that enclosed space the SEALs found eight dazed and confused men who had dropped their weapons and one man who had been blown into the swimming pool with his weapon on top of him. As he struggled to the surface his eyes cleared to find the barrel of an MP5 in front of his nose. All of the men were restrained and pushed down hard to the deck to await disposal later.

The side decks were a different matter. The grenades had less effect out here and although the men on the machine guns were surprised, they were recovering fast. The heavy weapons swung round on their mounting pintles toward the SEALs coming up the stairway. They were fast, but with the element of surprise in their favor, the attackers were faster still. The MP5s spewed their 9 millimeter rounds in a hail along the deck and on both sides of the ship the machine gunners were cut down before they could do any damage.

Forward of the bridge, the promenade deck curved round in a semicircle with a waist height safety bulkhead around it. Six men had been crouching behind this with rifles, waiting for a chance to cut down the men inside the cave mouth. There had been no way to drop any disorientating grenades on these and so they were a serious danger. One made the mistake of standing up to look back through the bridge windows after the flash bangs went off and received two bullets in the back for his trouble, from two sides of the cave. The rest learned fast and stayed low. They moved left and right to attempt to reach the side decks, but as they appeared around the corner of the bridge, they found themselves facing the steady barrels of submachine guns from the side deck and from the wings of the bridge above them. With nowhere to go they dropped their rifles and slowly put their hands behind their heads as they sank to their knees.

Inside the bridge, three of the group of SEALs moved to secure the communication room. As they entered the room the wireless operator made the mistake of turning toward the door with a pistol in his hand. The short burst from the silenced MP5 threw him back onto his radio equipment and removed any threat he might have been.

Moving aft the team emerged onto the top deck where the RIBs and other boats were stored. They spread to each side and using the cover available moved cautiously to deal with the last machine gun. As they emerged from behind the boats and looked down onto the sunbathing deck they found that the machine gunner had no intention of dying as a hero. He was on his knees facing them with his hands already behind his neck. Two SEALs came from the saloon on that deck, picked him up almost gently and secured his hands behind his back, before shepherding him into the main deck saloon to sit by the pool. By the time he arrived, most of the surviving crew of the yacht had been rounded up and were sitting in a row along the starboard side, guarded by the SEALs.

Martinez stepped in front of the group of prisoners and said, "So which one of you is Romanov?" Nobody answered and nobody moved. "Come on. I don't have time for games. Where is Romanov?" Again he got no answer. Even in this situation none of these men were prepared to cross the Mafia boss. Martinez turned to Andrei. "Which one is he?"

Andrei ran his eye along the line of bedraggled and subdued men. "None of these."

The door to the bridge opened and the four men who had been in there during the attack staggered in as they were pushed through, all with their hands firmly secured behind them.

"That's Romanov," said Andrei, pointing at the second of the four.

He was quickly pulled to one side as the other three joined the line of prisoners.

"Nice to meet you, Mr. Romanov," said Martinez. "You have an appointment with our justice system back in the States."

Romanov laughed. "Your so called Justice system cannot touch me. I was nowhere near New York and had no knowledge that the Arabs in my crews would hijack the U-Boats for a terrorist attack on the city. You on the other hand will be charged with piracy for attacking my boat."

"Mr. Romanov..." Martinez began, but Andrei stepped up beside him.

"I think you should let me speak to Mr Romanov, as one Russian to another. And if you look over there you will see that I am not the only surviving witness to what you did."

Romanov's eyes widened and his jaw sagged a little as he recognized the servant he had ordered to be killed, but he said nothing. He looked at Jim and the other two Britons and shrugged. Martinez stepped back and watched as Andrei led Romanov to a chair at the far end of the room. The difference in size between the two men was marked, but somehow Andrei had the more commanding presence. He sat Romanov down and then pulled another chair across to face him. Andrei leaned forward and spoke very intensely to his prisoner.

Jim looked at Ivan and said, "So was all that training at Beaconsfield any use? Can you tell what they are saying?"

Ivan nodded. "It's very fast Russian, but I am getting the drift. At the moment Andrei is calling him a number of extremely rude Russian names, he seems quite upset that Romanov tried to have him drowned. He is now saying that the Americans are a just and honorable people and do not understand what a low life and scumbag Romanov is. Now that's interesting. He is also saying that they do not understand what is being said so they can do a deal. Romanov has perked up and is interested in the deal. Andrei is saying that if he tells him where the bearer bonds are he will help him get away and they can split the profits. He is also demanding a senior position in Romanov's organization back in Russia. He also wants to know if there are any more Russian art treasures on board. Romanov wants to know what his alternative is and Andrei has offered to blow his kneecap off to show him. I think Romanov believes him. Yes, he is telling Andrei where they are. Didn't catch that bit."

Andrei glanced toward Jim and Ivan then turned back and spoke to Romanov again.

Ivan turned away from the two Russians and whispered to Jim, "The bearer bonds are in the safe hidden behind the paneling in the wardrobes in his state room downstairs and the best Russian paintings and icons are in the other wardrobe behind the clothes. Andrei has told Romanov they need to go outside to work out their escape plan. I think we need to secure those bonds, boss."

Leaving Ivan to keep an eye on the two Russians, in case Andrei needed help, Jim slipped out of the upper saloon and went down to the lounge area with the impressive bar and the glorious religious artifact. Geordie followed him. They moved forward to the main state room and checked in the wardrobes. They slid the paneling to one side and found the safe was there and locked. The glorious icons and painting were pushed into the other wardrobe in an untidy pile. They could not open the safe, but Romanov had said it was full of bearer bonds. They could not guess what that safe was worth at that point, but it was a big one and could clearly hold an awful lot of paper certificates. Geordie was left to check the artworks and to pack them somewhere more suitable. Jim returned to the saloon where the prisoners were being held.

As he entered he nodded slightly at Andrei who acknowledged with an odd smile.

Jim walked to Ivan and said, "How is it going?"

"Andrei has been stringing him along, negotiating the size of his cut and trying to work out a way for them to get away from us. He has been pretty convincing. Just now he demanded the safe combination as a sign of good faith and Romanov cracked and gave it to him."

Andrei spoke again to Romanov and told him to stand. Romanov did as he was told and Andrei took him by the arm and steered him out onto the sunbathing deck. As they stepped out onto the deck Romanov looked across at Jim with a smug smile. Together the two Russians walked to the safety rail and Romanov leaned against it smiling down at Andrei. Clearly he was feeling relaxed and confident. Martinez was watching all this and came across to Jim.

"What is going on with those two?"

Jim shook his head "Not sure yet. Romanov thinks he has an escape deal with Andrei but he doesn't know that Ivan speaks Russian and heard it all."

"Does Andrei know about Ivan's skill?"

"Oh yes. We spoke about lots of things to try and keep ourselves awake during our days and nights in that damned dinghy. We even had Russian singing lessons. I now know more Russian folk songs than I know English ones, a lot of them seem to be quite sad."

"So why are they out there?"

Jim shrugged. "Andrei will have his reasons, I have no doubt."

As he spoke, Andrei stepped away from Romanov raised the MP5 and fired half a magazine into the Mafia man's chest. The impact at such short range lifted Romanov over the rail and dumped him on the helideck below.

Martinez sighed, "Oh hell, the President issued instructions for us to take him alive."

"No," said Jim, "he said alive if possible. Andrei had no choice when Romanov made a grab for that machine gun."

"What grab? He was nowhere near the machine gun!" Martinez looked at Jim for a moment then said "Oh, I see. Yes. We are probably lucky Andrei was so fast or we could have lost some people."

Andrei came back into the saloon. Jim and Martinez walked across to meet him.

"Do you want to explain that to me?" Jim said. Andrei nodded and wearily sank into the chair Romanov had recently sat in.

"Romanov was right about the American justice system," he said. "He could have carried on running his empire from a jail cell and lawyers in the USA are very clever about manipulating the law no matter what crime the animal has committed. It was necessary to send a message to the Mafia in Moscow in a form they will respect and understand, or you would have seen more of these attacks on innocent civilians in the future. No city in America or Europe would have been safe."

He leaned forward and handed his weapon to Jim. "I surrender to you. I am ready to face the courts for what I have done. I have no regrets."

Jim handed the weapon back. "Martinez and I watched the whole thing. When Romanov made that grab for the machine gun on the pedestal out there he could have done a lot of damage. You saved our lives."

Andrei looked puzzled. "But Romanov's hands were secured behind his back he could not have …"

Jim smiled. "They aren't bound anymore. Ivan has just gone down to check, but I am pretty sure we will find that he had slipped out of the restraints without you noticing."

"That is good and there is something you should know. The last word that the animal heard in this life was Tatiana. I have made our revenge for her life."

At that moment Jim saw Martinez spin toward the rear of the saloon. He looked in the same direction as the SEAL and saw Smith scrambling up from behind an armchair in the corner that had been his hiding place throughout the action.

"You bastard Wilson! The payoff from this job would have set me up for life and you ruined it!"

Smith's hands came into view from behind the chair. He was holding a folding stock AK-47 assault rifle and was fumbling to cock it while turning it toward Jim and the others. With a speed that beggared belief, Martinez raised his weapon and fired a burst of three rounds across the saloon. Smith staggered back against the bulkhead and looked down at the spreading red stain across his chest. For a second he looked at Jim and then slid down the wall and back into his hiding place. The closest SEAL stepped to the chair and looked over the back. He straightened and turned to the others shaking his head.

Martinez looked across the saloon. "Major," he said, "any chance you and your two boys could get those engines running? It would be nice to take this boat back home without some regular Navy pogue getting all the credit. And Andrei, thanks for the assist back there, it could have been nasty."

"No sooner said than done," said Jim, "if you could send a man down to open the safe in the main state room and start sorting out the bearer bonds in there. Geordie can come and help me. Ivan! Andrei! Stop sitting about, we have work to do!"

As with most modern yachts the engine system was largely automated so starting up presented little difficulty with Andrei translating the labeling on the control consoles. They found the internal controls and closed the outer doors to the moon pool and then went back up on deck to help where they could. The two HALO jumpers had now come aboard and the lines securing the yacht within the cave were released. The SEALs proved to be expert boat handlers and eased the large vessel around the bend in the cave using the bow thruster to control the turn, then slowly nosed the yacht out to sea. As they emerged from the cave into the early dawn they found there were a number of large gray ships waiting for them. As a small celebration one of the SEALs attached a large US Flag at the stern post and when it unfurled in the morning breeze the ships saluted with deafening fog horn blasts, as a flight of USMC Harrier jets flew low overhead.

Chapter 54

The voyage back to the mainland was uneventful with calm seas for most of the way and an escorting frigate on each side. The prisoners were confined in the crew quarters with a pair of vigilant SEALs on watch at all times. For the rest they took great delight in trying the very fine array of food that Romanov had provided for himself. The supply of wine was also of a very high quality and there was also a case of Macallan 12 with most of the bottles unopened.

Jim said, "I guess that is how he rumbled your little game with the whisky, Andrei. So that must be why he tried to drown you with us."

Andrei sipped from his cut glass tumbler. "I think I told you he was not a nice person. He did not deserve such a fine whisky in the first place, but I suspect I also knew too much for him to risk me staying alive. That is probably why he had Tatiana killed as well. I think he was just cleaning house. I think the men he left on the island as a distraction were also intended to die."

The yacht approached Melbourne in Florida and slipped into the Indian River south of the Fort Pierce Inlet State Park. They made their way north up the broad waterway, with the British team and Andrei standing at the rail for most of the way watching the dolphins and the pelicans pass them by. The vessel passed under the Pineda Causeway and turned slowly right into a small marina. Standing on the deck they were surprised to see a large airfield beyond it. They all turned as Martinez came out on deck.

"What is this place?" asked Ivan. "It looks military."

"It is. That's Patrick Air Force Base and this is the marina that belongs to the base. It was the nearest military base where we could be secure, but where a boat like this would attract no attention. Plus with those long runways it's very handy for catching a flight to anywhere you want."

As the yacht came alongside the wharf in the Patrick Marina they saw three very shiny green and white helicopters swoop across the river to land on a broad area of grass. They carried on securing the boat without paying much attention. The prisoners were taken down the gangplank and handed over to a platoon of US Marines who were very quick to ensure that there would be no trouble from them. The bodies of Romanov's men killed in the securing of the yacht were taken off next and thrown, none too gently, into ambulances. The man who had been blown over the side had not been recovered and had been left in the cave for the fishes to explore when they next came out of their holes.

M113 Armored Personnel Carriers drew up along the quay with a cordon of Humvees around them, all with heavy machine guns mounted on the roof and alert gunners behind them. They were there to collect the material stolen from the bank vaults.

Before they could come aboard to start unloading it, a column of black Chevy Suburbans with smoked glass windows pulled up and disgorged their passengers. A very tall man with white hair strode purposefully through the cordon followed by a group of civilians and military officers who seemed to be having trouble keeping up. From the deck Jim and Martinez watched the soldiers in the security cordon move forward to stop them and immediately slam to a rigid attention and salute.

"Somebody important?" asked Jim.

"You could say that," said Martinez, "it looks like we are having a visit from the President of the United States and all sorts of other people I don't know."

As they came closer Jim said, "I can help you with one of them. That's David Orwell the British Prime Minister on the left."

"And the one at the right is the one and only Evgeny Zhukov, the President of Russia," said Andrei from behind them.

"Hmm, now we find out how much trouble we are in, I suspect, Andrei," said Jim.

"It does not matter, my friend. Romanov is dead and the Mafia did not succeed. They will get the message. Everything else is beneath notice."

The three men went down to the main lounge area to greet their distinguished visitors.

The Secret Service men accompanying the President rushed to disarm the three men as they came into the lounge. The President stopped them.

"When the Commander-in-Chief has to be protected from US Navy SEALs and our close allies, it will be a very sad day," he said, in that famous rumbling voice. He stepped forward and shook hands with the three men. "No speeches needed today," he said. "A fine job, gentlemen. A shame about Romanov, but I have read Lieutenant Commander

Martinez's preliminary email report and it told me there was no choice."

Martinez coughed. "Sorry, sir, but that's Lieutenant."

"Don't correct your Commander-in-Chief, son. Hand me the box," the President said, holding out his hand. A Naval officer stepped forward and placed a small blue box into his outstretched hand. He passed it to Martinez "Your new rank badges. There will be the customary pinning ceremony later, but I wanted to be the one that handed those to you."

Martinez snapped to attention and saluted. "Thank you, sir. I will make sure I am worthy of these."

"Oh, you're worthy already, son, you were going to be promoted on your record anyway, and this mission has just brought that forward a little." The President turned. "That's my man seen to, at least for now. So your turn," he said to the two men waiting directly behind him. "Lieutenant Commander, I think you ought to introduce me to your team."

Martinez led the President toward the staircase leading up to the saloon where the SEAL team were getting ready to disembark. The Secret Service moved to go with him.

The President stopped and said, "No need for you, gentlemen. I can't think of a safer place for a president than in the middle of a highly effective SEAL team."

The Russian President was the first of the rest to move forward to grasp Andrei's hand. Out of politeness to his hosts he spoke in English.

"Well done and I am glad it was you that shot Romanov, however that happened. The message to the Mafia at home has already been received and our police teams are moving while they are still off balance."

Andrei nodded, but did not speak. Instead he turned and pointed behind the bar. The Russian President's jaw dropped for just a moment as he turned.

"Can it be true? The one from the Cathedral of Christ the Savior, all these years?"

Andrei nodded and the two Russians clasped each other in a bear hug like two old comrades. Jim saw the tear in the eye of a President who was famous as a hard man.

"There are more icons in the cabin above us. I think the Hermitage Museum will be having a new exhibit of recovered art that the Nazis looted and sold."

The two Russians moved off together to examine the other icons on the higher deck, both wearing large grins. The Prime Minister stepped up to Jim.

"I do hope you don't expect any such displays from me?" he said.

"No sir. I don't expect anything from you."

The Prime Minister looked him in the eye and said, "I suppose I deserved that. The cutbacks in the manning in the Armed Forces were driven by politics and my hands were tied. Plus, they were handled badly and discharging you and your team from the Army was wrong. The mobilization for this crisis has allowed me to correct that. I apologise to you." He held out his hand.

Jim took his hand. "Big of you to say that, sir. I appreciate it." And he meant it. "So how much trouble are we actually in, sir?"

"A damn sight less than you deserve. The US Justice Department has determined that you are liable for prosecution on some pretty serious charges. However, in gratitude for the actions of HMS Huntingdon and a fisherman from the British Cayman Islands, President Barker has given all three of you an executive pardon. The German government has decided not to press charges so as not to publicize that war crime in the Kiel base and the Russians are keeping quiet so they can deal with their internal Mafia problem. So you three need to keep your mouths tight shut and you owe the skipper of the Huntingdon a beer or two, I think."

"Thank you, sir. May I show you some of the things we found when we took this yacht?"

They walked toward the bar and joined the two Russians who had returned and were admiring the glowing paintwork of the triptych behind the bar.

The US President came back into the cabin and took over again. "You three stay, but the rest of you give us the room. The President and the Prime Minister and I need to have a serious talk with these men."

He waited until the room was cleared, with the Secret Service standing guard outside the doors.

"Before we go any further, is Sergeant Peters available? We have someone who would like to see him."

Jim walked to the bottom of the staircase and called up for Geordie, who trotted down the stairs and followed Jim back into the saloon. By the time they got there a very attractive young woman was standing between the President and the Prime Minister. She saw Geordie and ran across the deck into his arms. They clung together for a few seconds and then started to walk out of the saloon together. They paused in the doorway and Geordie looked at the President over his shoulder.

"Thanks, Boss" he said.

The President had a smile on his face as he said, "We found that young lady working as a volunteer in one of the temporary first aid stations in the middle of Manhattan."

Jim turned to the President. "That was a nice thing to do, sir. Geordie has been worried sick about Sam, though he tried not to show it."

The President smiled, then turned to include the others. "Gentlemen, with all your adventures I suppose you are a little out of touch with what has been going on in the world. Now, as I expect you recall, the attack on the World Trade Center by Al Qaeda caused a mixed reception around the world. Our allies and friends sympathized and helped with the reprisals. Others rejoiced that we had been hurt. This attack has been differently received. A chemical attack on innocent civilians by an organized crime syndicate has revolted many people. Others were revolted by the use of Arab stooges to try and throw the blame on the Middle East again to try and damage our relations with the Muslim world. In any event, the huge support we have received from almost every country has been a significant step forward. Many nations have a problem with organized crime undermining their governments and victimizing their people. This attack will allow us to join forces and to take these people down, once and for all. We are forming a multinational task force to take the fight to the gangs wherever they are and we would like you to be the first three members of that task force." He looked at the three of them. "Well?"

"Yes sir, whatever you need," Martinez replied.

Andrei said, "If I can help them of course I would be happy to be part of this."

The Russian President patted his shoulder. "But not as a Special Investigator, you are now a Police Commander."

The Prime Minister looked at Jim with a raised eyebrow, but did not speak.

Jim said, "If I can bring my two men with me, then of course I'm in."

The Prime Minister said, "Conditions? Very well, they are in too. By the way, I know your two companions here have been promoted, but I suspect the German government would take a very dim view of me promoting people who tried to steal their property, even if it was out of date.

Plus, I had a word with the Commander Royal Engineers before I left the UK and he told me that if we promoted every Royal Engineer officer who did an exceptional job in difficult circumstances, he would have nothing but Generals in his Corps. You should be grateful to the President for issuing an Executive Pardon for your part in this, otherwise you could have been in very deep trouble."

He paused and looked Jim in the eye.

"However, I do have plans for you in addition to the task force the President is setting up. So you will get some exceptionally interesting jobs when you get home and so will your two pirates."

V4 Vengeance– Factual Context

This story revolves around the re-use of technology found in a secret base buried beneath a hill. Is this a fantasy too far? I don't think so. Let me give you a few facts and opinions and then you can make up your own mind.

First the V1 Flying Bomb. This did exist and it was successful. Taking off from short ramps located mainly in Occupied France, these early cruise missiles were mainly targeted on London and they worked. The fastest fighter aircraft of the time were only just able to catch them and some were shot down by aircraft and by anti-aircraft guns on the ground although they were a very small target and difficult to hit. Braver pilots actually flew alongside them and put their own wing below that of the V1, then lifted their wing and flipped the missile over so that it then plunged to the ground. Despite this bravery, many of these missiles got through to London and killed appreciable numbers of people. To give an idea of the scale of the problem, 9521 flying bombs were fired at South East England, including London. 2448 were fired at Antwerp and other targets when the launch sites within range of England were overrun by the advancing allied armies. In all they are thought to have caused some 22,892 casualties and done appreciable amounts of damage, as well as diverting scarce resources to the defense against them.

Less well known is that the V1, or more correctly the Fi 103, as it was designated by the Luftwaffe, had a number of variants. The E-1 model was designed with longer range to be launched from Holland after the launch sites in France were destroyed or overrun. The F-1 had even longer range. The B-2 had a more powerful explosive warhead and the C-1 carried a fragmentation bomb. The Fi 103 D-1 was designed to carry a chemical warhead, but it had not gone into series production by the time the war ended. The missiles could also be air launched from modified Heinkel HE111 bombers, although carrying the weapon degraded the already limited performance of these aircraft and made them extremely vulnerable to attack by allied fighters. A small book, "Meteor 1 vs V1 Flying Bomb" by Donald Nijboer gives more details of this weapon.

The V2 was a far more sophisticated missile that took off vertically and went high in the air before plunging down on its target. The target was often London and there was no defense against it and no warning. The damage done was quite extensive. The government of the time lied to the public about the cause of some of the explosions, blaming ruptured gas mains, etc. that had been supposedly damaged by previous bombing, in order to avoid panic.

The V3 was a large smooth bore cannon that was intended to bombard cities in southern England. It would have worked, but the advance of the allied armies after D-Day was too swift and the gun sites were overrun before they could be used as intended. One was used for a very short time, but to no great effect. This technology really was revived for Saddam Hussein of Iraq who was in the process of building such a cannon to bombard Israel. This scheme failed when some of the essential parts were intercepted by Customs Officers on the docks in the UK, before they could be shipped out.

Serious consideration was given to attacking New York during the Second World War as a reprisal against the Americans. The main method considered was to use the four engine Condor aircraft as a bomber, but these were in short supply and there were technical difficulties due to the range required. By that point of the war aircraft production had been concentrated on small defensive fighters to guard the homeland against the massive attacks of the RAF by night and the US 8th Air Force by day. Some startling designs were in use. In particular the ME262 twin jet engine fighter, which was arguably the most advanced fighter of the war, but was brought into production too late to have a major effect.

A large four engine bomber, known as the *Amerika* Bomber, was in early development and was intended to bomb New York and other cities with a useful bomb load. Fortunately the technology of the time was not quite up to the job. However a two stage version of the V2 rocket, known as the A10, was also in development and was intended to reach the eastern cities of the US but, luckily for New York, the Germans ran out of time and surrendered before it was ready.

German scientists were working on Nerve Gas and had developed at least three types, Sarin, Tabun and Soman. Although effective, there were difficulties with these agents, particularly in the storage and handling of such dangerous and corrosive fluids. Binary warheads, where the chemicals are combined at the last second to create the nerve agent, had been developed and manufactured. They were never used in Europe because it was believed in Germany that the Allies had an even greater capability for chemical warfare and the retributions would have been horrendous for the German people. It is also possible that Hitler was influenced by the horrors of Gas Warfare that he had seen during his service in the trenches of the First World War. In fact the Allies were taken by surprise at the large quantities of viable nerve agent munitions they found as they advanced into Germany. They did not develop nerve agents themselves until after the war and it seems likely that, had the Germans used these weapons, the war could have taken a different path with many more allied casualties.

Would chemicals from the Second World War still be viable and deadly after all this time? If stored properly, why not? Unexploded gas shells from the First World War and buried in the wet soil of Picardy are turned up by farmer's plows every year in France and there have been cases where the gas has leaked and killed or severely affected people nearby.

Germany produced a range of highly effective submarines during the war. These U-Boats came very close to forcing the surrender of Britain, before the USA entered the war, by strangling the supply of food and munitions being shipped by the Merchant Navy. Near the end of the war they produced submarines capable of traveling from Germany to Japan without refueling and were able to ship advanced German technology, by this method, to their Japanese allies. Luckily it arrived too late to have an impact on the Pacific War. Size was not a problem since Germany also produced the '*Milch Cow*' U-Boats that took fuel and food out to the wolf packs in mid Atlantic to increase their time on station. Submarine bases built on the Atlantic coast of France still stand, despite massive bombs being dropped on them by the US and British air forces.

I have made my U-Boats Type XXII. As far as I can discover no Type XXII were built although XXI and XXIII did exist and were quite advanced boats for their time. I have borrowed features from the Type XXI for my fictitious boats. A number of the Type XXI were built by Blohm and Voss. Equally the numbers U-3998, 3999 and 4000 were not used although numbers above and below these were. Nine different U-Boats actually used Dragons as their emblem although, as far as I know, these were not drawn in the way I have described.

"T-Force" did exist and took possession of a considerable amount of advanced technology and equipment that was shipped back to the UK as a part of war reparations. The USA and Russia did much the same in their occupation areas.

After the war the Allied powers experimented with captured German technology. The story of the V2 being the basis of the US Space Program is well known, with captured German scientists being used to give the US and Russia a major step forward in weapon design. What is less well-known is that the US Navy experimented with launching the V1 from ships. A ramp was mounted on the deck of an LST and successful launches were carried out. They also experimented with launching from the deck of a submarine with missiles that had been stored in waterproof containers on the deck. For more information on the technology that was found in Germany at the end of the war and removed, you may wish to read "T Force – The Forgotten Heroes of 1945" by Sean Longden.

The British Kiel Yacht Club still exists at the time of writing and for many years since the war soldiers stationed in Germany, as part of the British Army of the Rhine, have been able to use the sailing boats to cruise around the Baltic and the very pleasant Danish islands. The story of the hidden U-Boat base was told to me when I sailed from there and was widely believed. The reference to legends of hidden bases and secret rooms is also a fact. Almost every Army base I went to during my service had their own version. I can vouch for the mention of the secret room in Detmold, West Germany, as it was found in Hobart Barracks when I was stationed there. It is also true that large factories, munitions dumps and bases were constructed deep underground to avoid allied bombing.

It is sadly true that Russian prisoners of war, Jews and political prisoners were used as slave labor and were treated extremely harshly. The SS had no compunction in slaughtering these slave laborers and by the end of the war were equally cavalier in shooting their own people if they were in the way.

Could a submarine come within range of New York without detection? I believe the answer is yes. There is a huge amount of traffic up and down the Hudson River and even if SOSUS operators heard the submarine amongst that jumble of noise it would be seventy years out of date and would not sound like the modern boats they are trained to detect.

Would New York be able to handle a chemical attack delivered in the way I have described? Probably not. Despite the remarkable courage of the New York Fire and Police Departments, demonstrated during the attack on the World Trade Center, they are civilian organizations and not equipped to deal with the weapons of mass destruction from a war long since over. The people of New York are understandably nervous of further terrorist attacks and the confusion would only need to last for a few hours in this crowded city for this story to work.

The vengeance of the US Armed Forces would be swift and deadly, I have no doubt, but they too can be misled and their awesome power misdirected. I have huge respect for US Forces and having worked with them I find their senior officers to be thoughtful and intelligent, far from the "Gung Ho" reactionaries of popular stories and movies. I am certain that, after the attacks on the World Trade Center and the Pentagon, procedures will have been carefully examined and quietly changed. This happens in all Armed Forces after wars and damaging events.

Organized crime in Russia after the collapse of communism is a very real problem for the Russian government and these so called Mafia, or *Mafya*, gangs are ruthless and violent. Would they have the nerve to attack the USA? If they thought they could get the US to believe someone else did it, then I think they might. Would they use a luxury yacht? Why not? The extremely rich Russian oligarchs who have emerged as Russia embraced capitalism seem to have a fascination with building bigger and better ones than their rivals and they do give a flexibility of movement that is no longer available in air travel.

The Cathedral of Christ the Savior in Moscow did exist and was demolished by the communists to make way for the "Palace of the Soviets." This was never completed after the invasion by German forces put a stop to the construction. Following the collapse of the Soviet Union, the Cathedral has been rebuilt as an almost exact copy of the original. Considerable quantities of Russian art treasures were stolen by the Germans during the war and not all of it has been recovered.

I have mentioned that a cave would amplify the sound of helicopter rotors and would provide warning to those inside. This was a technique used by the Viet Cong during the Vietnam conflict to warn of the approach of US helicopters. A wide hole was dug and a person would sit in it listening for the echoing thump of rotor blades that they would otherwise not hear until the aircraft were much nearer. A crude but effective version of the 'Sound Mirrors' that were built on the south coast of England in the 1930's for long distance aircraft detection.

Does HALO parachuting exist? It certainly does and it is dangerous. It was developed originally by Colonel John Stapp of the USAF. Only experienced parachutists, mainly those in the Special Forces, are trained in its use as a stealthy insertion technique. Should there be any kind of failure there is little or no time for a reserve chute to deploy.

Bringing all these facts and legends together is the basis for my fiction.

Now if we could only find the hill with those U-Boats beneath it.

Photograph Courtesy of Grupo Bernabé of Pontevedra.

NIGEL SEED

Born in Morecambe, England, into a military family, Nigel Seed grew up hearing his father's tales of adventure during the Second World War which kindled his interest in military history and storytelling. He received a patchy education, as he and his family followed service postings from one base to another. Perhaps this and the need to constantly change schools contributed to his odd ability to link unconnected facts and events to weave his stories.

Nigel later joined the Army, serving with the Royal Electrical and Mechanical Engineers in many parts of the world. Upon leaving he joined the Ministry of Defense during which time he formed strong links with overseas armed forces, including the USAF, and cooperated with them, particularly in support of the AWACS aircraft.

He is married and lives in Spain; half way up a mountain with views across orange groves to the Mediterranean. The warmer weather helps him to cope with frostbite injuries he sustained in Canada, when taking part in the rescue effort for a downed helicopter on a frozen lake.

His books are inspired by places he has been to and true events he has either experienced or heard about on his travels. He makes a point of including family jokes and stories in his books to raise a secret smile or two. Family dogs make appearances in his other stories.

Nigel's hobbies include sailing and when sailing in Baltic he first heard the legend of the hidden U-Boat base that formed the basis of his first book some thirty eight years later.

ACKNOWLEDGMENTS

"We are all travelers in the wilderness of this world and the best that we can find in our travels is an honest friend."

—Robert Louis Stevenson

I have been blessed with a number of honest friends who have helped me by reading my book at the embryonic stages and giving me useful criticism. You know who you are and thank you all. I have also been privileged to have my book critically examined by the exceptional author, John Gordon Davis. I owe him a great debt for his advice and encouragement. Equally, I am indebted to David Lane, Robert Astle, Jillian Ports, Kate Murphy, and Brooke Kressel-Magin at Astor+Blue Editions for their support and considerable advice in editorial, layout and design.

The biggest debt though is to my wife who has lived this project with me and been supportive throughout, especially when I was struggling.

MORE NIGEL SEED FROM ASTOR-BLUE EDITIONS

V4 VENGEANCE

Desperately seeking employment, recently discharged Royal Engineer Jim Wilson takes on an impossible challenge with the help of his former army mates, Ivan and Geordie. Hired by a Russian museum, they are sent to the Baltic coast of Germany to find a rumored World War II U-Boat base. Their discovery is beyond shocking: not only does the base exist—it contains secret submarines full of V2 rocket bombs. And they are not working for a museum. They are at the mercy of a notorious group of Russian mobsters, the Romanov Gang.

GOLDEN EIGHTS

In 1940, the British army was in a state of disarray following the evacuation from Dunkirk, and invasion seemed imminent. As a precaution, the government sent the bulk of the national gold reserves to Canada via ships that ran the gauntlet of the U-boat fleets. Much of this treasure was hidden in England, only to vanish in the fog of war. Now, a clue has finally emerged that might lead to the treasure's long lost hiding place. Needing the gold back in order to prevent a massive financial crisis, the government tasks Major Jim Wilson with finding it. Wilson and his team start the search, unaware that there is a traitor watching their every move.

TWO INTO 1

The Prime Minister's behavior has changed following his return from Washington, and Major Jim Wilson is called in to investigate. Wilson's discovery threatens the peace of the world, and the major must find a way to put things right. With little time left, Wilson and his team set out on a dangerous quest that takes them from the hills of Cumbria to the Cayman Islands and Dubai. All the while, there are others watching and playing for high stakes.